SPIRIT OF THE NORTH

SPIRIT OF THE NORTH

A Novel

Valar Morghulis
Game of Thrones

Ian Thomson

Quirinal Press

Cover image (copyright pending) with thanks to
Blackburn with Darwen Library and Information Service
www.cottontown.org

DEDICATED TO

Blackburn Public Library
And its staff
Then and now

BY THE SAME AUTHOR

Martin, a Novel

Humphrey and Jack, a Novel

A Dish of Apricots, A Novel

The Northern Elements, A Novel

Northern Flames, A Novel

Cherries

Lord Lindum's Anus Horribilis

Lord Lindum's Anus Mirabilis

The Mouse Triptych

The Swan Diptych

Come Away, O Human Child

PART ONE

GLENDOWER: I can call spirits from the vasty deep.
HOTSPUR: Why, so can I, or so can any man. But will they come when you do call for them?

1 Henry IV
William Shakespeare

1 BLOOD MOON

MY GRANDMOTHER SAID she had seen a red Indian chief come floating out of the full length mirror of her wardrobe. He wore warpaint and a headdress bristling with feathers of many colours. Around his neck were strings of beautiful beads. He seemed to give off his own light, and his red skin was shiny and the muscles of his arms were powerful.

'Weren't you scared?' I said.

'Nay lad,' she said. 'There were no cause to be frit. I've never felt so safe in all my days. He was my protector, my spirit guide. His name was Blood Moon.'

I couldn't say whether I believed her or not at the time. I was probably only six or seven. I think I believed her as I believed in Jesus and Father Christmas, taking their existence for granted whilst having doubts at one and the same time. I remember being glad that there was no mirror in my parents' wardrobe at home.

I liked going to Grandma's house because she spoilt me rotten. She lived on Hope Street, off the top of Montague Street. Mum used to drop me off there for a whole day a couple of times a month.

'It's nice to have a break once in a while,' she would say. 'He's no bother, only he never stops talking.'

Gran used to call me Little Tommy Tittlemouse because my name is Thomas and I was such a chatterbox. She would sing to me:

Little Tommy Tittlemouse
Lived in a little house;
He caught fishes
In other men's ditches.

I was full of questions. 'What's this, Grandma?' and 'What's that, Grandma?' and she would often reply with, 'It's a layore to catch meddlers'. I would ask what it meant, but she would just tap her nose and say nothing. I still don't know. Blackburn friends of my own age remember the expression, but nobody can tell me what it means, or where it comes from. I've tried Googling it, and there are a number of variants suggested, but no satisfying answers.

'What's for dinner?' I would ask.

'A doll and a drum and a kick up the bum,' she would say.

'What's for afters?'

'Wait-and-see pudding.'

I would get so frustrated at her evasions that I would throw a cushion at her. There were cushions all over the house with covers she'd knitted, crocheted or embroidered. She would throw one back at me, and a full-blown cushion fight would follow, until she collapsed wheezing with laughter into her armchair by the range. Then I would climb onto her lap and snuggle into her ample bosom, and she would tickle me until I screamed at her to stop.

Mum was a good cook but Grandma was even better. Her pastry melted in your mouth and her Lancashire cheese and onion plate pie was fit for the gods. We were learning about Greek mythology at school and I thought they could have served this pie up on Olympus. I could imagine Zeus asking for second helpings - I certainly did - and sometimes thirds.

Something Grandma cooked often was Scotch broth. It seemed slightly exotic to me with its celery and barley - ingredients we never saw at home. I was a bit suspicious about it at first but soon came to love it. I would wolf it down with buttered slices of Mother's Pride bread. Sometimes she would send me to the pub across the road - I think it was called The Bank. I would take a jug and the landlady would fill it with mild beer. I was ridiculously underage, of course, but they thought I was cute and indulged me, and besides, Grandma and her chums were regulars.

Once in a while, these ladies would meet at Grandma's for tea and malt loaf. Sometimes they would splash out and there would be a box of Kenyon's cakes, vanilla slices perhaps, cream horns, wimberry tarts, or - my favourite - profiteroles, which Grandma called 'elephants' feet'.

The meetings would be held in the 'front room' which, in keeping with the traditions of many working class people throughout the country, but especially in the North, was kept 'for best' and hardly ever used. It would be kept spick and span, everything dusted and polished, rugs beaten savagely in the back yard, net curtains washed frequently, brass ornaments shone fit to dazzle, and yet - for most of the time - the room was unoccupied.

Grandma's front room normally dwelt in gloom, but on the occasion of her tea parties, she would turn on, not only the standard lamp with its huge fringed shade - depicting nymphs and shepherds in a pastoral dance - but also 'the big light'. Then you could see her ornaments clearly: a pair of pot dogs on the mantelpiece (black and tan Alsatians with lolling tongues); a pair of porcelain Chinese dragons on a bookcase; a serving dish on the dresser commemorating the coronation of George V and Queen Mary; a plate for the coronation of George VI and the Queen Mother; a china mug celebrating the wedding of Princess Elizabeth to Prince Philip of Greece, and a whole tea set commemorating the coronation of Elizabeth II. I thought it was like a history lesson in porcelain.

There were deep armchairs on either side of the fireplace, where a fire only burned on these occasions. The blue and white Delft tiles on either side would probably fetch a few bob these days. An uncomfortable chaise longue with green velvet upholstery, rubbed shiny in places, stretched under the window. Beside it the front door led straight into the street, though draughts were excluded by heavy velvet drapes in the same dark green. In the middle of the room was a round table with a beige lace-fringed cloth, embroidered with forget-me-knots at the centre, and in the middle of the table was a large oil lamp with a ruby-coloured glass shade fashioned like a large tulip. Around the table were four spoon back Victorian chairs. A battered chair was brought in from the kitchen for me and I sat on a cushion so I could reach everything.

I called Grandma's three friends 'auntie' though they were no relation. There was Auntie Doreen, Auntie Betty and Auntie Hilda. I thought that they would make a great comedy trio in the kind of films that we saw at the Saturday Matinee at the Star in Little Harwood. Auntie Doreen was very tall and thin; Auntie Betty was tiny with the delicate bones of a bird, and Auntie Hilda wore glasses with diamanté wings like an American actress. This look clashed rather with her black frilly blouse and the cameo brooch at her neck. Come to think of it, Grandma could have starred in my imaginary comic movies too, being larger than life and genuinely funny. All three of our visitors wore hats indoors.

Grandma wore an iridescent silk shawl over her shoulders with golden tassels. She also wore a man's wristwatch that had been her husband's. When tea was done and we were 'full up to t'gunnels', Grandma would read the tea leaves. She would swill out excess tea back into the teapot and tilt the cup so the leaves would make a significant pattern. I used to ask to see the dregs but I could never discern any pattern, significant or otherwise.

'That's because you don't have the gift, Tommy Tittlemouse,' she would say. 'Except for the gift of the gab, that is.'

I now know, though I didn't at the time, that the futures she predicted for Aunties Doreen, Betty and Hilda were packed with clichés such as tall dark strangers; unexpected journeys; lucky finds; objects, situations and animals to beware of, and talismans to cherish - the vague and random stock-in-trade of newspaper horoscopes.

Her predictions for me were more specific. She said that the tea leaves told her that I would be either a doctor or a policeman. I said I couldn't see a stethoscope or a policeman's helmet in the wet leaves but she just said, in a mysterious whisper, that you have to know how to read the signs. At the time I'd wanted to be a policeman on Mars so I was quite content with the prophecy. Eventually, as it turned out, I was to become both a doctor *and* a policeman, though not on Mars, and so, completely by chance, she'd made a lucky guess about my future.

She had other means of looking into what was yet to be. She read palms (I would be lucky in love - true) and she could read the bumps in your head (I was a near genius allegedly).

Or out would come the Tarot pack. I was fascinated by these well-thumbed cards. I thought they were very beautiful but also rather sinister. This was partly because the meanings were not quite what you thought they might be. Death, for instance, was not necessarily a bad card, and nor was the Devil. Death could mean transformation and change, new beginnings and release from old obligations. The Devil, if reversed, could mean independence and freedom.

I had my suspicions that, as far as the tea leaves and the palms and the head bumps were concerned, Grandma was making it up as she went along.

The Tarot was different. There seemed to be rules and there seemed to be power in the cards which you needed special skills to unlock. The cards meant different things depending on whether they were upright or reversed and depending on what other cards were turned up in the reading - and this is what I thought was sinister. The aunties seemed to like the Tarot. I was intrigued, but the cards also gave me the shivering habdabs.

2 IS THERE ANYBODY THERE?

'I'M GOING TO HAVE TO FIND another minder for him now, Dad. Either that or I'll have to give up work. I can't have your mother putting her crazy ideas into his head.'

I was used to Mum talking about me as if I wasn't there, but at that precise moment I was wondering, not for the first time, why she always called my father 'Dad' when he wasn't her dad but mine.

'What's to do now?' Dad said, lowering the *Lancashire Evening Telegraph* and looking over the top. 'Can a man not get a minute's peace in his own house? What are you on about "crazy ideas"? What "crazy ideas?"'

'You know very well what I'm talking about, David Catlow. Telling fortunes. All that nonsense.'

'Get away with you. It's harmless. It's just party tricks, that's all.'

'It's not harmless. Dabbling in the occult - it could be dangerous. Filling his head with tea leaves. I won't have it.'

Mum was tidying up with savage ferocity.

'Is your head full of tea leaves, Tommy?' Dad said.

'No, Dad,' I said.

I didn't really want to contradict Mum but it was true. My head wasn't full of tea leaves.

'Tea leaves, palm readings, reading your bumps, horoscopes, Tarot cards,' Mum went on. 'I don't want his head filled with all that nonsense. He has too much imagination as it is. Honestly, he's too young for all this stuff.'

'You never know, there might be something in it.'

Dad winked at me.

'It's superstition and it's unhealthy,' Mum said. 'I love your mother to bits, honest I do, but I'm telling you straight, if she'd lived a hundred years ago, she'd be burnt as a witch.'

'I think you'd have to go back more than a hundred years, love.'

'Did I ask for a history lesson? Did I? No. Well, think on.'

'And where do you think you're going to get another minder?'

'Oh, I don't know. Somewhere.'

'You'll have to pay, you know. By the time you've shelled out, it'll hardly be worth your going to work. And Mother would be heart-broken, you know. She lives for looking after Tom.'

'Oh, I know, Dad, bless her - but you'll have to have a word with her. She's to stop this black magic rubbish. Are you listening to me?'

Dad had lifted his paper up again and was hiding behind it.

'Yes, love.'

'I mean it, David.'

You could tell she was dead serious when she used his real name.

'I know you do, love.'

'You'll talk to her then?'

'Aye, I will if you'll only stop moitherin',' he said. 'How about a brew while you're on your feet?'

'What did your last slave die of?' Mum said.

'Kindness,' Dad said.

Mum harrumphed, but put the kettle on all the same. Dad risked another wink at me over the top of the paper.

'Would you like some Ovaltine, Tommy?' Mum said over her shoulder.

'I would an' all,' I said.

Whether Dad ever did speak to Grandma, I don't know, but it would have been too late anyway.

Because a fortnight earlier, Grandma had held a séance and I was there. After all the fuss about the fortune telling there was no way I was going to tell my parents about it now, and anyway, Grandma had said: 'No need to tell your Mum, is there, Tommy Tittlemouse?'

'No, Grandma,' I'd whispered, excited by the secret.

'Good boy,' she said. 'They can sense these things on the other side, you know.'

What 'these things' were, I wasn't sure, and I had only a vague notion of what 'the other side' was either. I thought it must be some dim region of mist and shadows behind the dresser in the front room, or maybe behind the enormous gilt mirror over the fireplace whose reflections were dusky with tarnish.

Anyway, on the occasion of the séance, I was staying at Grandma's for a whole weekend while Mum and Dad attended a wedding somewhere down south. This was always a great luxury and I was particularly looking forward to sleeping in the old-fashioned bed in the back bedroom.

It was really high and I had to sort of climb into it. The bedstead was iron-framed with brass bed-knobs; the mattress was deep and soft and made me think of a gigantic marshmallow; the sheets smelled of lavender; on top of the blankets was a bedspread of knitted squares, and on top of that was a blue silk quilt. I would be near-buried in comfort and warm as toast.

Best of all Grandma would tuck me in, and tell me stories from Hans Christian Andersen or the Brothers Grimm. She didn't need a book - she knew the stories off by heart. Looking back over the years, I am struck by how dark some of them are and, though I was freaked out by the dog with eyes as big as saucers in *The Tinder Box* and the poor child freezing to death in *The Little Match Girl*, I always slept well enough.

Come to think of it, I was even more freaked out when Dad took me to see *Pinocchio* at The Royal when I was about the same age. I was just about all right when Pinocchio lied to the Blue Fairy and his nose grew and grew, but I really didn't like it when it grew leaves and a bird nested on the end of it. I got very fidgety indeed when Pinocchio and Lampwick were given donkeys' ears and tails and started braying. But when Geppetto and

Pinocchio were swallowed by the whale I burst into floods of tears and begged Dad to take me home.

I don't think I ever found out what happens at the end until my wife and I took our own kids, Michael and Lisa, to see it when they were small. Needless to say, neither of them was the least bit fazed, though they did say that they were irritated by Jiminy Cricket.

'He's supposed to be Pinocchio's conscience,' I said.

'Why would you want an insect to teach you right and wrong?' Lisa said.

'I know,' Michael said. 'I mean, what do insects actually know?'

'I think he's a smug bug,' Lisa said, and they both squealed with laughter at the daft rhyme.

I mention my squeamishness about a wooden puppet because it contrasts starkly with how undaunted I was by the dark mysteries of the séance.

The aunties arrived in a state of great excitement and Grandma dispensed glasses of QC British sherry to relax the 'sitters' beforehand. I was given a tot of Ribena.

'Are you off to bed now, Tommy, lad?' Auntie Hilda said.

'He's going to join us, aren't you, Tommy?' Grandma said.

'Isn't he a bit young, Daisy?' Auntie Betty said. I always had to fight the giggles when somebody used

Grandma's first name. It reminded me of the song about the bicycle made for two.

'He'll be an asset,' Grandma said, in a tone forbidding contradiction. 'He has the gift. I can feel it in my water.'

Nobody seemed to remember that Grandma had denied my having any supernatural talents only days before.

The ladies set about preparing the front room. The wick of the oil lamp in the middle of the round table was trimmed, lit, and turned right down. Grandma threw a red silk scarf over the tasselled lamp shade in the corner. Then she produced from a drawer in the dresser a Chinese fan and a music box with a ballerina in a blue tutu on top. These were laid on the table beside the oil lamp with great ceremony.

'Have you got anything of *his*?' Grandma said to Auntie Betty. I assumed she was referring to Betty's recently deceased husband.

'He treasured this,' said Auntie Betty, producing a little silver snuff box from her handbag. 'Look, it's from the Liberal Club. They engraved it for him. He was in the billiards team.'

'That'll be perfect,' said Grandma, placing it very precisely on the round table and giving it a little pat with her fingertips.

'Mind you, he never took snuff,' Auntie Betty said.

'And he weren't that good at billiards neither,' said Auntie Hilda.

'You're not wrong there, Hilda, if truth be told, but, ey, he *did* enjoy it, bless him.'

'God rest his soul,' said Grandma.

'Amen,' said the aunties.

'Now, then, sit you down,' Grandma said, as she turned off the big light. 'Tommy, here, next to me.'

So we sat in our little circle in the dim red light, holding each others' hands and Auntie Doreen led us in a hymn:

Shall we gather at the river?
Where bright angel feet have trod
With its crystal tide forever
Flowing by the throne of God

We joined in the chorus with great gusto and swung our joined hands to the beat, smiling at each other:

Yes, we'll gather at the river
The beautiful, the beautiful river
Gather with the saints at the river
That flows by the throne of God

Grandma then said a prayer which I don't remember, but it was something to do with asking Jesus to let light shine through a chink in the door to 'the other side', and for Satan to bog off and mind his own business, or words to that effect.

And then we sat there in silence for half an hour.

And nothing happened.

Every so often, Grandma would say: 'Is there anybody there?'

And nothing happened.

Just as I was getting a bit fidgety and almost on the point of saying, 'Can I go to bed now?' Grandma asked again: 'Is there anybody there?' There came three loud knocks.

Were they from under the table? Or on some other piece of furniture? Or at the doors? It was hard to say, but the vibrations seemed to fill the room.

Grandma and Auntie Betty to my left tightened their grip on my hand.

'Is that you, Blood Moon?' Grandma said. 'Knock once for yes and twice for no.'

There was a long pause and then again three really loud bangs.

'Don't be afraid, Blood Moon,' Grandma said. 'We're all friends here. Is that you?'

And immediately there was a single rap.

'Is all well with you, Blood Moon?' Grandma said. 'Do you walk in the light?'

A single rap.

'We sense your presence here, Blood Moon,' Grandma said. 'Do you feel our love?'

There was a long silence, then a subdued rumbling, like a heavy truck passing by and at last a single loud knock.

'Will you help our friend Betty, Blood Moon? Will you help ease her troubled heart? She wants to know how her husband, Theo Hardcastle, is faring on the other side. Will you not speak through me, Blood Moon?'

There was a series of more subdued knocks.

'Put your fingers on the snuff box and close your eyes,' Grandma said to the aunties and me. I sneaked a look at her. She had leaned her head right back and was breathing steadily but audibly.

'Will you help me comfort Betty Hardcastle, Blood Moon?'

Single knock. Gasp from Auntie Betty.

'Hush,' Grandma said. 'Join hands again.'

We did so. Nothing happened for a few minutes. I was conscious of the ticking of the carriage clock and Grandma's deep breathing. Suddenly she spoke.

'Blood Moon says Theo is happy, Betty. He is waiting for you on the other side.'

'Will it be long before I join him?'

'Blood Moon says there are things you cannot ask,' Grandma said.

'But I will see him again, won't I?' Auntie Betty said with a quiver in her voice.

'You will,' Grandma said. 'He is glad you are looking after the snuff box. He says you should go easy on the gin. He says he plays billiards on the other side sometimes and that he is better now than when he was among us. He says you're not to forget to water his roses.'

'Oh, Daisy, I won't,' said Betty, weeping happily now. 'Tell Blood Moon how very grateful I am.'

'He knows,' Grandma said.

Suddenly, I felt her hand go very cold. She seemed to go into a spasm. I cried out: 'Grandma!'

'Keep hold of her hand, Tommy,' said Auntie Doreen. 'It's all right. She's going into a trance.'

Almost immediately Grandma was still again though her head remained thrown back in an unnatural way. Then she spoke in a voice that was not her own. It seemed far back in her throat.

'LET ME GO NOW,' the voice said.

'Soon, Blood Moon.' This was Grandma's own voice. 'First answer me one more question.'

The strange voice replied: 'LET ME GO. I AM IN PAIN. I CAN STAY NO LONGER.'

'One question,' Grandma said.

'ONE QUESTION. BUT QUICKLY NOW.'

'What does the future hold for this boy?'

Grandma let go of my hand and placed hers on my head.

'THIS BOY WILL DO GREAT WORKS IN THE HOUSE OF DEATH. HIS JOY AND SOLACE WILL BE THE EIGHTH BOOK.'

There was a series of raps; the clock chimed, though it was not the hour; the Chinese fan opened of itself; the music box began to play *Frère Jacques*, and the ballerina began to twirl; the oil lamp went out, and a pot dog fell off the mantlepiece.

3 IN THE ADELPHI

'WERE YOU SCARED?' Will Melling said, over sixty years later.

'No,' I said. 'I don't think I was. Fascinated more like. Thrilled even. Strange, isn't it?'

Will and I were sitting in the Adelphi pub, near Blackburn railway station. We had taken to meeting up once a week for beers and talk ever since we had solved the mystery of 'the skelly in the bog'.

When we were kids my dog unearthed a skeleton of a little boy on a demolition site where the Larkhill flats are now. It was what remained of a child thrown into a midden by his panic-stricken friends, after a tragic accident on the Leeds and Liverpool canal. He had lain there since Victorian times and the riddle of who he was and how he came to be there remained unsolved until Will and I revisited the case a year or so ago and gained a certain amount of notoriety as a result.[1]

My name is Tom Catlow, by the way. I was Senior Scientific Officer (Forensics) with the East Lancs and Ribble Valley Police Force until my recent retirement. Will and I had been members of the same gang as kids and I tracked him down as I was working on the case. He had had a successful career in sports journalism and his knowledge of print media had proved helpful in our research.

'Obviously that famous forensic brain of yours had not yet been fired up,' he said.

'Well, I wasn't analysing the situation as it unfolded if that's what you mean,' I said.

'Yeah, but you must have had some idea that your Gran had rigged things up. How old did you say you were? Six?'

'Or seven. I didn't think about it rationally. It was more of an emotional experience. Do you member that stunt that Peter Shawcross pulled on us in the cellar of that empty house behind St Urban's?'

'When he lit up those abandoned statues with his torch so that it looked as if they'd come to life?'[2]

[1] See *The Northern Elements* by Ian Thomson (2019)

[2] *The Northern Elements*, p.107

'Yeah,' I said. 'Did you stop to analyse what was going on then? No, you didn't. You freaked out and shot off like shit from a goose.'

'I was younger than the rest of you.'

'Only by a couple of years.'

'Exactly, you'd have been about the same age as I was at the séance.'

Will laughed.

'All right, *touché*,' he said.

'Anyway,' I went on. 'Who said that Grandma was cheating?'

'Oh, come on, Tom. Leave it out,' Will said. 'You might have fallen for it at the time but there have to be simple explanations for all these phenomena.'

'"There are more things in heaven and earth, Horatio, than are dreamt of in your philosophy."'

'Horatio, who?'

'It's from *Hamlet*, you illiterate git.'

'Smarty pants,' Will said. 'But you've got to be pulling my leg. You are not seriously trying to convince me that a scientist like you really believes in this hokum?'

'Is you disrespectin' my gran?' I said.

'Yes,' Will said. 'Sounds to me like she was an accomplished conjuror.'

'All right,' I said, 'I'll give it to you straight. Even at the time, I might have had some doubts, I admit. For instance, I thought Grandma might be doing the knocking - but how? We were holding hands, remember.'

'Was she using her knees?' Will asked.

'Well, that did cross my mind,' I said. 'But consider this: like many women of her generation Grandma was scrupulous about keeping the street in front of the house clean. She would sweep it twice a day. Sometimes she would even mop it!'

'You're joking!' Will said.

'I am not,' I replied. 'What's more, the line between her wet pavement and the dry flags in front of the houses on either side was as sharp as if a line had been drawn with a ruler. It was as if she was making her virtue obvious to her neighbours whilst showing them to be slovenly by comparison.

'But the front step was Grandma's ultimate indication that if cleanliness is next to godliness, she was Hope Street's number one angel. When the rag and bone man came round with his horse-drawn cart, he would give you, in exchange for your newspapers and outgrown woollies, either a goldfish in a plastic bag, or a donkey stone for the front step. Obviously I was desperate for a goldfish (I was going to call it Huckleberry Hound - which is not very fishy I'll admit) but Grandma always opted for the stone - and it had to be a white one, not a yellow one.

'Then, she would take the stone and a bowl of warm water out to the front step. She would get down laboriously to kneel on a cushion and scour the step like a maniac. The stone and water would create a kind of thin paste and when it dried you could polish it with a cloth. God help you if you trod on her step before Grandma had finished. Her step had to be the best in the street.

'But here's the thing: once Grandma was down it was a hell of a job for her to get back up again. It was a kind of three-stage operation. She would kneel up and sit on her heels, resting for a moment or two with her hands in the small of her back. Then, with one hand leaning against the door jamb she would creak to a kind of crouching position. And then, very slowly, she would straighten up. Grandma was a heavy woman and riddled with arthritis.

'So no, I don't think she was using her knees. What's your next theory, Mr Sceptic?'

'Oh, I don't know,' Will said. 'I'm thinking pulleys, levers, springs, timers - that sort of thing. An accomplice maybe?'

'If you're thinking that there might be somebody else in the house, you'll have to think again. It was just too small. There had been nobody upstairs when Grandma and I went up there before the séance to put a hot water bottle in my bed and to lay out my pyjamas.'

'I bet your pyjamas had aeroplanes on them,' Will said.

'Correct,' I said.

'Bingo!' Will said. 'Were they Winceyette?'

'Correct again,' I said. 'Maybe you have the gift yourself, Will Melling?'

'Or maybe I just know you very well, Tom Catlow. What about the front bedroom.'

'No, we went in there to pick up the silk scarf for the lamp downstairs. Look, the idea's crazy. What would be her motive?'

'Just mischief?'

'Oh, you've got her right there. I'm sure Auntie Betty's dead husband telling her to lay off the gin was Grandma having a laugh.'

'And that bit about not forgetting to water the roses.'

'That bit too. And Theo playing billiards on the other side.'

'Do you think that Blood Moon stuff might have been a kind of misdirection?' Will said. 'You know, where a conjuror's patter draws your attention away from what he's doing in plain sight?'

'Could be. Now I think about it, she had an impressive repertoire of card tricks and she could pull shillings out of my ears, which was pretty good because I got to keep them.'

'Your ears?'

'No, the money, you cloth head.'

'Which must have been a pretty good incentive to believe in magic, I suppose.'

'Exactly. But look, even if the séance was just a clever box of tricks, and I'm not saying it wasn't, you're missing out the importance of the ambience, the "vibes" if you like.'

'What is a hyper-rational, evidence-based forensic scientist doing talking about "vibes"?' Will said in mock horror. 'Are you going soft in your old age?'

'I don't think so,' I said. 'It's the rationalist in me that tells me I have to take the atmosphere into account. It was carefully curated, as the pretentious wallies on the telly would put it. Granny the medium and Blood Moon the spirit guide, dim lighting, holding hands, the hymn, the prayer, the ritual, - it was all part of the mesmeric effect. Whatever shenanigans my gran might have been up to, the fact is that the aunties desperately wanted to believe in it, especially Auntie Betty. She really needed to believe that the connexion with her dead husband was real.'

'OK,' Will said, 'but, with respect, Tom, wasn't your grandma taking these old dears for a ride?'

'Maybe, but if Auntie Betty got genuine consolation from it, where's the harm? I suppose you could call it a sort of "pious fraud". In any case, I have a strong feeling - and I can't prove this - that even if the props were rigged, and even if the guttural voice was a bit of performance art, she really believed that she was making contact with the spirit world.'

'Maybe,' Will said. He didn't sound too convinced.

'Now then,' I said, 'it's your round. Get the beers in and I'll tell you about another séance that really was one hundred per cent fixed.'

'You know, there's one thing that really troubles me,' Will said, standing and picking up the empty glasses.

'What's that?'

'What kind of fruitcake would call a goldfish Huckleberry Hound?'

And he went off to the bar.

4 OUIJA

'RIGHT,' WILL SAID, returning with a couple of pints of Thwaites' bitter and two packets of pork scratchings, 'tell me about this séance. How do you know it was rigged?'

'I know,' I said, 'because I was the one who rigged it.'

And this is the story I told Will:

'I took a first degree in Biochemistry at Bristol. Then I moved to Cambridge to follow a programme of nine years' study which involved preclinical training, another bachelor's degree and then a doctorate in toxicology. My friends at the time weren't just the medics from my own college, St Catharine's, but also a bunch of law undergraduates from Corpus Christi across the road. We had a number of things in common. Both medicine and law require a vast amount of rote learning, and it was especially true in my case, as a future forensic scientist.

'We also played hard. Typically, we would meet in The Eagle (which was actually owned by Corpus) for a couple of beers before dinner in our own colleges. Then a couple of hours of hard swotting before meeting up in the pub again for as much Greene King bitter as we could sink before closing time. All the same, we were never late for nine o'clock lectures the following day.

'The other thing we had in common was a black sense of humour. The practice of medicine and the law takes you into some pretty dark places at times and you could argue that a twisted sense of humour is a survival mechanism.

'In the summer of my second year as a graduate student at Cats, I was awarded a research fellowship and decided to throw a dinner party to celebrate. With the fellowship came the option of a set of rooms in college or a college flat out on Barton Road which had a study with a walled garden accessed through French windows. There was also a sizeable kitchen. The garden cinched it really. I had most of my meals in college and worked in the college library but it was nice to have a bit of privacy when I wanted it and to cook for myself occasionally. It was a bit of a way out but there was always my trusty bike, which I called Bucephalus, after Alexander the Great's favourite steed.'

'Pretentious or what?' Will said.

'Ironic.'

'Oh, get lost.'

'Fair enough. The dinner party was actually *very* pretentious. There were eight of us, four of each sex - back when there were only two sexes. I can't remember all their names now but my good friend Fergus Reilly was my partner in crime in the Great Séance Fraud. He was from Liverpool, back when it was still part of Lancashire - still is, as far as we're concerned. We're still in touch. He lives in County Kerry, has a large family, and they keep a cow in the kitchen.

'Each of the chaps was responsible for a course and the girls chose the wines because we were into busting gender stereotypes. I still have the menu which I had typed up on college crested cards. Here it is:

Fergus Reilly's Original Dublin Bay Soup
Chicken Curry à la Wigan Pier
Sorbet au Manège Enchanté
Cherubs on Horseback
Toast: The Duke of Lancaster proposed, by Thomas Catlow, B.Sc. (Bristol), B.A. (Cantab.)'

'Shouldn't you have toasted the Queen?' Will said.

'I did,' I replied. 'As a good Blackburnian, I toasted her according to her title as Duke of Lancaster.'

'Don't you mean "Duchess"?'

'No, she holds the title in her own right, so she's the Duke. Don't interrupt.'

'Look, just what are you up to?'

'What do you mean?'

'You're working up to something, Tom Catlow. I know you of old. Why are you showing me a menu from half a century ago? What's with all these stories about séances?'

'You'll see. Am I boring you?'

'No, on the contrary.'

'Well, shut up and you'll find out.'

'Go on then.'

And I resumed my account of the dinner party.

I can't remember exactly what the girls brought, but they chose some pretty impressive wines. Charlotte, Fergus's girlfriend, also brought a litre bottle of Scotch and I had plenty of gin and vodka. By the end of the meal, we were pretty mellow and I have to say my Magic Roundabout sorbet might have contributed to the general feeling of boozy geniality. I made it with cherries that had been soaked in Kirsch and added a few generous slugs for good measure. I daresay you could have got pissed on the pudding alone.

Anyway, once the table had been cleared, I proposed a séance as an after-dinner entertainment. I wrote the letters of the alphabet on index cards plus the numerals one to nine and a zero. There was also a card with YES written on it and another that said NO.

We pushed in the leaves of the table so we could sit round it more closely and I arranged the cards in a circle. Fergus placed an upturned tumbler in the middle and we all placed the tips of our right forefingers lightly on the base. Then, Fergus began an incantation which went something like:

> *Timeo Danaos et dona ferentes benedic domine nos et haec dona tua retro me Satanas adeste fideles Caesar adsum iam forte mugistusque boum mollesque sub arbores somni non absunt.*

This nearly reduced me to giggles which would have given the game away. Both Fergus and I had done Latin up to the fifth form. Maybe the others had too. If so they hadn't been paying attention because what this nonsensical patchwork of Latin rags really meant was:

> *I fear the Greeks especially when they bring gifts - bless us and these thy gifts - get thee behind me, Satan - Come all ye faithful - Caesar had some jam*

for tea - and, the lowing of cattle and gentle slumbers under the trees are not absent.

Fergus and I had worked everything out in advance, you see. For a long time nothing happened because that was the way we'd planned it. We sat there in candlelight with the curtains closed, joss sticks burning on the mantlepiece. From time to time, I would say the classic: 'Is there anybody there?' And nothing happened except a bit of giggling from the girls.

Suddenly, the glass began to move. It went to the letter A, then X, returned to the centre and stopped. After a minute it began to move again and rapidly spelled out:

AXJIVLR

And then it stalled again. After a few moments, in fits and starts, the glass spelled out random clusters of letters.

Then I said: 'Who are you spirit?'

The glass eagerly spelled out:

I AM MXRTHX

'It's "Martha",' said one of the girls excitedly. 'Are you Martha?' she said.

I could almost sense Fergus's glee. Charis had taken the bait.

The glass shot to YES.

'Fergus is pushing the glass,' Simon Lawrence said.

'I am not,' Fergus said, lifting his finger from the tumbler.

I AM NOT

said the glass as if in mockery.

'It's Tom then,' Simon said.

'Shut up, Simon.' said Charis. 'You'll frighten Martha.'

'It really isn't me,' I said, and lifted my finger from the glass. To my intense surprise the glass moved a little even though Fergus had not replaced his finger. Whether I had inadvertently given it a little shove when I lifted mine or whether there was a change of temperature and pressure inside the glass I don't know. You know when you put a glass down on a wet surface it can slide along as if of its own accord. Maybe it was something like that, although the physics was beyond me. Or maybe, I remember thinking for a microsecond, maybe Martha is real.

'Yes, shut up, Simon,' Charlotte said. 'Come on boys, complete the circle.'

And Fergus and I put our fingertips back on the glass.

'Are you dead?' Charis said.

'That's a bit tactless, don't you think?' Simon said.

'Oh, do shut up,' Charlotte said. 'Or sod off.'

'Sorry,' Simon said in a baby voice.

Charis repeated her question: 'Martha, are you dead?'

Fergus and I left it for quite a while before the glass moved to the YES card.

Slowly, with agonising pauses, and with some garbled replies and bouts of nonsense words, Martha began her tragic tale.

Of course Fergus and I had been pushing the glass all along. Sometimes I would be the motor force and sometimes Fergus would be the agent. The only thing that was magical was the unspoken synergy between us. If I felt the slightest resistance, I would let Fergus take charge of the narrative and vice versa. The silent communication between us which decided when we would pause and when we would introduce distractions was close to telepathic. We could sense that the others were being drawn into the spell we were weaving.

Naturally, we had worked out the rather hackneyed story in advance. Martha had been born in 1872 or 1873 (she wasn't sure) in the Union Workhouse on Mill Lane. At ten she had found a place as a scullery maid in the kitchens in Pembroke College. The work was hard, the hours were long, and the pay negligible but she had been happy.

At thirteen, she had fallen in love with an undergraduate called Miles de Broughton. (I know, I know, it's dreadfully Mills and Boon.) He had promised to marry her in Little St. Mary's and said she should have a carriage and pair and as many silk ribbons as she liked. Besotted, she let him have his way with her one summer evening in the long grass on Sheep's Green near the mill race.

When Martha discovered that she was 'in the family way' she approached Miles and asked him to marry her immediately to save her from disgrace, but he laughed at her and said that she had been a pleasant enough diversion for a summer evening but that she was to trouble him no more.

Martha continued to work in the kitchens until she could no longer disguise her condition. As her belly grew bigger, there could be no doubt, and her employment was terminated. She was thrown without ceremony out into the street, and was forced to beg for a living outside the newly built Fitzwilliam Museum until she reached full term when she had no option but to return to the workhouse to have her baby.

Rather than stay in that place of grim regulation, she left as soon as she was able, and the baby strong enough to survive. It was a girl, and she had named it Florence.

Thanks to sympathy for the child, her revenue from begging was enough for food, and sometimes shelter in the doss house on East Road.

One day, Martha was crossing Trumpington Street to her station on the steps of the Fitzwilliam when a runaway horse which had broken its traces, came galloping towards her. It knocked her sideways and she dropped the child. Horrified, she saw baby Florence roll over twice under the horses' hooves and receive a lethal kick in the head.

At this point in the story, there was an anguished scream.

It was Charis.

'Noooo!' she screamed, 'not the baby. Get me a Bible. I want to hold a Bible.'

The hairs on the back of my neck bristled and my heart was banging. Charis had frightened the living crap out of me.

This was not part of the plan.

5 SUPERSTITION AND RAIN

'BLOODY HELL!' WILL CRIED. 'Was she the hysterical type then, this Charis?'

'Not that I knew of,' I said. 'Not till she started shrieking. She was pretty drunk, I suppose, but even so, I had her down as stable and level-headed. She was a natski, for heaven's sake.'

'A what?'

'She was reading Natural Sciences. I mean how much more down to earth can you get?'

'Archaeology?' Will said.

'Haha. Very droll. Funny thing is, I was working myself up to asking her out. She was really fit.'

'And did you?'

'Not on your Nellie. After that freak-out? You must be joking. It was a lucky escape. I realised that I didn't want to be tied down to somebody who could be wholly taken in by a prank that was so obviously fraudulent.'

'It can't have been that obvious, if the others fell for it too.'

'I'm not sure if they did. It was never mentioned again. I think everyone was really shaken up by Charis's anguish.'

'So what happened?'

'Well, I found her a Bible and she sat there clutching it with tears dripping off her chin and her long hair all over her wet face. There were gut-wrenching sobs and little whimpering noises and every so often she would shudder.

'Fergus and I took a couple of tumblers of Chivas Regal into the garden. He thought it was absolutely hilarious. "Hook, line and sinker!" he kept saying. "Hook, line and sinker!"'

'What about you?' Will said.

'Me? I felt incredibly guilty. That poor girl. For all I knew she was scarred for life. You do realise, of course, that we could never confess to our trickery now. I still feel guilty when I think about it. Am I blushing?'

'No.'

'It feels as if I am. The shame, the shame.'

'Serves you right for being so cynical.'

'Ah, but there's another weird thing. I'm not cynical about it.'

'How do you mean?'

'There's this film by Polanski, I forget what it's called. *Repulsion*, was it? He's very good at making everyday things seem really weird. And there's a wall with dingy wallpaper and it seems to become less solid and a fist seems to be pressing through from the other side. I felt a bit like that. As if the interface between what we know and what we don't had become porous. As if there really was another world, running parallel, and for a moment it had leaked through into ours. As if that, not our silly games, was what had terrified Charis.'

'Oh, leave it out, Tom,' Will said. 'You don't expect me to buy that.'

'Oh, I know what you're thinking. You've said it already. Somebody who has spent his career in the company of corpses must know what *dead* means. You'd think so wouldn't you? Bodies with one hundred per cent burns, bodies perforated with a hundred frenzied stab wounds, bodies with organs missing, drowned bodies bloated with gas, bodies shrivelled with poisons, severed limbs, torsos, decapitations, the torn mess of bomb victims, cadavers with entry wounds and exit wounds - I've seen it all on my autopsy table - and you'd think, wouldn't you, that dealing with all this, this *meat*, that there would be no escaping the fact that death is final? You would, wouldn't you?'

'Steady on, our Tom. You'll have me gagging on me scratchings.'

'But sometimes, just sometimes,' I continued, 'as you put your saws and your scalpels and your forceps in the steriliser, and your stoppered chemicals back in the cupboard and you sluice down the table, you can't help thinking that there *must be* a ghost in the machine. The butcher's meat you've returned to the mortuary, can't be all there is.'

'And is that what you believe?'

'No, not really. The scientist in me says that we are bio-chemical entities that have evolved over millennia and that our thoughts and feelings and our literature and philosophy are the products of electro-chemical pyrotechnics in our brains. It is also highly probable that nothing we say, or think, or feel, or do is brought about by our free will, but is the product of a determined chain of cause and effect going back before we were born.'

'This is getting a bit depressing,' Will said.

'Not really,' I said. 'All that is what my head says - which is the same as what my education has led me to understand - but another part of me, in an unspecified location, can't quite accept that we will be totally annihilated. As my dad used to say: "You never know, lad, there might be summat in it."'

'I never know with you, Tom Catlow, whether you're leading me on or not.'

'I'm not, as it happens. However, as the Walrus said, "the time has come to talk of many things" - but not before I get another pint in. Same again?'

'Sure,' Will said.

When I returned with a pint in each hand and two packets of scratchings between my teeth, Will looked pensive.

'I suppose,' he said, 'if we're talking about spirits and stuff, we come from the right part of the world.'

'You've been thinking, haven't you?' I said.

'I have,' Will said, sipping the foam from the top of his pint.

'You want to be careful about that,' I said. 'Your brain could spontaneously combust.'

'Lancashire, I mean,' Will said, ignoring me completely. 'A county that remained Catholic in the Seventeenth Century despite the threat of dire persecution. Have you ever been to Samlesbury Hall?'

'Course I have. Ruth and I had Sunday lunch there not very long ago. Jolly good it was too.'

'Yeah but the rest of it is pretty spooky though, don't you think? It feels like it hasn't moved out of Elizabethan times.'

'I'll give you that,' I said. 'It is pretty eerie.'

'You must have heard about the ghost?'

'The White Lady, you mean? To be fair, I reckon every stately home or manor house in England has a ghost.'

'Ah, but Lady Dorothy's one of the best,' Will said. 'She's supposed to have had a secret tryst with the heir to Hoghton Tower. Now, her family were Catholic and the Hoghtons were Protestants. Apparently, Dorothy's brother found out about the liaison and murdered young Hoghton. Dorothy topped herself and has often been seen floating about in flowing white robes.'

'Well, she didn't come floating around the refectory when we were there,' I said.

'I'll tell you what I thought was spookier than any ghost,' Will said. 'The priest hole. Did you see that?'

'We didn't do the tour. To be honest, we were just there for lunch. Ruth had an appointment in Preston and we couldn't stop.'

'You missed something there, mate. There's this beautifully ornate fireplace and the hidey-hole is ingeniously concealed behind it. It's really cramped. It must have been horrendous to be holed up there in terror of vicious marauding Prots bent on torturing and killing you. One priest was discovered towards the end of the Fifteenth Century. They dragged him out and executed him on the spot.'

'And he haunts the place as well, does he?'

'Probably. And then there was William Harrison. The Harrisons owned the place in Victorian times. I can't remember why, debt probably, but William blew his brains out with a pistol and he haunts the upper rooms. He's not a pretty sight allegedly.'

'Of course,' I said, 'while we're at it, Lancashire is witch country, isn't it? You can see Pendle Hill from our bathroom window on a clear day.'

'Hey, can you remember that school trip to Pendle Hill from St. John's?'

'I certainly can. We were excited about it for weeks before.'

'Yeah. Do you remember, Mr Butterfield told us all about these poor families who accused each other of witchcraft till it became a kind of contagion. Rivalries were blown out of proportion and there were attempts to settle old scores - until loads of them were imprisoned in Lancaster Castle in terrible conditions until they came up before the Assizes.'

'And ten of them were hanged.'

'And we all drew pictures of witches on broomsticks and they went up on the wall.'

'Except mine was of Granny Demdike making a potion,' I said. 'She had a pointy hat and was throwing up into a big cauldron with multicoloured flames underneath. On one side of her was an enormous marmalade cat and on the other a golden toad which was the same size as the cat. Do you remember it?'

'No,' said Will.

'Well you should. It was a masterpiece. Mr Butterfield said so. He gave it pride of place in the display.'

'And your head doubled in size that very day.'

'Exactly. Mind you, the trip was a bit of a washout in the end, if I remember correctly.'

'It was, wasn't it? We set off in glorious sunshine and must have driven the Buttercups bananas in the coach by singing "Ten Green Bottles" over and over. And then again, the climb was a bit wearing - not that it was particularly steep - it wasn't - but the grass was really tussocky so it was hard going for our little legs.'

'You particularly,' I said laughing. 'You were a midget in those days, weren't you?'

'I was two years younger than you, and you know it.'

Actually, Will had been quite small for his age, though he'd kept up with us in all the antics of the Brookhouse gang. He must have shot up like a hothouse plant in his teens, because when I caught up with him decades later, and we solved the mystery of 'the skelly in the bog' together, he was taller than me. Looking at him now, in the Adelphi, he still looked fresh-faced despite the years.

'We stopped halfway up to eat our butties,' I said. 'It was still sunny but there were big clouds. You could see their giant shadows passing over the patchwork of fields below us.'

'That's right,' Will said, 'and, as we carried on, the clouds got thicker and darker and by the time we reached the top we were *in* one - dense, wet mist. "Stick together, boys and girls," Mr Butterfield said, "or the boggarts will get you." Have you ever seen a boggart Tom?'

'No. Have you?'

'No. I always imagined they were green and covered with warts - oh, and they had hooves instead of feet.' Anyway, there we were on the top of Pendle Hill with not a witch in sight. In fact, there was nothing in sight. No view. Nothing. Sod all.'

'I remember,' I said. 'Half an hour earlier we'd been sweating and now we were shivering. You could only see a couple of yards in front of you, it was so dense. I remember we spent some time looming out of the mist at each other, pretending to be witches, but we soon got fed up of that. Mr B hoped it would pass, but it didn't, so we started the descent. And it rained all the way back to the coach.'

'We were drenched,' Will said. 'And when the driver started the engine and turned the heating up, the windows steamed up immediately, we were so sodden.'

'Well,' I said, 'that's Lancashire for you: superstition and rain.'

6 THE EIGHTH BOOK

'WERE YOU SUPERSTITIOUS as a kid, Tom?' Will asked.

'No more so than most,' I said. 'Actually, I think I was pretty fearless - or I wouldn't have climbed the mill chimney or encountered the rats in the canal tunnel or been fazed when my dog dug up a human skeleton.[3] I'd have been deeply unsettled by Grandma's séances if I'd not been pretty tough, wouldn't I?'

'I suppose,' Will said.

'I *was* frightened by some pretty weird things when I was little though.'

'Like what?'

'OK, well, when I was no more than a toddler, it was trains - well, not trains exactly - it was the noise of trains in the shunting yard. I would be lying in bed with sheets pulled up to my chin and I could hear clanking and banging and rattling and the shriek of metal on metal. Brookhouse Lane was not too far from the yards but all the same the noises were kind of echoey. I was terrified

---

3 *The Northern Elements*, p.129

and would cry my eyes out until Mum or Dad came to console me.

'One night, Dad had had enough. He opened the bedroom window wide, lifted me out of bed, and thrust me bodily through the window and out into the night air where I could hear the shunting noises, unmuted, as it were, without the echo effect. "See, Tommy, it's just trains. No need to be frit, cock." And do you know what?'

'What?'

'I was cured! For life. Never frightened of trains again. Loved them ever since. I used to get Dad to take me on his bike to Daisyfield Station to watch the steam trains from the level crossing.'

'I think I'd have been traumatised for life,' Will said.

'By the steam trains?'

'No, you barmpot. By being stuck out into the night air naked. He could have dropped you.'

'No way, he had a good grip. And I was only little, remember. Besides, it worked didn't it? And any road, I wasn't naked. I was wearing my 'jamas.'

'Well, thank God for that,' Will said.

'On the other hand, there was one phobia my dad couldn't cure,' I said.

'Which was?'

'Muffin the Mule. I was terrified of Muffin the Mule.'

'What the hell is Muffin the Mule? It sounds like some kind of deviant activity.'

'It was a wooden string puppet. This woman called Annette Mills used to sit at a grand piano and she used to talk to Muffin the Mule who would dance about on top. He lived in a caravan and was very naughty.'

'I never saw it,' Will said. 'We didn't have a telly till 1960.'

'Ours was really old-fashioned. It was in a huge carved wooden cabinet but the screen was tiny - about the size of a small microwave. I used to rush home from school to watch *The Woodentops* and *Bill and Ben*, but whenever *Muffin the Mule* came on I was terrified shitless. I used to hide behind the curtains and scream for Mum to turn it off.'

'What were you scared of?'

'God knows,' I said. 'To this day, if there's one of those TV archive programmes on the box and she comes on with that bloody piano and that *thing* clattering about on top of it, I can still feel the old terror rising.'

'You big girl's blouse!'

'I know. It's sad, isn't it? Do you think that counts as a superstition?'

'Mental deficiency more like.'

'I did have a religious phase, you know.'

'Surprise me,' Will said.

'I'd be eight or nine, about the same time as Grandma's séances, and I made a kind of shrine in my bedroom. There was an altar made out of an old wooden wireless casing with a fancy carved sunburst on the front. I put a lace-edged tray cloth on top, nicked from the sideboard downstairs. There were Price's candles in little brass candleholders which I'd bought at the bric-a-brac stall on Blackburn market and there'd be flowers - not lilies and roses like in St John's church - but buttercups and bluebells, even dandelions. But the crucifix - oh, the crucifix - that was something else.'

'Go on.'

'It came from the market as well, from that Catholic stall on the Victoria Street side. The crucifix was plastic and the body of Jesus was luminous: it was green and it glowed in the dark. I would lie there in bed at night and contemplate the body of Our Lord which seemed to be floating in front of me. So here was a boy who was afraid of Pinocchio and Muffin the Mule but not the pale green image of the crucified Christ hovering near his bed every blessed night.'

'You were obviously a very spiritual child.'

'Obviously.'

'Well, now, suppose you tell me what you're working up to with all this talk of the occult and "the other side" and the things in heaven and earth that I'm not aware of. You said you'd explain.'

'OK, I'll stop beating about the bush and come straight to the point. How would you feel about joining me in a bit of sleuthing again?'

'You mean detective work?'

'Yes, I suppose so. I was a bit hesitant about asking you straight out because - well - even though we got to the answers about the skeleton in the midden, it did involve a measure of emotional cost.'

'More so for you than for me,' Will said. 'I mean, finding out that your great grandfather was involved in the death of that poor lad must have been pretty gruelling. And then that letter from the Somme before he was shot to pieces - that was really hard.'

'Yeah, well, I know it got to you too - because of the silver cross and that.'[4]

'It was pretty moving, if I'm honest,' Will said.

'You can say no if you want to,' I said. 'I'll quite understand. I'll follow up the case myself if you're not interested. It's just that I thought we made such a good team.'

'We'll see, but you haven't told me the story yet.'

'Yeah right,' I said. 'Well, it's another cold case. Back in 1980, I'd just moved back to Blackburn and was a junior member of the forensics team under Walter Avery, now Sir Walter. He was a brilliant man and I learnt a lot from him.

'Anyway, we were called out to one of those massive mansions on East Park Road, you know where I mean.'

'Alongside Corporation Park? Yes, I know.'

---

4 *The Northern Elements*, p. 164

'Well, this house had been bought in 1980 by some middle-eastern chap and he'd sent builders in to refurbish it from top to bottom. In the basement, where the kitchens had been in Victorian times, there was a massive fireplace and a cooking range which he wanted taken out and finally the whole thing filled in and plastered. When the workmen removed the range, they found a much smaller alcove or recess behind it that had already been bricked up. It looked to them like a pretty amateur job. The mortar was crumbling and some of the bricks were loose. The men were curious. One of the builders told me later that they had fantasies of buried treasure. They were in for a shock.'

'A body?'

'A skeleton.'

'Murder?'

'Well, it wasn't suicide, was it?'

'Now, now,' said Will. 'It could have been somebody covering up an accident like last time.'

'Excellent, Watson,' I said. 'This is why I want you on board.'

'Patronising git. What did you learn from the body?'

'Well, the rats had been at it. It had been laid in there on its back and some of the bones had been dislodged. There was still some hair on the scalp. There were fragments of clothing and a pair of boots which the rats had gnawed at but which were mostly intact. We gathered all the evidence we could, but we would have to get it back to the mortuary and reassemble the skeleton. The clothing and boots would have to go off to the lab along with hair and bone samples. This was before DNA, of course.'

'Any theories at the scene?'

'Sir Walter surmised that the body was that of a girl, past puberty, but not much. Because of the disturbance of the remains, it wasn't possible at the site to confirm whether the victim was alive or dead when she was bricked in, but Sir Walter was inclined to believe that she was already dead. If she'd been alive, you'd have expected to see signs of struggle inside the enclosure. There would also be signs of bodily fluids and well, excrement, if she'd been there for some time. We carried out tests, but there was nothing. The builders had disturbed the bricks, of course. Nevertheless, they were carefully numbered and taken away for further analysis.'

'Time of death?'

'Date of death, you mean. You've been watching too much *Endeavour*. This was back in 1980.'

'Date of death then?'

'The remains of the boots suggested Victorian times. The post mortem and analysis of the fabrics might enable us to be more precise.'

'Wow!'

'And that, in the end, is why the case was eventually suspended. There was enough going on in the area as it was. Two of the Yorkshire Ripper's murders had been in Manchester and police forces on both sides of the Pennines were on high alert. He wasn't caught until the following year. We had no time to follow up a historic case going that far back.

'It's been at the back of my mind since then and, well, after the "skelly in the bog" case, it moved to the front. Cases are never really closed. Something terrible happened to that poor girl. I want to follow it up. Are you in or not?'

'I'm in.'

'Excellent.'

'What I don't get though is what spiritualism has to do with it.'

'Ah, but you see, I think it may have a lot to do with it. When the builders were redecorating an upstairs room which had been a study, they removed layers and layers of wallpaper. On the ceiling they found writing which alluded to the spirit world.'

'I don't believe you.'

'You will. It was photographed. I'll show you,' I said. 'Oh, heck. Is that the time. I've got to meet Ruth at the station in ten minutes. Sup up.'

Ruth is my wife. She'd been shopping in Manchester as she often did when Will and I met up for a few beers.

'There'll be hell to pay if I keep her waiting. Now here's what I propose. Why don't you come to our place for Sunday dinner. We can go to the Feilden's Arms while Ruth cooks and I can fill you in on what we discovered before the case was suspended.'

'You're on,' Will said.

As we stood in the booking hall waiting for Ruth, Will said: 'You know that séance of your grandma's?'

'Yes. What about it?'

'Well, what was that about "the house of death"?'

'"This boy will do great works in the house of death" you mean?'

'Yeah that. Well that came true, didn't it?' Will said.

'You could say that performing autopsies fits the bill for the house of death, I suppose. I don't know about great works, though.'

'False modesty,' Will said. 'And what was that about the eighth book?'

'"His joy and solace will be the eighth book."'

'Did you crack that?' Will said. 'Did you ever find out what the eighth book was.'

'No,' I said. 'I did think about it. Grandma didn't have a lot of books. There was a pile of *Reader's Digests* in a corner table in my bedroom and there was a little bookcase in the front parlour. Granny was a member of the *Companion Book Club* which was really popular in the sixties and seventies. It was mostly mysteries and thrillers, though I remember being intrigued by one title: *The Shrimp and the Anemone*.'

'Did you read it?'

'No, I keep meaning to.'

'And did you find the eighth book?'

'No, I told you. I counted to the eighth book from the left on the top shelf.'

'What was it?'

'It was *Mrs Beaton's Book of Household Management*,' I said.

Will burst out laughing.

'And what did you learn about yourself from that?' he said.

'I flicked through it. What did I learn about myself from recipes for beef tea, lark pie, ox ears, and tips for the management of servants? Not a lot.'

'What about the Bible?' Will said.

'I don't know. What about the Bible?'

'What's the eighth book?'

'Do you know - it's not exactly on the tip of my tongue,' I said.

'Hang on,' Will said. 'I'll Google it.'

Will took out his mobile phone and tapped the question into the keypad.

'Bloody hell!' he said. 'It's Ruth. It's the Book of Ruth.'

'Well,' I said, 'I'll go to 't foot of our stairs.'

7 BRIEFING

MY JOY AND SOLACE came down the ramp from the platform bearing several colourful carrier bags.

'O lord,' I said, kissing her, 'I hope you haven't bankrupted me again.'

'Don't be such a misery guts,' Ruth said. 'Hello, Will. He's not as tight as he pretends, are you, darling?'

'Who's pretending?' I said.

'Now, I hope you're not too pissed, Tom. I want you to run along to Morrisons and get a few things before we get a taxi. I'll get a cup of tea here with Will. I've made a list.'

'Tell her nothing,' I hissed to Will as she groped in her bag for her shopping list. He winked back.

'I've invited Will to dinner on Sunday,' I said. 'I hope that's all right?'

'Of course it's all right,' Ruth said. 'I've been telling you for ages to bring him over.'

'Be warned,' I said to Will. 'She'll try to mother you.'

'I think Will is quite capable of looking after himself,' Ruth said. 'Off you go - and no daydreaming.'

'What on earth do you mean?' I said.

'Would you believe it, Will?' she said. 'I once sent him off with a shopping list with Paxo on it and he came back with Tampax. Was I supposed to stuff a chicken with tampons? I ask you.'

'I was thinking about a case,' I said.

'No doubt,' she said. 'Now hurry up. It's only a few things.'

'If you're so worried about my capacity to do a bit of elementary shopping, why don't you go yourself?'

'Because I want to talk to Will.'

'O my days,' I said. 'William beware! She doesn't want to mother you. She wants to flirt with you!'

'Go on, bugger off,' Ruth said.

'You've bought more shoes again, haven't you?' I said. 'I can tell.'

'You heard what I said,' Ruth replied. 'Get on with it.'

The following Sunday, I drove out to Cherry Tree and picked Will up and took him back to our house at Mellor. There was no point in his catching a train into Blackburn and there were no buses on a Sunday. It had been agreed that he should stay at ours overnight and I would drive him back on Monday morning. That way we could have a few beers before lunch and a decent wine with the joint. When I'd parked the car we went inside.

Everything was under perfect control in the kitchen which was rather different from my style of cooking.

'What are we having?' I said.

'Lamb,' Ruth said.

'My favourite,' Will said.

'Mine too,' Ruth said. 'Right, you boys. Run along and play. Where are you going?'

'The Feildens Arms, I thought. It's a lovely morning for a walk,' I said.

'Good idea, Tom' Ruth said. 'Lunch is at three. Don't be late. And don't be plastered.'

'It seems a bit unfair to leave you with all the work,' Will said.

'She prefers it,' I said.

'You chauvinist pig!' Will laughed.

'No, really I do,' Ruth said. 'I won't let Tom into the kitchen when I'm cooking. He has a tendency to taste things and add ingredients I don't want him to add, and get underfoot generally.'

'And, conversely,' I said, 'she is not allowed in the kitchen when I'm cooking. She has a tendency to start tidying up and stifling my creativity.'

'Only because you use up every single implement in the house to even boil an egg.'

'Outrageous slander!' I said.

'Go on. Get out of here!' Ruth said, waving a tea cloth at us.

It was indeed a glorious spring morning. We walked along Mellor Brow from Mellor itself to the smaller village of Mellor Brook. To our right lay the Ribble Valley and beyond the purple-green edge of Longridge Fell with the darker scarp of Pendle behind.

'Incredible view,' Will said.

'Yes,' I said, 'the Romans had an observation post up here attached to the Roman settlement at Ribchester. You can see why. Nothing moves for miles in any direction without its being visible from up here.'

White blossom covered the hawthorn hedges like snow along our route. There were bluebells in the hedgerows. Fat buds were unfurling on sycamore and beech trees although a mighty ash standing in the middle of a field would be a while yet before it came into leaf. Lambs ran to their mothers as we passed and their cries were strangely like the cries of human babies. There was real warmth in the sun.

And all this was in sharp contrast to the dark tale Will and I were about to explore.

There was a little fire in the hearth in the pub despite the sunshine streaming through the windows - an insurance policy against the Lancashire weather which can change at the drop of a hat. I have known many a day of dazzling sunshine eclipsed quite suddenly by black rain clouds boiling down from the fell.

But for now the atmosphere in the pub was convivial, what with the fire and the sunbeams. I was greeted by the regulars around the bar as one of their number. I was accustomed to referring to them as 'amiable old middle class buffers' when talking to Ruth.

'Like you,' she would say, and I would have to concede the point.

We took our beer to a quiet corner of a side bar, away from the pool table and the restaurant area. Sunday lunches here were good - but not on a par with Ruth's.

'Now then, Watson, to work,' I said. 'Where were we?'

'Did the autopsy tell you anything new?' Will asked.

'Not a great deal in terms of her identity,' I said. 'It confirmed that the remains were those of a girl in her early twenties - older than we thought at first. This was largely based on dentition but we also took into account the development of the skull and pelvic girdle. We had better luck in identifying the cause of death.'

'Tell.'

'Under magnification, we observed a fracture in the hyoid bone and x-rays confirmed that to be the case.'

'And what is the hyoid bone, if you please?'

'The hyoid bone is a small u-shaped bone at the root of the tongue in the front of the neck. A fracture is usually a sure sign of strangulation, though whether manually or with a ligature we weren't able to tell.'

'Murder then?'

'Well, like you said, 't could have been suicide by hanging or some kind of accident. Whatever the case someone needed to conceal the body. We need to ascertain a motive. What is certain is that the poor girl died before she was immured.'

'Immured?'

'Walled up.'

'You don't half come up with some posh words.'

'Comes with the job.'

'Did you get any closer to a date of death? Do they use carbon dating?'

'Archaeologists have been using it for some time to find the age of fossilised bones but we don't use carbon dating for the recent present. It's based on the decay time for Carbon 14 and the error for less than 500 years is too great. You could be eighty to a hundred years out either way, which is no use to us. And that's if there was no modern day contamination.

'But there was another factor which suggested the later Victorian era and which might prove to be important.'

'Which was?'

'The boots and the clothing. The style of the boots confirmed our late Victorian diagnosis. Even better, on the instep of one of the rat-nibbled boots, we could just make out this...'

I grabbed a beermat and scribbled:

...DLE & SONS
ESTER
EST 1873

'A bit of research came up with:

WM. BRINDLE & SONS
BOOT AND SHOEMAKERS
MANCHESTER
ESTABLISHED 1873

- which gave us a "not before" date.'

'Brilliant!' Will said.

'What's more,' I said. 'There were fragments of a pinafore made of Holland cloth which would once have been white. Holland is a cheap, relatively coarse-woven cloth. There were also shreds of a black French twill dress. Again cheap and serviceable. Taken together the fabrics are indicators of class.'

'Sounds like a maid's uniform,' Will said.

'Watson, you are the wonder of the age!'

'OK,' Will said. 'I get that all this is really creepy: "Servant Girl Walled Up In Victorian Mansion" is a terrific headline - but what's the spiritualist link? You still haven't told me. What was the bit about the writing on the wall?'

'On the ceiling, not on the wall. The decorators found writing on the ceiling, written with paint, probably linseed oil paint. The colour is red ochre - looks a bit like dried blood. Here - take a look.'

I took a number of large photographs from the document case I'd brought with me and laid them out on the table for Will to study.

'What are these symbols?' He asked pointing at a cluster of glyphs:

♏☿♒♎♋♊♓

'Signs of the zodiac,' I said. 'The first one is the symbol for Mars and Scorpio. I don't think they stand for anything much to be honest. Look, they appear in several places, in a different order each time, which suggests that they aren't in code, which is what we first thought. It's more like an attempt to create an atmosphere, a sense of the occult. At the time you could have found the symbols in any almanac.'

'Like *Old Moore's Almanac*, you mean?'

'Exactly,' I said.

'They used to sell that on the newspaper stand in the station,' Will said. 'I bought one once, out of curiosity. It was all cobblers but fascinating cobblers all the same.'

'What do you make of these inscriptions then?' I said, pointing to different parts of the photograph. 'This:

Mt 1914

And this:

Mk 1014

And this

Lk 1816?'

'Dates?' Will said.

'No,' I replied. 'Try again.'

'I get it. Matthew, Mark, Luke. Bible references.'

'Excellent, Watson,' I said.

'So: *Mt 1914* is Matthew, Chapter 19, Verse 14?'

'Correct.'

'And I suppose you looked them up?'

'Of course,' I said. 'They all refer to the incident where the disciples want to prevent the little children approaching Jesus.'

'"Suffer the little children to come unto me..."' Will said.

'"And forbid them not..."'

'"For of such is the Kingdom of God,"' Will concluded. 'They taught us well at St John's.'

'They did. What about this one? Mt. 2820.'

'St John's didn't drill us in chapter and verse. You'll have to enlighten me.'

I pulled open the little reporter's notebook with its elastic band to mark the next blank page and flicked through it.

'Here we are,' I said. '"Lo, I am with you always, even unto the end of the world."'

'There's something a bit sinister about that,' Will said. 'A bit chilling.'

'It's not meant to be. It's Jesus speaking. It's meant to be comforting. It's at the very end of the gospel.'

'I always found that post-resurrection stuff a bit weird,' Will said. 'You know Jesus suddenly appearing on the road to Emmaus, or materialising in time for a fish supper.'

'It's meant to be mysterious.The resurrection is a *mystery* in the spiritual sense.'

'But what does it mean? All this writing. What's the relevance?'

'I haven't the faintest idea,' I said.

'It all seems a bit random.'

'I think that may be the point.'

'I mean look,' Will said. 'WINGS - WATERS - SHADOWS - RIVERBANK - GO BACK - UNDER THE TEMPLE - ONLY SURRENDER - SPEAKING IN TONGUES - SORE AFRAID, etc. etc.

'It's gobbledygook. And what do you mean: that's the point?'

'I think it might be automatic writing, sometimes known as passive writing or even spirit writing.'

'What's that?'

'It's when a medium goes into a trance and begins to write, sometimes at speed. She (it's almost always a woman) is not conscious of what she's writing - she is just the conduit. The writing comes from the spirit world. Sometimes it's garbled nonsense, like the rubbish we put into the Cambridge séance, but there may be more lucid messages. Now, when it's all over, the medium will remember nothing and what she has written will be as strange to her as anyone else. She will not be able to decipher the gibberish or explain its significance. She will, however, experience a profound exhaustion.'

'Did your team manage to squeeze any sense out of this mumbo-jumbo?' Will asked.

'Not really. We puzzled about it for days. The vocabulary comes from the same linguistic field. It's apocalyptic. It seems like the language of the Book of Revelation.

'But it wouldn't compose. We got a maths boffin from Manchester University to run it through a linguistics computer programme but we got next to nowhere. There was one breakthrough, however. Look at the photographs again. Look at the corners.'

'The paint is a different colour.'

'Exactly.'

'And the words are in sequence. They make sense.'

'Right. And what do they say?'

Will pointed to one corner.

'It says: FATHER WEEP NO MORE. And here it says: ALL ARE HAPPY ON THE OTHER SIDE. And this one: WE LOVE YOU THROUGH ETERNITY and the last one says: WE WATCH OVER YOU. Wow!'

'What do you make of that?'

'Well, it seems as if the spirits are dead children contacting their living father.'

'That's what I thought too.'

'But who was the medium? And why write on the ceiling? How was it done?'

'My questions too.'

'It's not getting us anywhere.'

'On the contrary. Asking the right questions is what detective work is all about.'

'I still don't see the connexion between the servant girl in the cellar and the spirit writing upstairs,' Will said.

'Neither do I,' I replied.

8 HOWEVER IMPROBABLE

'WELL NOW, MR HOLMES,' Will said. 'If you cannot perceive a connexion I do not see how we are to proceed.'

'Not so fast, Watson,' I said. 'Just because we can't see the connexion doesn't mean to say that there isn't one.'

'It doesn't mean to say that there is either.

'True, but think about it: a servant girl appears to have been strangled and bricked in behind a fireplace. Strange spirit writing appears on the study ceiling which seems to be from dead children reassuring their father that all is well on the other side. Don't you see? The two scenarios occurring in the same house are so weird that they *must* be linked.'

'But that's just a hunch, isn't it?'

'Yes, it is, but that's how a detective moves a case on. We need more such hunches, Will. When I had my forensic scientist hat on, I had to limit myself strictly to observable facts and inductive logic. It wasn't my job to interpret those facts, though of course you couldn't help speculating. It was the detectives' job to construct the narrative and to test its probability. It's the improbability of this case that intrigues me.'

'So, how do we proceed then?'

'Like the original Sherlock Holmes, Will: "Once you eliminate the impossible, whatever remains, no matter how improbable, must be the truth."'

'OK, let's get to the division of labour. What do you propose? I know. You're going to send me back to researching old newspapers again, aren't you? Pages and pages of advertisements for trusses and ladies' corsetry.'[5]

---

[5] See *The Northern Elements*, p.175

I couldn't help laughing at Will's forlorn expression.

'Well, sort of. We need to build up a sense of context. I want you to find out everything you can about spiritualism, anything at all, but more specifically in Blackburn and East Lancashire, and particularly in, say, the last twenty years of Victoria's reign.'

'That should keep me busy and off the streets,' Will said. 'What are you going to do?'

'I am going to follow a hunch. I think the answers are going to be in that house somehow. Believe it or not it's on the market. I am going to see if I can have a look around. When I've dropped you off tomorrow morning, I'm going to call in at Higson and Ingham's Estate Agents at Sudell Cross.'

'You're not going to pretend you want to buy it, are you?' Will said laughing.

'I certainly am,' I said. 'You don't know about my acting talents, do you? I was a member of Blackburn Arts Club for a while.'

'Chief spear carrier, were you?'

'I'll have you know I played a number of lead roles, including Prospero in *The Tempest*. I was "commanding" according to the *Evening Telegraph*.'

'Can I come with you?' Will asked.

'Where?'

'House hunting.'

'No you cannot. You'll give the game away.'

'I won't. I'll be as good as gold.'

'No, I don't trust you,' I said. 'You have enough to do as it is.'

'Slavemaster.'

'Correct. Hey, look at the time. We won't even get a doggy bowl on the back step if we're late. Sup up.'

As we walked back I said: 'Ruth will want to know about our little project, you know.'

'Is it a secret?'

'Well no, not really, but she was very moved by the "skelly in the bog" case.'

'We all were. It was the stuff of tragedy.'

'Exactly, but, you see, I'm not sure I want her involved in such dark material.'

'She seems pretty robust to me.'

'Well, maybe. I don't know. If she asks, shall we tell her?'

'I'd say "yes",' Will said.

'OK, we'll see how it goes.'

On our return the house was full of the savoury smells of a good old English roast dinner. Ruth, unflappable as ever, was making gravy in the roasting tin.

'That smells fabulous,' Will said. 'What's the secret?'

'You put it in the roasting tray and bung it in the oven. After a while you take it out again,' Ruth said.

'That's what passes as Ruth's sense of humour,' I said.

'Open a bottle of wine, Tom, there's a good boy.'

'It shall be as you say, Memsahib,' I said.

'Actually, it's not quite as simple as that,' Ruth said to Will. 'I make a paste with oil, salt and pepper, and mustard powder, make some slits in the skin and rub the paste all over it. Then it goes in a very hot oven for fifteen minutes and then on a low heat for a long time. You can get timings on the internet. Do you cook for yourself, Will?'

I could hear the conversation from the dining room. I'd briefed Ruth about Will's failed marriage and hoped she wasn't going to put her foot in it by being too solicitous.

'I get by OK,' Will was saying. 'I rarely do a full Sunday lunch, though. I sometimes think it must be one of the most difficult things to get right. It's all about the timing, isn't it? I mean getting everything to the table while it's still hot. It's just not worth the hassle for one. And then there's so much washing up, it takes the pleasure out of it.'

'Well, you must come here more often then,' Ruth said.

'I told you she'd try to mother you,' I said, coming back into the kitchen.

'I sometimes let Tom do the roast,' Ruth said. 'He does it the French way with sprigs of rosemary and slivers of garlic slipped under the skin.'

'It's good,' I said.

'It *is* good,' Ruth said, 'but I prefer it *à l'anglaise*. And I'm not ashamed to put redcurrant jelly and mint sauce on my table no matter how much a French housewife with a baguette up her bum might sneer.'

'Mint sauce is terrific with roast potatoes,' Will said.

'It is,' Ruth said. 'Now if you boys want to go and sit up at the table, I'm about to dish up.'

The roast shoulder was everything the savoury aroma had promised, sweet and tender; roast potatoes were crisp on the outside, fluffy on the inside; roast parsnips and buttered carrots melted in the mouth; cauliflower cheese was rich and creamy, and the fruity Chinon I served up slightly chilled was the perfect accompaniment. For afters Ruth produced a bread and butter pudding made with hot cross buns.

'That was excellent, Mrs Catlow,' Will said when he could eat no more. 'I'm fair pogged.'

'Thank you, Mr Melling. Seconds?'

'I couldn't eat another morsel. I'd explode like Mr Creosote. Can I help you clear up?'

'Good lord, no. You're a guest.'

'That's as well because I'm not sure if I can move yet.'

'Coffee?'

'Yes, please.'

'Take Will through to the sitting room, Tom. I'll bring the coffee in there.'

It was over coffee that Ruth dropped her bombshell.

'Right. Out with it,' she said. 'What are you two up to?'

'Who says we're up to anything?' I said.

'Oh come off it, Tom Catlow. The whiff of conspiracy is coming off the pair of you in waves.'

'I suppose we'll have to let her in on it,' I said.

'I reckon so,' Will said.

'Are you going to explain or shall I?'

'You tell her,' Will said. 'You started it. It was all your idea.'

'Yes, but you're not married to her,' I said. 'If she doesn't like it, I'll get the rap.'

'Oh, for heaven's sake,' Ruth almost shouted. 'Grow up - both of you. And stop talking about me as if I wasn't here. Now spill the beans.'

So, taking turns, we explained the situation and what we had learned about it so far.

'That poor girl,' Ruth said. 'All this is fascinating. What do you propose to do about it?'

Will explained our proposed division of labour.

'OK, Tom,' Ruth said as she poured herself more coffee and stirred it slowly. 'I see why you want Will to provide some background, and I see why you need to get into the house to make it give up its secrets, but I think there's something else you need to be doing from the start.'

'What's that?' I said.

'Well, think about it. You don't have much of a *dramatis personae* yet, do you?'

'What do you mean?' I said.

'Well, what've you got? A dead maidservant, the father and some dead children. Well, yes, the father might be the murderer - if a murder was committed. The dead children might have some bearing on the case but can't have carried out the action.'

'Unless you believe in the supernatural,' I said.

'And do you?'

'I have my doubts sometimes.'

Ruth harrumphed.

'Well look,' Ruth said, 'a house that size must have had quite a household. Your skeleton can't...'

I interrupted.

'We should give her a name,' I said.

'Why?'

'It reminds us that we are dealing with a once sentient human individual and not a fiction. Any suggestions?'

'What about Adele?' Will said. 'It's a good Victorian name.'

'I like it,' Ruth said.

'So do I,' I said. 'Unanimous.'

'Right,' said Ruth, 'as I was saying, Adele cannot have been the only servant in a house that size. Besides, what about the mother? And were there other siblings who survived? Other relatives? Was there a nanny? And here's an awkward thought: What if the story of the dead girl happened at a different time from the narrative behind the ceiling messages?'

'I have to admit I hadn't thought of that,' I said.

'We have to interrogate not just the house,' Ruth said, 'but its population over time. We have to look at the census data: you can check it online. I can do that now I have more time. All right? Am I in?'

Ruth is a primary school teacher who recently decided to go part time.

Will and I looked at each other. This was like deciding whether to let a girl join your gang, long ago, when we were kids. Usually the answer was No, because they often wanted to play games where they snogged you, like *What's the time, Mr Wolf* and *Kiss-Catch*. The difference of course was that we were in our sixties and Ruth is my wife.

'She's good, she is,' Will said.

'She is good,' I replied.

I left a slight pause for dramatic effect.

'You're in, kid.'

'Right,' she said. 'I'll get on to it. Oh, and by the way, I'm coming with you.'

'What? Where? When?'

'Tomorrow. To the estate agents.'

'Why?'

'To lend you a bit of class. Otherwise they'd take one look at you and decide that no way are you the type that could afford to buy a property on East Park Road. I can wear my new shoes.'

9 A SUBTERFUGE

'DIDN'T I SAY AT THE STATION that she'll have bought new shoes?' I said to Will. 'She probably has more shoes than Imelda Marcos by now.'

'I think you sometimes forget that you are on a pension while I'm on a salary,' Ruth said.

'Are you planning on wearing anything apart from your new shoes?'

'I think I'll wear the navy suit I got for Nicholas's wedding. It cost the earth and I've only worn it once.'

Nicholas is our son.

'And don't think you are going to be accompanying me in that moth-eaten, out-at-elbow cardigan. I'm surprised they even serve you at the Feilden's Arms. Out of pity probably. You can wear your court suit.'

I have three or four serviceable off-the-peg suits and one bespoke one, beautifully cut and very expensive which I had made for court appearances when I was still in post, and which has never left the wardrobe since I retired.

'And don't bother rolling your eyes at Will,' Ruth said. 'Whoever heard of someone enquiring about the purchase of a house worth nearly two million *wearing a cardigan*?'

'I should think a man with that kind of money could afford to wear whatever he liked at a mere estate agent's,' Will said.

'He has a point, Ruth,' I said. 'Do you know, I think I'll wear a snorkel and flippers - and speedos.'

'In Blackburn? In April? You're off your chump.'

'I wasn't serious.'

'No, but I am. Court suit. End of.'

'As my liege lady commands.'

'Show Will the print-out,' Ruth said, clearing up the coffee things and heading for the kitchen. 'It's pretty impressive.'

I had looked up the house on Zoopla and printed out the details. I don't have a colour printer but all the same the black and white photograph was, as Ruth said, 'impressive'. It had been taken from a low angle to enhance its imposing nature, a massive Victorian mansion of yellow brick with all manner of gothic ornamentation: finials on the roof ridge; mansard windows below the roof; various turrets and stone cornucopia; an octagonal belvedere, and a deep balcony with wrought iron railings in front of three of the enormous windows overlooking the park.

It was strange to be looking at a building where I had spent many hours in 1980 trying to unravel its dark secret.

Higson and Ingham's literature read:

> ***Wastwater House*** *(built 1873) 4 Recep. Large dining room. 8 Bedrooms (2 ensuite). 2 bathrooms. First floor study. Very large kitchen (with dumb waiter) in basement. Park view. Large garden at rear with gazebo. Orchard. Coach house with parking for three vehicles. £1,778,000.*

'It's a blooming palace,' Will said.

'It must have been quite something in its heyday,' I said. 'It would have taken a number of servants to keep it running. But just think of the heating bills.'

'I'd really like a look around,' Will said.

'And so you shall - if we get lucky with the keys tomorrow.'

However, the following day things did not exactly go to plan.

Will asked to be dropped off at the Library rather than the railway station.

'As good a place as any to start my menial researches,' Will said. 'Give me a ring tonight and let me know how you get on.'

'Will do,' I said.

We found a parking space at the Richmond Street car park and walked the short distance to Sudell Cross. Only the day before, Will and I had been enjoying bright spring weather. Now Ruth and I had to walk with our heads bowed against a brisk wind which threw gusts of chilly rain into our faces.

The estate agents' offices were on the ground floor of a building which had once served a more dignified purpose judging by the grand architecture of the upper storeys. On the ground floor, however, there were only the plate glass windows, with their racks of photos of properties for sale or rent, such as you might find on any high street in the country. The only difference, I supposed, was that the asking prices were likely to be very much lower than in many other areas.

We weren't going to stop to find out as a flash of lightning, followed by a bang of thunder, turned the thin drizzle into a proper April downpour. My best suit, so fresh and crisp this morning, probably looked less pukka now and it crossed my mind that Ruth was probably regretting wearing her new shoes.

We stepped inside to a warm fug which immediately subjected my specs to a total white-out. Taking them off to wipe them, I could see that there were four desks in the reception area. At one of them was a tall thin girl with a cherry red blouse and a grey-blue cashmere cardigan draped over her shoulders. She looked as if she had just walked out of *Country Life*. She had an accent to match as she talked in an animated way on the phone, presumably to a client. Occasionally a flattened 'a' or a rounded 'u' gave away her Lancashire origins.

At the desk in front of her was a younger red-cheeked girl, with a hand-knitted jumper in multi-coloured stripes. She had spiky ginger hair and hooped earrings. The two other desks were unoccupied.

'Take a seat, please,' the younger girl said, barely looking up from her keyboard. 'Mr Frost will be with you in a moment.'

We sat down on the functional padded chairs. My wet clothes were sticking to me and felt cold, especially across my chest and the top of my thighs. The expensive college cufflinks with the wheel of St Catharine in gold against a crimson background looked a little silly in the floppy wet cuffs which had been so dapper in the morning. I sneaked a look at Ruth who looked very cross. Her coiffure was rather dishevelled and a strand of hair hung over one eye.

Mr Frost appeared after a few minutes through a door at the back of the office, carrying a batch of cardboard folders. He was a good-looking, fresh-faced young man of about twenty with thick, floppy blond hair and a lightweight pale blue suit which seemed ever so slightly too big for him.

'Oh dear,' he said. 'Is it raining?'

I could have hit him. Given that we were as sopping as if we had been left behind by the ark on the last sand-bank on earth; given that outside it had gone as dark as at the crucifixion and rain was beating against the windows, and given that he was unflustered and unforgivably dry, I had to restrain myself. Ruth held my wrist. She has a knack for intuiting my feelings.

'It is a trifle moist,' I said.

The mild sarcasm went right over his head.

'What can I do for you today?' he said.

I expressed an interest in Wastwater House.

He whistled.

'Much as I would like to get my hands on the commission for making a sale on that little property,' he said, 'it's way beyond my pay grade. Our Mr Higson is dealing with that baby in person. If you hang on to your horses a minute, I'll see if he's free.'

He disappeared through the rear door again. For some reason, Ruth was still holding my wrist in a tight grip.

'He looks about twelve,' I said.

'He's eighteen,' Ruth said.

'How do you know?' I said. 'O Lord, do you know him?'

'I used to teach him. Tom, we can't go ahead with this.'

'He doesn't seem to have recognised you.'

'We don't know that. For all we know he might be telling Mr Higson that his old primary school teacher wants to buy a two million pound mansion. It's ridiculous. You'll have to come clean, Tom.'

'How do you mean?'

'Tell the truth.'

'We'll look foolish.'

'Not as foolish as we'll look if Nick Frost *has* recognised me.'

We had dropped our voices almost to a whisper, but it was hardly necessary. The rain was still rattling on the window, the posh girl was still on the phone, and the other girl was now wearing headphones as she typed.

Just then the boy returned.

'Mr Higson is with a client at the moment. He wondered if you wouldn't mind waiting a little while. He reckons he won't be more than ten minutes.'

'That's fine,' I said.

He turned to Ruth.

'It *is* Mrs Catlow, isn't it?'

'It is, Nick.' Ruth was smiling.

'I thought so. You haven't changed a bit, Miss.'

'Neither have you,' Ruth said.

'Don't be daft, Miss,' he laughed. 'I was what - seven or eight when I was in your class?'

'You look the same to me - only bigger.'

'Get away with you, Miss. You're pulling my leg.'

'Only a bit, Nick. And don't call me "Miss"; it's embarrassing.'

'Oh, sorry.'

'How long have you been doing this job?'

'Nearly a year.'

'And do you like it?'

'Love it. I get a company car soon. For taking clients to view properties.'

'Brilliant. And are you behaving yourself?'

'What do you mean, Miss? I mean Mrs Catlow?'

'Tom, this is the boy who declared to me: "They all said I daren't lick a glue stick without feeling sick. They said I couldn't but I SHOWED THEM."'

'O God, now it's my turn to be embarrassed.'

The phone on Nick's desk rang and he answered.

'Mr Higson will see you now,' he said, 'if you'd like to follow me.'

'Told you,' Ruth whispered as we followed him down a corridor to a plush office at the far end.

'Nice to see you again, Miss,' Nick said opening the door. 'Oh shit, sorry. I mean, Mrs Catlow.'

He withdrew blushing furiously.

'What was that about?' Mr Higson said, rising from behind a large uncluttered desk and shaking hands with us.

'Oh, nothing,' Ruth said.

'Now, I believe you've expressed an interest in Wastwater House?'

'Indeed,' I said. 'But first I have to confess to a little subterfuge.'

10 KEYS

WITHOUT BEATING ABOUT THE BUSH I came out with the whole story. Mr Higson listened attentively, nodding from time to time.

'So, you see,' I concluded, 'it would be most helpful if I could gain access to the house, however briefly.'

'Are you looking for anything in particular?'

'I'm afraid it's a case of: "I won't know what it is until I've found it", though I have an instinct that the secret of what happened to that young girl is hidden within the house.'

'He says these mystical things,' Ruth said, 'and you might think he's crackers - but then events prove him right.'

'Oh, I'm sorry, darling,' I said. 'I didn't introduce you, did I? How rude. Mr Higson, my wife, Ruth.'

'Delighted. Shall we have some coffee?'

Ruth said it would be appreciated and Mr Higson rang through to Nick.

'I think something might be arranged,' Mr Higson said. 'I'm always happy to help the police.'

'Well, as I said, I'm retired and this isn't official business, but I could give you a couple of numbers at the station so you can check on my credentials.'

'Oh, I don't think that will be necessary, Dr Catlow. You see, your reputation goes before you.'

'What do you mean?' I said.

People didn't usually employ my academic title.

'You were involved in that case of the little boy's skeleton found up by Holy Trinity Church, weren't you?'

'Well, I may have...'

'Yes, he was,' Ruth said.

'I read about it in *The Lancashire Telegraph*. To be honest with you, I'm a bit of a fan of detective fiction - you know, Colin Dexter, Margery Allingham, P.D. James, Agatha Christie, Simenon, etc. - and to have a real murder mystery on one's own turf, as it were, quite fascinated me.'

I decided on the spot that I quite liked this chap - a tad pompous, perhaps - but with good judgement.

Young Nick came in with a tray of coffee and some Nice biscuits. He looked rather sheepish. Ruth gave him a conspiratorial wink as Mr Higson was pouring coffee which cheered him up at once.

'Have a biscuit,' Mr Higson said, proffering the plate. 'They are indeed "nice" biscuits but they should really be pronounced "Nice" like the French town where I assume they originated. I think I learned that from a P.D. James story. I also learned that Nice itself was named after *Nike*, the Greek goddess of victory. Of such obscure detail is the stuff of fiction woven.'

'No doubt,' I said. 'But as you pointed out yourself my field is in the realm of fact rather than fiction.'

'Quite so,' Mr Higson said. 'Thank you, Mr Frost, that will be all.'

Nick, who had been hovering, took his leave.

'Now, Wastwater House,' Mr Higson continued. 'There is quite a story there, I can tell you, and it's a story which explains why I might be able to help you.'

He paused - a little theatrically, Ruth said later.

'Actually, we do have a potential buyer. In fact, we had a number of enquiries but in the end they baulked at the price, which I couldn't lower, for reasons that will become clear. For one thing, the whole place was redecorated from top to bottom and various modern conveniences installed, and the whole plumbing and heating systems comprehensively modernised.

'Sadly, the proposed buyer is a property developer, who wants to turn the building into luxury flats. I say "sadly" because it is a fine building with a great deal of character. The vendor, a Mr Rafiq, is perfectly happy with the proposal, but there will be delays.

'We are waiting for surveyors and an architect to draw up proposals for the conversion. Like solicitors, these are people who like to take their time. When they are ready, they will have to submit their designs for planning permission. This could also take some time.

'Even then, there may be a final barrier. The building is Grade II listed. Any substantive and irreversible alterations may well be out of the question.'

'Is Mr Rafiq still living there?' Ruth asked.

'No, and that is another very curious thing about the situation. Mr Rafiq is in Iran.'

'But, I thought you said that the whole house had been redecorated,' Ruth said.

'The work was done decades ago, wasn't it?' I asked.

'That's correct. As long ago as the 1980s. You've done your homework,' Mr Higson said. 'In fact, Mr Rafiq has never lived there. He set the work in train and only visited once to inspect it, thirty-four years later. This was last November and it was raining much like today. It was also much colder. Mr Rafiq decided he didn't like the North West of England and his agents instructed us to put the property on the market. A bizarre tale, is it not? He has houses in the States, in Europe and the Middle East. He can afford to buy and sell on a whim.'

'Fancy being rich enough to buy a ruddy great big mansion, renovate it, and then sell it again because of the weather,' Ruth said.

'Exactly,' Mr Higson replied. 'And it's not as if he will be making a profit out of the sale, even if it does go through. Few people can afford to buy and inhabit a property like that these days - and fewer still could afford to run it. The fact is, he bought it one summer, because he was enchanted by the view from the balcony of the lake in Corporation Park, and when he saw it again in the cold and the rain he was immediately disenchanted.'

'It's a crying shame,' Ruth said.

'It is indeed, Mrs Catlow, but, that said, things are to your husband's advantage. Whilst plans are quite literally on the drawing board, I see no reason why you should not take a look around. No-one need know that you are not altogether genuine viewers and you would be in nobody's way.'

'That would be very much appreciated,' I said.

'Don't mention it, Dr Catlow. I do have a couple of provisos, however. I don't think that they will inconvenience you very much.'

'Fire away.'

'Firstly, I should be very grateful if you would keep any findings to yourselves. For the time being, at least. The press have a tendency to sensationalise everything - their job, I know, but we are in the business of selling properties, and there are plenty of potential clients out there who would not care to live in a house where a murder has taken place - if that is indeed the case - no matter how long ago.'

'I have absolutely no problem with that. While I was still in post I never briefed journalists, if I could help it, especially if a case was incomplete. There is always the possibility that journalists may prejudice enquiries. It's a habit I've kept up. I agree: we don't want any HAUNTED HOUSE FOR SALE headlines, do we?'

'Certainly not.'

'And your other proviso?'

'What? Oh yes, this one is of a more personal nature.'

'Go on.'

'I wonder if you could let me know how the case progresses. You could rely on my total confidentiality. You might think it a bit silly but I am immensely fascinated by this sort of thing and, you never know, I might be able to help you with further information. I can't think what but, as I say, you never know. Would that be a reasonable *quid pro quo*?'

'Absolutely fine,' I said.

'Splendid. Now, you won't want to go up there in this filthy weather. Let's just look at the forecast, not that the Met office is particularly reliable in this part of the world.'

He pulled up the forecast on his computer screen.

'Ah yes,' he said. 'It should brighten up considerably later in the week. How would, say, next Monday morning suit you?'

I looked at Ruth, and she nodded.

'Perfect,' I said.

'Well, I don't see why I shouldn't send young Mr Frost to meet you with the keys. He's been nagging me about a company car for some time and I think the time is probably right. Besides...' - and he turned to Ruth - '... something tells me you already know each other.'

'He's an ex-pupil,' Ruth said.

'Really? How charming. He's a good lad, very keen. Now, I won't keep you. Ten o'clock at Wastwater House. Mr Frost will be there already.'

He showed us out through a door in the corridor so that we needn't pass through the reception area again. The door led into Simmons Street. It had stopped raining but it was still very gloomy and we were eager to get home and have some lunch.

'Didn't you find him just a little bit absurd?' Ruth said.

'Who?'

'Mr Higson. All that "Mr Frost" stuff and his "*quid pro quo*" and his obsession with crime fiction and did you notice the paisley hanky flopping out of his breast pocket? He was like something out of Dickens.'

'I thought he was perfectly decent,' I said. 'And besides - we got the keys.'

'True.'

'And you met up with your amiable ex-pupil.'

'Very true,' Ruth said.

11 CENSUS

AFTER A LUNCH OF COLD LAMB and salad, Ruth went up to her study to see if she could find out who had lived in Wastwater House in the Victorian era. My own study is a shed at the bottom of the garden. I like it that way.

After changing into the much derided cardigan, I pootled down there with *The Times* and a flask of coffee. There was something slightly hypnotic about the rain crackling on the fibreglass roofing, and I must have dozed off over the crossword. The sun was shining when I woke up. Walking back to the house, I noted that the lawn needed cutting sometime soon.

As I came through the door I heard a scream from above. Fearing something dreadful, I rushed up the stairs. Actually, because the old knees are playing up a bit these days, I hobbled up the stairs - but I hobbled as fast as I could. As I burst into Ruth's study she was waving some printouts at me.

'What on earth is the matter?' I cried. 'Are you all right?'

'Eureka!' she shouted, swivelling round and round on the desk chair as if it were a fairground ride of some sort. 'Bingo!'

'What have you found?'

'Well, Mr Plod, I have found Wastwater House and its inhabitants in 1881 and 1891. I hope you're proud of me.'

'I most certainly am, you clever girl.'

'It wasn't straightforward. I found a free historical site after a bit of fiddling but you could only summon up the census record by surname rather than address. I reckoned that if you could afford to live on East Park Road you must be stinking rich. But how can you tell from a name if its owner is wealthy? So I experimented a bit with your surname. I know you like *Who Do You Think You Are?* on the telly.'

'All right. Spill the beans. Are the Catlows royalty? Or are we axe-murderers?'

'I doubt very much whether an axe-murderer would list the fact as his occupation. And there don't appear to be any dukes in your lineage either. I am afraid the truth is much more mundane. I seem to have married beneath me. Your ancestors all seem to have been involved in the cotton trade in fairly lowly roles: weavers, spinners, carders, winders, overlookers, power loom operators, and poor honest labourers. Even Washington Catlow of Tontine Street in St John's parish was a poor loomer. There is one exception.'

'Don't tell me. Let me guess. I know: Theophilus Catlow was Archbishop of Canterbury!'

'In your dreams! But Arthur Catlow, of Dandy Walk, St Mary's, was a muffin and crumpet maker!'

'Hooray! That's more important than royalty.'

'I didn't know there was a St Mary's in Blackburn,' Ruth said.

'You *do* know,' I replied. 'It must be the cathedral.'

'Of course. Anyway, all this was getting me nowhere. And then I had a brainwave. I guessed that the mayors of Blackburn must have been blessed with dosh back then, so I googled a list of them and started working through the Haydocks and Hornbys and Tattersalls. Even these chaps had weavers and spinners as namesakes.

'But then I struck gold with Cornelius Pickup. Take a look at this:'

CENSUS 1881 Municipal Borough of BLACKBURN St James's

SUR-NAME	Fore-names	Relation-ship	Sex	Age	Occupa-tion	Address
PICKUP	Cornelius	Head	M	44	Banker	Wastwater House East Park Road
PICKUP	Louisa	Wife	F	34		Wastwater House East Park Road
PICKUP	Fanny	Daur	F	13	Scholar	Wastwater House East Park Road
PICKUP	Charlotte	Daur	F	11	Scholar	Wastwater House East Park Road
PICKUP	Eliza	Daur	F	9		Wastwater House East Park Road

PICKUP	Alice	Daur	F	5		Wastwater House East Park Road
YATES	Benjamin	Visitr	M	37	Captain of Steamer	Durham
YATES	Dora		F	38		Durham
USHER	Letitia	Gvrnss	F	23	Gov-erness	Wastwater House East Park Road
FOSTER	Millicent	Servnt	F	41	Housekpr	Wastwater House East Park Road
FOSTER	Betty	Servnt	F	39	Cook	Wastwater House East Park Road
DUXBU RY	Mary A	Servnt	F	14	House-maid	Wastwater House East Park Road
GREEN	Jane	Servnt	F	23	House-maid	Wastwater House East Park Road

'Wow! Amazing work, Mrs Hudson. So what do you notice?'

'What do I notice, you patronising so and so? I notice that there is an age gap between Cornelius and his wife, and that she has been bearing children at roughly two year intervals, all girls.'

'Remember,' I said, 'that the entry only records those present in the house on the night of the census. There may have been boys, for all we know. The Head of a household like that may have chosen to send any boys away to public school.'

'True. Now, presumably "scholar" means simply that the older girls were of school age, while the younger ones had a governess.'

'Agreed.'

'Now the Pickups must have been rolling in it to afford a household with five servants.'

'And there may have been more who did not "live in" - gardeners, for instance, charwomen, a groom, a scullery girl?'

'Could be. They could afford to play host to guests of a respectable social station.'

'My guess is that there was room for quite a house party, if they wanted - beyond a single couple. I wonder what kind of steamship Captain Yates was master of.'

'Have I missed anything?' Ruth asked. 'Have you anything to add?'

'Nothing of any great moment,' I said. 'It may or may not be significant that, guests apart, Cornelius is head of an all-female household. I also noticed elsewhere that Louisa is from Kendal on the doorstep of the Lake District. The house is called Wastwater House. Wast Water is the deepest and most-isolated of the lakes. Is there any connexion? Just a thought.'

'OK, plenty to go on. Now take a look at this. Ten years later:'

CENSUS 1891 Municipal Borough of BLACKBURN St James's

SUR-NAME	Fore-names	Relation-ship	Sex	Age	Occupa-tion	Address
PICKUP	Cornelius	Head	M	54	Retired Banker	Wastwater House East Park Road
PICKUP	Alice	Daur	F	15	Housek-pr	Wastwater House East Park Road
DUXBURY	Mary Ann	Servnt	F	24	House-maid	Wastwater House East Park Road

'Good grief!' I said. The difference was shocking. 'What can have happened?'

'That's what I thought,' Ruth said. 'Some kind of financial crash?'

'Possibly,' I said, 'but I have a gut feeling that something much more sinister was involved. Only the youngest daughter and the youngest servant are left. The daughter is also acting as her father's housekeeper where once there was a full-time paid employee.'

'Where do we go from here?' Ruth said.

'We hypothesise, like good scientists. Now a financial crash would mean drastic economies which would shrink the household. It would explain why some of the servants had to go, but I think it's a pretty weak explanation for the shrinkage of the family.'

'What about the Spanish Flu?'

'Well, it did affect a third of the world's population and go on to claim fifty million lives - but that was just after the First World War. Incredibly contagious, but the wrong time frame for us.'

'Coo! You do know a lot of things, my dear.'

'Now who's being patronising? Let me remind you, my dear wife, that I have a degree in medicine.'

'So you do. Go on.'

'Less well known is the outbreak of influenza in 1889 that became known as "Russian Flu". It hit England in waves, each more devastating than the last. It even hit the royal family and carried off Victoria's eldest son, so it was no respecter of persons. A disease as infectious as that could lay waste to a household as grand as the Pickups, just as easily as a family in a labourer's cottage.

'Then there was smallpox, typhoid fever, yellow fever and scarlet fever, and, although hygiene for the middle and upper classes was improving and the quality of drinking water much better, cholera was still a constant threat.'

'So how do we find out if it was some lethal disease that was visited on the Pickups?' Ruth asked.

'The Registry of Births, Marriages and Deaths.'

'Is it online?'

'It is, but it's back to needle-in-a-haystack work and an encounter with some pretty gruesome handwriting.

Which brings me to another hypothesis: we need to check whether the daughters married. All of them were of marriageable age by 1891. Come to think of it, young ladies were married from their home parish back then. It might be quicker to check the register at St James's church. But even if they were all married off, that doesn't explain why the two remaining members of the family made do with just one servant in a vast house like that, and why Alice was acting as housekeeper.'

'Well, at least we have a plan of action,' Ruth said. 'Hang on. Just a minute, Tom - another brainwave. There might be a family grave at St James's or - given that the Pickups appear to have been very grand - maybe there's even a family vault at Blackburn Cemetery?'

'Genius. If there is it could have evidence of any family members who were not resident for the census. It looks like you've got your work cut out.'

'Excuse me. I have thoroughly enjoyed being your unpaid researcher but I am still a busy teacher, part time or not, and I have lessons to prepare this evening.'

'I thought the bug had got you, that's all.'

'Let's just say that I get the appeal but, no - this all seems like work for Will, though I might be available for menial tasks on occasion, if you treat me nicely.'

'What if I made supper?'

'It would be a start.'

As my signature chicken in cider was simmering away, I rang Will.

'Oh boy,' I said, 'have I got news for you!'

12 WHAT WILL FOUND OUT

'I HAVE SOME MATERIAL OF INTEREST to relay myself,' Will said after I had told him about our visit to the estate agents and Ruth's discoveries. 'But listen, I want to invite you both to lunch next Sunday to thank you for yesterday.'

'Oh Will,' I said. 'There's no need for that.'

'Of course there isn't - which will make it all the nicer. I thought we could go to the Inn at Whitewell. The food is amazing, if you've never been.'

'We haven't but I know it has a fantastic reputation.'

'I will be your designated driver.'

'That's very generous of you,' I said.

'Well, look at it like this. It wouldn't be much of a thank you present if one of you had to do the driving and couldn't have a drink.'

'We will be deeply honoured,' I said.

And this was true, for few got to ride in Will's pride and joy, a champagne-coloured Alfa Romeo Giulia, which he kept in tip-top condition in his garage. He loved it even more than rugby league and cricket, which was saying something. When he was teased about the fact that it appeared hardly ever to be on the road, he would say: 'Look: I can get from Cherry Tree to Blackburn by train in six minutes - five, if it doesn't stop at Mill Hill. There are sixteen trains a day in that direction and sixteen trains back. Why should I risk getting her scraped in a car park by some biddy who can't manoeuvre, or a hoodie with a grievance and a set of keys?'

You didn't press it too much or he'd get touchy. I knew he liked to go for long drives in the countryside and I suspected he looked for quiet B roads where he could indulge the car's capacity for speed. So, when I said we would be deeply honoured, I meant it.

'But let's meet up for beers as usual during the week,' he said. 'Bring Ruth's printouts. I've got quite a bit of stuff on spiritualism. Thursday as usual?'

'Fine. Where?'

'What about The Postal Order?'

'On Darwen Street?'

'That's the one. 12.30?'

'Done.'

The Postal Order is a Wetherspoons with substantial food and cheap beer. It is sited in the old General Post Office, a building of magnificent Edwardian grandeur, with a spacious interior where it would be possible to find a relatively quiet corner for a chat. There were paintings and photo displays everywhere featuring the town's history so it seemed quite appropriate in a way. As with all Wetherspoons pubs you needed oxygen and sherpas to get to the toilets.

Will was already there when I arrived. We ordered burgers and beer and set to. I showed him the printouts and outlined the action plan Ruth and I had evolved.

'Makes sense,' he said. 'Looks like Births, Marriages and Deaths is my line.'

'Hatches, Matches and Dispatches? Yes. We hoped you'd say that.'

'What about you?'

'I'm going to try and see if I can get a look at the BMD register at St James's. Do you remember, with the last case, Will, we kept coming up with dead ends? We seem to be making better progress with this one.'

'Well yes, but, if I dare say it, I think you may have missed out one rather obvious step.'

'Go on, say it. I triple dog dare you, as we used to say.'

'Well, shouldn't you have checked the next census? In 1901, presumably? To see if Pickups were still living in the house?'

'Of course we should! 'Ecky thump, of course we should! We were so excited by what we'd found we didn't follow up on the next step. Like you say: obvious.'

'Easy done.'

'Only if you're a bit retarded. I feel a right plunger-head. Hang on though. I can do this on my phone.'

I'd remembered the site Ruth had been using and did a search for Cornelius Pickup in 1901.

Nothing.

'No show,' I said to Will.

'Maybe he moved out of town? Or maybe the upkeep of the house was proving just too much?'

'Maybe. Or maybe he just died. He'd have been getting on after all. I'll tell you what we'll do. I'll get in touch with Mr Higson at the estate agents and see if we can get a gander at the history of the house between the Pickups and Mr Rafiq's purchase in 1980. His solicitor will have the deeds but Higson might have a copy.'

'That makes sense.'

'OK Will, what have you found out?'

'Right, given that my brief was very broad and given that I've only had a few days to get started, I have some interesting bits and pieces for you.'

'Fire away.'

Will produced his reporter's notebook and undid the elastic.

'In no particular order then. First: your grandma's red Indian - what was his name?'

'Blood Moon.'

'Right. Well Blood Moon was in no way unique. In fact, red Indian spirit guides were coming out of the woodwork all over the place, especially in the West Riding of Yorkshire, Lancashire and the West Midlands.'

'I suppose we should really call them "Native Americans",' I said.

'Do you remember when we used to go to the Saturday matinée at the Star in Little Harwood?' Will said. 'We'd play "Cowboys and Indians" on the way home. You'd make a gun out of two fingers and a thumb and you'd hold your wrist with your left hand and go *kchoo, kchoo* and blow the smoke away from the muzzle.'

'And if you were being shot at, you'd hurl yourself to the ground and roll over a couple of times to dodge the bullets.'

'Well, "Cowboys and Native Americans" doesn't quite work. It doesn't have the same ring to it, does it? Anyway, the point is that the craze for spiritualism in the nineteenth century was an American import. Perhaps it came over with the raw cotton. Some Americans - and Canadians - were impressed by the earth-water-sky religions of the Indians and by their reverence for the ancestors. It became a sort of cult.'

'Like proto-hippies, you mean?'

'In a way, yes, though they didn't see any clash with fundamentalist Christianity - you know: the resurrection of the dead, life everlasting, and Jesus's back to basics menu.'

'Got you,' I said. 'That explains Grandma's mixture of hymns and prayers and the occult.'

'Exactly,' Will said. 'Anyway, the fashion crossed the Atlantic.'

'That sort of explains why it hit the western counties first, right?'

'Yeah, but also London, inevitably.'

'Another sign of the trend was the massive popularity of *The Song of Hiawatha*. Remember chanting that at St John's?'

'By the shores of Gitche Gumee,' I began, 'By the shining Big-Sea-Water...'

Will continued: 'Stood the wigwam of Nokomis, Daughter of the Moon, Nokomis.'

'Et cetera,' I said.

'Et cetera. Now the point is that Blood Moon is a bit of a stereotype, a cliché. Thanks to Longfellow, native Americans came looming out of wardrobes all over the North.'

'Had they been living in wigwams in Narnia?' I said.

'Don't be facetious,' Will said.

'Sorry. Go on.'

Will consulted his notebook.

'Now, spiritualism was at its height in England in the late Victorian period, the nineteen-twenties and thirties, and in the fifties. Can you think why that might be?'

'Well, in the aftermath of the two world wars, I suppose people wanted to believe that their loved ones were not wholly annihilated.'

'That's right,' Will said, 'and after the Great War especially, when a generation of young men was wiped out in four years, mothers and sisters and daughters and sweethearts desperately wanted to believe that the carnage wasn't final, and that they would meet again in the "sweet by and by".'

'That's from a hymn, isn't it?'

'Yup. And a very popular one with spiritualists for obvious reasons. Now, why the late 1800s, do you think?'

'High mortality rates?'

'Right. Especially infant mortality rates. Family bereavement was a fact of everyday life. Childbirth was a perilous business, both for mother and baby. You can see why a movement that seemed to offer proof of immortality would bring with it profound consolation.'

'And this fits in with our speculations about the writing on the ceiling.'

'Indeed it does,' Will said. 'Now, are you ready for my *pièce de résistance*?'

'Bring it on.'

'*Meine Damen und Herren, Mesdames et Messieurs, Ladies and Gentlemen!*' Will said. 'I give you...Pocahontas!'

13 POCAHONTAS

'WHAT?'

'Pocahontas.'

'Yes. The native American princess. What about her?'

'You asked me what I could find out about spiritualism in Blackburn. Well, firstly, it was rife and, secondly, there were sceptics about. There's a bit of a paradox here, you see.'

'How do you mean?'

'I mean that while the Victorian period saw an upsurge in the popularity of spiritualism - even the Queen herself was known to have dabbled...'

'Albert, are you there?' I squeaked in falsetto.

'Exactly. Now at the same time it was the Age of Science - and the scientists disapproved of what they regarded as medieval superstition. Oddly enough, Freud was very interested in the spirit world and Conan-Doyle was wholly convinced. The creator of Sherlock Holmes even believed in fairies. Meanwhile Harry Houdini was contemptuous. He spent a lot of time exposing fraudulent mediums. After all, this was a man who knew every illusion in the book. In fact, he invented most of them. He'd have smoked out your gran in no time.'

'Fascinating, but what's this got to do with Blackburn and Pocahontas?'

'Patience, patience. I'm coming to that.'

'Go on.'

'Thing is, these mediums could become quite famous. They would put on elaborate stage shows featuring telepathy, telekinesis, healing and even materialisations.'

'What's that?'

'The medium actually caused the spirit guide to appear in person, as it were, usually from some kind of curtained cabinet.'

'Like a conjuring trick?'

'Presumably. Now these performing mediums attracted large audiences, paying audiences, and they went on tour. They even had managers.'

'And one of them came to Blackburn?'

'I should think lots of them came to Blackburn, but, more importantly, one of them was exposed as a fraud in Blackburn.'

'Tell, tell.'

This was genuinely exciting.

'Enter Miss Wood, a young medium whose spirit guides were "Maggie", "Benny" and "Pocahontas", a native American child who was usually referred to as "Pocha" or "Pocka".'

'Aha!' I said. 'Now I'm with you.'

'Aha, indeed,' Will said, blowing on his finger nails and polishing them on his lapel. 'In the summer of 1877, Miss Wood was caught out whilst masquerading as the spirit of Pocka at a séance. I couldn't find out where, but my guess would be the Theatre Royal or the Exchange, opposite the Town Hall. She had emerged from the usual cabinet in diaphanous clothing and eerie lighting. Unluckily for her she was physically seized and exposed as being all too mortal.'

'Where did you find out about this?'

'It seems she was contacted by *The Blackburn Times*. She may even have sold her story to them.'

'Bravo! Well done, Will!'

'Oh, there's more. She was unable to get back to the safety of the cabinet and (I quote) "the medium was found on the floor, near the curtain of the recess, in an attire which was confined to chemise, stockings, and a pair of ...."'

'A pair of what?'

'What do you think?'

'Knickers?'

'The *Blackburn Times* just has a line instead of the unmentionable word.'

'I suppose her career was ruined?' I said.

'It looks like it, although she tried to get out of the situation by speaking in the voice of the child, Pocka. She said she had been controlled by an evil spirit who had (and I quote again) "all but stripped her naked and sent her out of the circle".'

'Did people buy it?'

'Nah, not really. Hang on.'

He flipped through his notebook again.

'Here we are,' he said. 'This is from *The Medium and Daybreak*.'

'Visionary title. What is it?'

'As far as I can tell, it seems to be the principal periodical for followers of spiritualism. Here goes: "If Miss Wood will sell herself to the degrading manipulation of newspaper reporters, that they may, through her disgrace, earn a small pittance by writing special reports of their ignoble triumphs, she must be content with the wages of such conduct."'

'That's a pretty haughty tone, isn't it?'

'Yeah, it is,' Will replied. 'It sounds like a kind of excommunication, doesn't it? Actually, in later issues, the writer, a Mrs Burns, evolved a pretty clever slant on the affair. The suggestion was that Miss Wood had been reduced to this fraud by a decline in her powers. It was well-known that mediumship put a strain on both body and mind and that any medium's powers would weaken over time. A month later, Mrs Burns argued that Miss Wood *should* share her story for the good of others.'

'So Miss Wood is being painted as a kind of exception, a medium who was cheating because of the decline of her powers?'

'That's right. Here's another excerpt that intrigued me. It's a clever slur on Miss Wood. "Drink," Mrs Burns declares, "is often to be found to be at the bottom of the trouble. It is my experience that intemperance has the direst consequences for a medium's powers."'

'What happened to Miss Wood?' I asked.

'I don't know,' Will said. 'She never performed again in Blackburn, that's for sure, or anywhere where the *Blackburn Times* is read. I suppose there was nothing to stop her decamping to some other part of the country where she was unknown and materialising as Pocahontas to Geordies or Brummies.'

'Did that put an end to the credibility of these performances in Blackburn though?'

'It seems not. In the autumn of that year a Miss Guppy promised a display of levitation by spirit hands and claimed that if the ambience was right she could sometimes cause the spirits of dead relatives to speak through her or even to materialise. Apparently, some spoilsports claimed that these materialisations were identical to each other, but the bereaved welcomed the apparitions with passionate recognition. So, no to your question. The game wasn't up. Halls and theatres and churches continued to be packed. You've got to remember that this was superb theatre and audiences loved it, whether they believed in it or not.'

'And I suppose,' I said, 'that the believers were motivated by a need to deny the finality of death and that they continued to believe even in the face of evidence that seemed to disprove their faith.'

'Not surprising,' Will said, 'when the established religion of the country urges us to believe in the resurrection of the dead.'

'Was there a spiritualist church in Blackburn?'

'There was a Spiritualist Temple on St Peter Street. I'll bet your gran and the aunties will have attended. It's not far from Hope Street. It wasn't built until 1901 so it wouldn't have been available to the Pickups but perhaps there was a predecessor, though I haven't found one so far. But then, there was no objective need. Jesus said: whenever two or three are gathered together in my name, you've got a church, or words to that effect. I imagine that was very much the attitude. People held séances in each other's houses, like your gran, or in hired rooms - and then there were the big theatrical extravaganzas like Miss Wood's.'

'Is it still there?'

'No. It was demolished. In the slum clearances of the sixties, I think.'

'Was there a replacement?'

'Yes, there is and it's still functioning - on Prince's Street off Montague Street. It's called The Spiritualist Centre and it has healing rooms and mediums' rooms. It also has a website.'

'Can you consult the departed online?' I said.

'Not yet,' Will laughed. 'No doubt that will come. Actually, it's quite an attractive modern building.'

'I wonder what goes on in there.'

'Well, Mr Holmes, you are about to find out. I am going to attend a meeting this very evening. I telephoned the number on the website and a very nice lady said I would be most welcome. I did explain that I was not exactly a believer but I would give the proceedings my utmost respect. See what I am prepared to do in furtherance of the cause. Do you want to come?'

While I can see that any ritual which can bring solace to the bereaved or to the lost cannot be bad, the idea of a séance gave me the creeps. Perhaps it was a result of my subliminal shame for my behaviour at that fraudulent séance in Cambridge all those years ago. Who knows?

'Not on your nelly,' I said.

14 THE INN AT WHITEWELL

I WROTE SOMEWHERE[6] that detective work on a murder case is like watching a video in reverse. You have the cadaver and you work backwards through the *who*, *what*, *where*, and *when*, uncovering the means and opportunity as you go, until you arrive at the event itself, and the *why* - the motive.

That all makes it sound very orderly whereas in fact it's usually a messy and random business, with many a false lead, twisting paths culminating in dead ends and

---

[6] *The Northern Elements*, p. 157

lots of red herrings. I realise I'm mixing my metaphors. Let me try again.

Perhaps it's more like moving through concentric circles. You start off swinging wide and the evidence you've gathered seems random and distant from your aim, but as more evidence comes in, as hunches are followed up, and things begin to interlock, the circles tighten until you arrive at the centre.

I was explaining these thoughts to Will and Ruth as we sat with our apéritifs in the Inn at Whitewell.

Will had said that he felt that, although we seemed to be making fast progress with the case, the facts that we had gleaned so far seemed to be haphazard.

'Is there any way you can move across the circles faster?' Ruth said.

'Not really. Each case is different,' I said. 'I suppose a certain doggedness helps. And don't forget the colossal importance of luck. Remember Aunt Cassie's legacy? Maybe we'd never have got to the bottom of the case of "the skelly in the bog" if we hadn't found Daniel's letter.'

Great Aunt Cassandra's 'legacy' had been three dusty boxes of memorabilia left to my father and passed on to us when he died. We had looked through it in a cursory sort of a way at the time, and consigned it to the attic for years. Our researches on the earlier case prompted us to retrieve it, and a more careful examination turned up a letter, hidden behind a photograph of my great grandfather in military uniform, written the night before he was killed in the Battle of the Somme. In it he confessed to my great grandmother, Maisie, that as a child he had been involved in the accidental death of a playmate. He went on to describe how he and his friend had hidden the body in an outside privy near Larkhill.

This anguished confession had helped us solve our case, but it had moved my wife and me very deeply, and Will too, I think.

The Inn at Whitewell is a delightful rural pub and restaurant in the Trough of Bowland. Professional Yorkshiremen may drone on about 'God's Own County' but Whitewell is as pretty an unspoilt village as any you might find anywhere in the Ridings. The Inn itself was once a manor house and parts of it go back to the fourteenth century. The white gabled frontage looks out over the village green, and the Orangery at the rear, where we were having lunch, has a vista of rich green pasture, sloping down to a bend in the River Hodder with dense woodland beyond.

The food is sublime. I was going to start with homemade black pudding and follow up with a whole roasted grouse from the Lancashire moors. I wasn't particularly bothered what the others were having.

'How was your visit to the Spiritualist Centre, Will?' I asked when the starters had arrived.

'Very strange,' Will said. 'In some respects it was like any old church service. In other respects, it was quite different. There were hymns and prayers, often for members of the community who were not present. But the highlight was the presence of Mr Walter Backhouse, the visiting medium.'

'Did he have magical robes?' Ruth said. 'Like Dumbledore?'

'Not at all,' Will said. 'In fact, he was an ordinary little man in a cheap suit and specs. He looked like a clerk - perhaps he *was* a clerk in everyday life - but the distinctive thing about him was his voice. It was a great booming bass voice which you wouldn't have expected in such a little man.

'Well, he came onto the platform and started talking to the congregation in a conversational tone. Every so often he would turn to one side and address something invisible in that great voice. He did this with such conviction you could almost swear that there *was* something there. Those sitting around me were staring as if they could see it.

'"Zachary," he cried, "Go stand in yonder corner and WAIT."

'He repeated this until there were about a dozen spirits in attendance at the back of the stage. The names were a curious hodge-podge. I can't remember all of them and it seemed a little rude to get my notebook out, but there were: Imhotep, Malachi, Anushka, Pixie and Betty. It all sounds preposterous but the performance was so hypnotic that I was intrigued.

'Mr Backhouse called Imhotep forward.'

'Wasn't he a Pharaoh?' Ruth said.

'An Egyptian court official at any rate,' I said. 'Go on, Will.'

'He had a brief conversation with the spirit in some language I didn't understand and then turned to the congregation. "Is there anybody here called George? Imhotep has a message for someone called George." Everybody looked around at each other but there was no George. It's a common enough name in Lancashire and the hall was quite full, but no - no sign of a George.'

'This sounds like a common magician's con trick,' I said.

'That's what I thought,' Will said. 'I had to suppress the giggles when he said, "Come on now, surely you remember. He had a dog called Patch. Surely someone knows George and his dog, Patch?" People around me were shaking their heads.

'This routine went on. He called other spirits forward who suggested other names, both male and female, but he had no luck with the congregation. By now he was tearing his hair out with frustration and began shouting at the spirits and abusing them, sometimes in the strange language and sometimes in English. Whether this was genuine rage or part of the act, I'm not sure.

'Eventually, he called Betty forward and spoke to her, or rather the space where she was supposed to be. He turned to the congregation.

'"Is there anybody here called Will? Betty wishes to know if there is anybody here called Will."'

Ruth burst out laughing.

'Oh Will,' she cried. 'Whatever did you do?'

'There was nothing for it, I had to stand up. I'd told the lady on the telephone that I would treat the service with respect and I'd given her my name.

'"Have we ever met, Sir?" he said.

'"We haven't."

'"Your surname is Melling, is it not?"

'"It is."

'"And you are a reporter, are you not?"

'"I'm a retired journalist, yes."'

The congregation burst into thunderous applause. What they didn't know was that I'd given this information to the lady on the phone as well.

'"And Betty tells me that you recently lost your wife. Is that so?"

'"I'm divorced as a matter of fact, and when I last checked, my ex-wife was alive and kicking."

'I thought this would put a dampener on the proceedings but no, more wild applause.

'Mr Backhouse went on: "Well, a divorce is a kind of parting, is it not? My commiserations, Mr Melling."

'More crazy applause. For some reason people around me were patting me on the back.'

'I suppose they believed what they wanted to believe,' I said.

'Evidently,' Will said. 'Anyway, this carried on with precious little success until Mr Backhouse turned on the spirits cowering in the corner - I *imagined* they were cowering because nobody could see them - and he said in the booming voice: "Depart ye whence ye came, ye naughty spirits. DEPART! Learn what it is to languish on the other side unloved and unremembered." The congregation were silent for a long minute and then there was prolonged applause.

'This seemed to exhaust him and he stood there swaying and mopping his forehead with a handkerchief. A lady with a floral hat brought on a chair.

'"When Mr Backhouse is recovered," she said, "he will see members by appointment in Healing Room 2. The roster is posted on the noticeboard at the back of the hall. Meanwhile tea and biscuits will be served in the vestibule."'

'Did you hang around?' Ruth asked.

'You bet I did,' Will said. 'It was really interesting. And to be honest I was gagging for a cuppa. What surprised me was that everybody was really friendly, and quite a lot of them seemed to want to talk to me, mostly women. I haven't been mobbed by the ladies like that since I was in my teens.'

'In your dreams,' I said.

'Shut up, you,' Ruth said. 'I bet Will was quite a catch in his day. Go on, Will.'

'The general feeling was that the meeting had been a great success. I said I couldn't really understand that because there didn't seem to have been any successful contacts or messages passed on.'

Will consulted his notepad again.

'A Mrs "Call-me-Ada" Sowerbutts of Copy Nook said: "Oh that happens, chuck. Them spirits is very playful tha' knows. Dead mischievious. But Mr Backhouse knows how to keep them under control. Otherwise there'd be 'avoc. They've been known to tie men's shoelaces together and loosen ladies's corsets."

'"I know," said Mrs Nellie Drummer of Addison Street. "That happened to my sister Barbara at a séance in Accrington. She were falling apart when she left the room. Her stays had been unlaced and her bra undone at the back. Her bosoms were all over the place. And all her hairgrips had been pulled out. Our Barbara would never tell a fib, you know."

'I asked what they thought about Mr Backhouse's healing powers and why he hadn't done a healing session in public. "Oh, he usually does," I was told. "Only when the spirits start misbehaving, it takes it out of him, don't you see?"

'Then I asked them whether his healing record was any good and there were all sorts of good reports. I think the best was from Miss Flood of Pump Street. "I had this goitre on my neck," she said. "Big as a rugby ball it wa'. Doctors could do nowt about it. It were there for years and one day I had a private session wi' Mr Backhouse and he prayed a bit, and then he passed his hands over it like, and it went overnight. Just like that. It went down like a bust balloon."

'Well, who was I to suggest that there might be some other explanation, especially as Miss Flood received ringing endorsements from some of the other ladies.

'Mind you,' Will continued. 'Not everybody was positive. One or two of the chaps told me, out of the hearing of their wives, of course, that they'd only come along because they'd been press-ganged.

'"I don't mind," Mr Wolfenden said. "It gives her a bit of consolation. The cat died recently, d'you see. Kidney failure. Dandelion, it were called. She loved that cat."

'Mr Pike was a bit less charitable:

"Man's a bloody fraud," he told me. "A fookin' charlatan."'

15 WASTWATER HOUSE

AFTER LUNCH, WE ASKED if we could take our coffee and liqueurs on to the terrace outside. There was still a slight chill in the breeze but it was pleasant enough to sit out there and look out over the field where sheep, dotted about like balls of fluff, were grazing contentedly. The sun had hit the river and it wound like a ribbon of bronze. Crows argued in the woods beyond and a blackbird sang nearby.

The fabulous meal had brought on that sense of wellbeing that makes you glad to be alive. The grouse had been magnificent and the sticky toffee pudding celestial. I felt incapable of moving for a while. I thought I might even nod off.

Somewhere, below the level of the decking, unseen, a sheep coughed loudly.

'What in the name of all that's holy was that?' Ruth said. 'It fair made me jump.'

'Sheep,' said Will, laughing.

'One of the Were-Sheep of Bowland,' I said. 'They suck your blood if you come across them at night.'

'Silly sod,' Ruth said.

I thought it was time to review what we'd learned so far and to think about what our next move should be.

'*Revenons à nos moutons,*' I said.

'What?' Will said.

'It's French. It means: let's get back to our sheep. Let's get back to business.'

'OK, but what've sheep got to do with it?'

'It's a French idiom. From a play. Oh, never mind. Let's just recap on what we know.'

Will looked at Ruth, inclined his head in my direction, and did the twirly finger at his forehead gesture.

'Screw loose?' Ruth said. 'Yes, from birth.'

I ignored them.

'Right Will,' I said. 'Pen and paper - time for your summative skills with bullet points. Heading: *What We Know*.'

Will found a clean page in his notebook. This was the entry he arrived at. Ruth and I added reminders as he wrote.

- Remains of girl found in basement of Wastwater House
- Walled up behind range
- Aged 23-24?
- Asphyxiated - Hyoid bone fractured
- Probably strangled (with a ligature?)
- No signs of struggle
- Died elsewhere and moved
- Date of death: not before 1873, probably not after 1891
- 'Spirit' writing on ceiling of study

- Suggests dead children 'comforting' father
- Census of 1891 indicates rapid reduction of household
- Spiritualists continue to believe despite evidence contrary to their beliefs

'Does that about cover it?' Will said.

'I think so,' I said.

'So what's the action plan?' Ruth said.

'The question should be - what do we need to find out next?' Will said.

'Well, tomorrow we are going to visit the house,' Ruth said, 'to check out Tom's hunch that it holds the secret to the girl's death.'

'And this time I'm coming,' Will said.

'I don't see why not,' I said. 'We've already dropped the charade that we want to buy the place.'

'We need to find out what happened to the mother and missing children,' Ruth said.

'And why the domestic servants were culled so drastically,' Will said. 'So: I am going to consult the Births, Marriages and Deaths register.'

'And I am going to try and check out the register at St James's,' I said, 'and consult Mr Higson about the deeds to the house.'

'And I propose a visit to the cemetery,' Ruth said, 'to see if there's a family grave. We could go after school on Wednesday if that suits you?'

It did and, after Will had paid the bill, we began gathering our things ready to make our way home.

Monday morning was bright with brittle sunshine. We'd agreed to meet Will in the memorial garden near the gates of Corporation Park and he was there before us. The flower beds were well tended and brilliant with freesias, pansies, peonies and iris, overlooked by the pietà, with the virgin holding up the dead Christ - or was it a soldier? There were poppy wreaths at the foot of the statue. Sadly the little lion's head fountains that fed the pool weren't working and there was litter in the water.

'Whenever I come here,' I said, 'fifty years seem to vanish. That little path behind the benches was my route up to school throughout my teens. Come on, before I start blubbing with nostalgia.'

We didn't take the little path but walked instead up the broad avenue where trees were coming into fresh green leaf. Blackbirds ran about on the grass verges and there was birdsong in the trees. We went up past the statue of Flora and turned to walk alongside the lake.

Just before the gate on East Park Road, the railings curved around a little promontory jutting out into the water. We paused for a while to watch the ducks. Every so often a female, harried by male suitors, would take to the air, followed by the drakes. They would circle over the park and then come skidding back over the water leaving v-shaped wakes behind them. They would quarrel for a bit and then calm down, bobbing under the water with their tails in the air and then resurface, shaking their feathers. Swans sailed by, as if above all this.

'It'll be my turn to start skriking in a minute,' Will said.

'How come?' Ruth asked.

'This spot is one of my earliest memories. This very spot. My mum used to bring me here to feed the ducks when I was just a toddler. She used to push me in my pram all the way up Earl Street - and you know how steep that is - and all the way along London Road. It would have been too far for me to walk. When we came to Park Road I used to marvel at the trees around the big houses.'

'I know what you mean,' I said. 'There's not a lot of foliage down Brookhouse Lane, is there?'

'Right. Anyway, when we got here, Mum would produce half a Wonderloaf and I would feed the ducks. I liked the way they would come swimming as fast as they could paddle, from every corner of the lake, and the swans came too. I tried to get my bread to the swans and the little Chinese ducks but it was a total free for all. Every so often a swan would bend its neck and snap at a duck, which would skitter away quacking like crazy and then come straight back.'

'That's really sweet, Will,' Ruth said.

'It's nearly ten,' I said. 'Let's go and look at the house, shall we?'

Nick Frost was standing on the steps leading to the front door which had been painted a gleaming pillar box red. An equally shiny BMW was parked in the drive.

'Wow!' Ruth said. 'Is that your company car, Nick?'

'I wish,' he replied. 'No, it's Mr Higson's. I'll be getting mine soon. It'll be a Fiesta though. Shall we go in?'

After Nick had disabled some complicated alarms behind the door, we followed him through a wood-panelled anteroom into a spacious entrance hall. A grand staircase with carved wooden griffons at the foot of the bannisters led up to a gallery on three sides of the first floor. There was another gallery around the floor above. And above that there was a polygonal lantern set with stained glass which threw lozenges and roundels of coloured light onto the parquet floor.

'I expected masses of advertising leaflets behind the door,' I said, 'and dust everywhere.'

'Ah, no,' Nick replied. 'Mr Rafiq has a cleaner come in twice a week.'

'And it's been decorated again,' I said, looking through open doors into the reception rooms. 'That's not the wallpaper they put up in the eighties.'

'That's right: he ordered the whole house to be done up again before he made a visit last November.'

That explained a faint smell of plaster, gloss paint and overtones of wood polish.

'I can't get over the staggering wealth of this man,' Ruth said. 'He has this house redecorated twice and leaves it empty for nearly forty years. Mind you, I'm not impressed with his taste. A bit too Laura Ashley for me.'

'Where do you want to start?' Nick asked me.

'Oh, the cellars I think. Don't you?'

16 THE BUREAU

BEHIND THE GRAND STAIRCASE were stone steps leading down to the cellars. There was a strong smell of white-wash and it was distinctly cool. I had a little trouble locating the spot where Adele had been found because the whole chimney breast had been demolished and the range was gone. There was the ghost of an outline on the ceiling which showed where the brickwork had been and new plaster applied. Thanks to strip lights the rooms were very bright. There was nothing spooky about it at all.

Otherwise it was very much as I'd remembered it, except that where there had been stone scullery sinks, there was now a stainless steel double sink with gleaming draining boards, and alongside there was a large dish-washer, a fridge, and a chest freezer. Against the opposite wall was an eight-hob cooker with double oven. All this was evidently brand new and the fridge was still in its cardboard packaging. Will lifted the freezer lid.

'Any bodies?' Ruth said.

'Nah,' Will replied. 'Empty.'

Nick Frost gave them a strange look.

'Anything to report?' Will asked me.

'I didn't really expect to find anything down here. The SOC team went over every millimetre of the basement.'

Another room was lined with racks for storing wine but they were empty and dust-free. In the furthest room another set of steps led up to a heavy door. Nick fumbled with his bunch of keys and managed to open it. We went up the steps into the back garden.

It was vast. From the road you would never have guessed that there was so much space behind the house. At the front, where black metal railings topped with gold-painted spikes rose from a low brick wall, there were just rhododendron bushes and a monkey puzzle tree. Behind there was a lawn, mowed short with a criss-cross pattern. There were trellises down the high red brick walls on either side, thick with roses, clematis, honeysuckle and fuchsias. A large magnolia tree glowed in a corner of the lawn with its mass of white waxy flowers. At another corner stood a gazebo in the rustic style, and beyond all this was an orchard, where the trees were throwing chequered shadows in the morning sunshine.

'Oh, it's beautiful!' Ruth exclaimed. 'All this and no-one to enjoy it. Such a sad, sad waste!'

We returned to the cellars, and, as we trooped back to what was once the kitchen, where Adele had been found, Ruth noticed a pair of double doors halfway up a wall. She touched Nick on the shoulder.'

'What's this?' she asked.

'Ah, now this,' Nick announced, 'this is your dumb waiter, recently electrified. Give me your handbag.'

'No, why?'

'Trust me.'

Reluctantly, Ruth handed over the bag. Nick placed it, along with a handful of brochures he'd been carrying, in the space behind the double doors. Then, he pressed a green button with 2 on it and the compartment, along with its cargo, glided smoothly upwards.

'That is a very expensive bag, you know,' Ruth said to Nick.

'Don't worry, Mrs Catlow. It's quite safe.'

Next, we inspected the reception rooms on the ground floor. The one on the right of the vestibule was an enormous space, a noble space. Nick called it 'the salon'. The windows reached from floor to ceiling and there was a view of the east gate of the park and the shimmer of a corner of the lake beyond. The white wallpaper featured little pastoral scenes etched in blue such as you might find on crockery. It was pretty but seemed out of tune with the grandeur of the salon. There were no curtains at the window and the floorboards were bare.

We inspected the other rooms on the ground floor, and they were much the same, if not quite so grand. To be honest, I was beginning to feel that - palatial as all this was - we were not going to find out anything we didn't already know.

Nick led us up the stairs and along the gallery to the room above the salon.

'The dining room,' he said, throwing open the doors with a flourish. This was even more imposing than the room below. Tall French windows opened on to a wrought-iron balcony. Nick unlocked them and we stepped out.

The view of the park was magical. We could see the lake clearly now and the smaller one beyond it. In the distance was the conservatory, long neglected now, though you could not tell that from here. We could see how lawns led up to formal gardens and the bowling green, and then up to the Broad Walk, running the width of the park. The steep slope above was thickly wooded and stretched up to the cannons.[7]

'Oh, my word, I could live here,' Ruth said ecstatically. 'You wouldn't have a couple of million quid about you, would you, Tom?'

---

[7] See *The Northern Elements* p. 29

'I would have had several million if you hadn't spent it all on your shopping trips to Manchester.'

'Which reminds me,' Ruth said to Nick, 'where's my handbag?'

Nick pointed to double doors in the wall opposite the windows. Unlike the functional doors in the basement, these had been painted white, and featured rococo designs picked out in blue and gold. We stepped inside, and Ruth retrieved her bag from the dumb waiter, and handed Nick his brochures.

'The view from the study is also stunning,' Nick said. We walked round the gallery to the room at the top of the staircase. Again Nick threw open the door with a theatrical gesture.

'Good God!' I said.

What I saw knocked me for six - and it wasn't the view.

In all the rooms we had visited so far we had not seen a single stick of furniture, but here, facing us, between two windows, was a colossal Victorian bureau.

If you were to film this moment, everything except the bureau would go out of focus and start to rotate, and the bureau, in high definition, would come looming out at you, full of menace.

'What on earth's the matter, Tom?' Ruth said. 'You've gone quite white.'

'Are you all right, Mr Catlow?' Nick said.

'Look at the size of *that*!' Will said.

'*That*,' I said, '*that* was here the last time I was in this house. I'll bet it's been here since Pickup's time.'

'It's hideous,' Will said. 'How the hell did they get that thing up here and through the door?'

'Mr Higson reckons it must have been built here,' Nick said.

'And I should think it will stay here until the crack of doom,' I said, 'unless someone unbuilds it.'

'I don't think it's hideous,' Ruth said. 'It has a certain gothic grandeur.'

I was inclined to agree with her. Grand it certainly was. Three people could easily have sat at it side by side. It was made of mahogany though the sloping panel at the front was inlaid with patterns of some lighter wood. On top there was a kind of miniature balustrade. There were a number of drawers increasing in size: four, two, one. You could have hidden a body in the bottom drawer; it was as big as a coffin. Each drawer had a key hole with a brass surround and a handle with a brass tag. None of the keyholes held keys. The bureau was highly polished and the brass was as bright as new.

'Is it locked?' Ruth said.

'The drawers aren't,' Nick said, 'but they're empty.'

'This is locked though,' Will said. He was trying to open the sloping panel but it wasn't budging. There were three keyholes along the top of the panel, again with brass surrounds and no keys. 'Someone was keen to keep things secure.'

'This is how it was in 1980 when we had to abandon the case,' I said. 'We have to get into that bureau.' I turned to Nick. 'I don't suppose Mr Higson has the keys?'

Nick shook his head.

'I thought not. Too much to hope for. I suppose Mr Rafiq is its rightful owner? He doesn't have the keys by any chance?'

'I couldn't say,' Nick replied.

'Is this where the spirit writing was?' Ruth asked.

'On the ceiling, yes,' I said. 'Once we'd photographed it, the decorators were free to go ahead.'

'I wonder how it was done,' Ruth said.

'So did we,' I said.

We trooped up to the floor above. Here the rooms were smaller.

'I suppose the servants lived up here?' Will said.

'When there *were* servants - plural,' Ruth said.

I sat on the windowsill in one of the rooms, and looked out over the town. We were high enough to look out over the tops of other houses lower down East Park Road. I could see the Town Hall Extension (known as the Y-front building when we were at school) and over to Brandy House Brow and Whinny Heights.

I tried to imagine the house when Cornelius Pickup and his family lived in it - and failed.

We have to get into that bureau, I thought.

By fair means or foul.

17 TEA IN THE CEMETERY

THE FOLLOWING WEDNESDAY, I parked the car on Bank Hey Lane, and Ruth and I entered the cemetery through the gate on the Arterial Road. It is built on a hillside and there are a few thousand graves. Sadly, some of them had been vandalised and wild grasses were growing everywhere. On the other hand, it was ideal for wildlife: flowers, birds, rabbits and even deer finding sanctuary on its quiet slope.

'We used to play here when we were kids,' I said.

'Weren't you spooked?' Ruth said. 'All the legions of the dead under your feet?'

'Never gave it a thought. It was just an amazing place to play hide and seek.'

Recently there had been a clearance and reclamation campaign run by volunteers with help from the army, and the place was looking better. Because of the slope the vista was particularly dramatic. There were ranks of headstones whose sheer number was astounding. Some of the older ones were at crazy angles and some of them had fallen over completely. The last resting places of the town's wealthier citizens were impressive in their lugubrious pomp. There was a variety of monoliths: pillars, needles, spires and obelisks. There were many crosses - plain and Celtic. There were funerary urns, carved sepulchres, and elaborate mausoleums for whole families. Angels pointed heavenwards, or held out the book of life, or simply wept. There were small temples in the classical style and gothic vaults with many arches resembling small churches.

Before long we came across the grave of Frederick Kempster, the so-called Blackburn Giant, although the inscription on his grave called him 'The British Giant'. The grave was about ten feet long.

'I read about him in the paper quite recently,' I said. 'He was a showman. He died at Queen's Park Hospital. Apparently it took fourteen men to lower him into the grave.'

'Too many potato pies?' Ruth said.

'Pies don't make you grow taller,' I said. 'You can be remarkably callous, you can.'

We wandered about in a desultory sort of way inspecting graves and reading inscriptions.

After a quarter of an hour or so, Ruth sat on a low tomb which afforded an excellent view out towards Wilpshire. She produced a flask of tea and a couple of pastries.

'Isn't this a bit sacrilegious?' I said.

'I hardly think the dead will be offended by a mug of Typhoo and a couple of Kenyon's custard tarts,' she replied.

'I think,' I said as we sipped the tea, 'that we need to be a bit more systematic with this search. How about you take the area to the left of the main path, and I take the right, and we work out and in again along roughly horizontal lines. No need to go out to the edges where the more recent graves are, just this cluster of bigger graves. If you find anything, just text me.'

'Makes sense.'

'Got any more custard tarts?'

'No. You'll spoil your dinner.'

We began our search. Sometimes I'd come across a patch that hadn't been restored and I'd have to be careful of nettles. Sometimes, I'd find a grave that had been carefully cleared and occasionally there'd be fresh flowers. This was usually where the remembered ancestor had been in the military.

I was tramping through an uneven patch where some of the monuments were leaning precariously owing to subsidence when I heard a shrill whistle, and I could see Ruth in the distance, waving her arms at me frantically. It was a football supporters' whistle produced with two fingers in the mouth at either side. I'd seen Ruth do it before and pronounced it unladylike. She said it was handy for getting the children to line up at the end of playtime.

I joined her as quickly as possible. She was standing in front of a majestic monument. On top of the huge sarcophagus was a colonnade of gothic arches. Above them was a statue of Jesus himself, his head covered with his robe, his left hand extended, and the right pointing at the sky. In front of the tomb, two kneeling angels supported a stone tablet on which was inscribed:

Here Lie
The Mortal Remains
of
CORNELIUS PICKUP
1837-1894
and his beloved wife
LOUISA
1847-1890
also his longed-for son
HORACE
who breathed the air of this world for but a few hours before he was taken, along with his mother, into the care of ALMIGHTY GOD

"The LORD giveth and the LORD taketh away"

also his cherished daughters
CHARLOTTE
1870-1887
&
ELIZA
1872-1888

The trumpet shall sound
Then shall they

WAKE ETERNALLY

"Beloved, believe not every spirit but try the spirits whether they are sent of GOD, because many false spirits are gone out into the world"
1 John 4, i,ii & iii

We stood in front of the tomb for several minutes in what I can only describe as awe. The family suddenly became more real, much more so than in the dry records of a census.

'Oh Tom,' Ruth said. 'There *was* a boy. Poor little Horace. It looks as if Louisa died in childbirth. Oh, Tom, how very sad.'

I thought she was going to cry.

'It was very common at the time,' I said.

'I doubt if that was much comfort to poor Cornelius,' Ruth said.

'No.'

'And the daughters. Already dead. Within a year of each other.'

'It could have been only months, or even weeks. If one died at the end of the year and the other at the beginning of the next.'

'True.'

'That suggests illness to me. Maybe Will can find out the causes of death from the BMD register.'

'That poor man,' Ruth said. 'He loses two teenage daughters and then his wife and "longed-for son". We're talking about a house of tragedy - enough to make a grown man run mad.'

'Or into the arms of spiritualism?' I said. 'Remember the writing on the ceiling.'

'You're not saying that you believe the dead children were responsible for it?'

'No. I'm saying that it's understandable that, after these terrible bereavements, Cornelius would want to believe that the children were trying to contact him.'

'Do you think that the writing appeared up there all at once?'

'No. My hunch is that the messages appeared over a period. If we had had the time, we could perhaps have proved that forensically.'

'But why the ceiling?'

'Perhaps there was a simplistic notion that the difficulty of writing on the ceiling rather than on the walls was less likely to be fraudulent, or seen as fraudulent. I don't know.'

'This is quite a find, Tom. It still doesn't explain what happened to the servants, though, does it?'

'Perhaps they were taken off by whatever killed the daughters. Typhus, perhaps? Or cholera?'

'All of them?'

'Oh yes. Both are very infectious and highly virulent.'

'I don't feel like cooking tonight, Tom. This has quite got to me. Let's pick up fish and chips on the way home.'

'Sure.'

'And then let's watch something completely vacuous on the telly.'

'That shouldn't be difficult. We'll have plenty of choice.'

'I want to forget about Wastwater House for a bit. Come on. Let's get out of this place.'

And we left the dead to their dreamless sleep.

18 AT THE BROWN COW

SINCE I WAS IN MY TEENS, 224 pubs have been lost to Blackburn. Back then there seemed to be a pub on every corner, all different, reflecting the locality and the clientele. They ranged from sticky-floored dives in the town centre to the plush new Clarendon in the Precinct or the upstairs bar in St John's Tavern.

It was in the latter that I had a job during university vacations. The Tavern had four bars. The décor in the Vault (a northern term for the public bar) was spartan and meagre. It was understood that this bar was for men only and it was assumed that any woman daring to enter and install herself on one of the barstools was on the game. There were a dartboard, dominos, draughts, cards and cribbage boards and a lot of foul language. The Market Bar was very busy, especially at lunchtimes on market days and on Saturdays. It would fill up with market traders who were pretty rowdy but very genial. The Lounge Bar was more genteel. It was where husbands would take their wives on a Saturday night. I used to be amused by older couples sitting side by side, not saying a word to each other all night. Maybe everything they had to say to each other had been exhausted years before. They didn't look unhappy - just a bit blank. Sometimes there'd be a works 'do' or a hen 'do' and the atmosphere would be livelier - well, deafening really. The upstairs bar aspired to be posh: we served morning coffee and ham sandwiches sprinkled with cress.

I started off 'waiting on' in the Lounge Bar. I had my tray, my cash float, and a special station at the end of the bar. I was expected to remember quite large orders and do calculations in pounds, shillings and pence in my head. I doubt if I could do it now. Eventually, I was promoted to working behind the bar and later still to running the upstairs bar on my own. There were no computerised tills in those days; again, it was all down to mental arithmetic. My tips were good - the upmarket punters liked my bow tie and BBC pronunciation and I made a point of being exquisitely courteous to the ladies.

But it's all gone. There are scarcely half a dozen pubs still going in the town centre. The whole demographic has changed: young people prefer clubs to pubs; orthodox Islam forbids alcohol; it's cheaper to drink at home; public health drives mean many drink much less. All the same, a little bit of me dies whenever a pub closes. I feel another bit of the culture of my youth has gone. All the same, perhaps it's not so much the changing face of the town that I am lamenting, as the passing of youth itself.

Tempora mutantur, nos et mutamur in illis. Times have changed and we have changed with them. There you go. The benefits of a grammar school education.

Will and I met up in The Brown Cow near Ewood Park. Rovers' fans had made sure that the Cow and The Aqueduct were still going concerns. On match days you couldn't move in either, before or after a game. This morning the Cow was quiet - one of the reasons for choosing it. It was convenient for Will - just one stop on the train to Mill Hill and then a short walk. I had taken a taxi.

I told Will about the tomb in the Old Cemetery and the inscriptions.

'I had only limited luck at St James's,' I said. 'I rang up the vicar earlier in the week and she put me in touch with Richie Earnshaw, a churchwarden who has an interest in local history and particularly the history of the church. She gave me his number and we met up at the church this morning. He's a lovely man and couldn't do enough to help.

'As we'd guessed, the two older Pickup girls were married from St James's. Fanny married Arthur Gleeson, a mill owner from Manchester in 1888, and Charlotte married Simon Street, Rector of St Chad's in Rochdale just months later. They'd have left Blackburn to set up their own homes with their husbands.'

'Good marriages,' Will said. 'Cornelius would have been very proud.'

'Now, get your hanky out,' I said. 'The baptism of baby Horace is recorded on October 5th, 1890. The vicar must have rushed to Wastwater House and baptised the infant before it died. However, any funeral service for mother and baby wasn't held at St James's. There isn't any record of Cornelius' funeral either.

'As for any entries before these, I hadn't taken account of the fact that the foundation stone for St James's wasn't laid until 1874. We are so used to seeing the spire on the skyline, I think I sort of half-believed it was always there. Before then, East Park Road was part of St John's Parish. In fact, the bottom of the road is still in St John's. Heaven knows where their register is. The church was desanctified - or whatever the word is - in the seventies and now it's burnt down.'

'Well, it doesn't really matter for our purposes, does it?' Will said. 'It's not as if we are trying to build a complete family tree.'

'True.'

'Now,' Will said. 'I think I can help a bit here. I had some luck with the Births, Marriages and Deaths register in the Town Hall. A press pass can sometimes speed things up a bit, you know. As far as Charlotte and Eliza are concerned your speculation is correct. The cause of their demise on both death certificates is recorded as smallpox.'

'How dreadful. A cruel death. Thank God, it's been eradicated.'

'So that accounts for the disappearances in the census - for the family, at least,' Will said, 'Apart from Cornelius himself and Alice.'

'Is there no record of their deaths?' I said.

'No. I presume they must have died elsewhere. Cornelius' body must have been brought back for burial.'

'Are you sure there's no record of Alice's death?'

'Quite sure. I found the registration of her birth in 1876. No record of any marriage in Blackburn at least, unlike her sisters.'

'I suppose it was often the case that the youngest daughter would end up looking after an ageing parent?'

'Possibly,' Will said. 'As far as her death is concerned, I checked right through to 1980, which would have made her 105. You can't accuse me of a lack of thoroughness.'

'No,' I said. 'No, I can't. But don't you think it's really strange that Alice is the only family member who is not mentioned on the inscription on the tomb?'

'She might have died elsewhere - abroad perhaps - and it was impracticable to bring the body home,' Will said.

'Or maybe there was some rift?'

'Maybe.'

'I have this gut feeling,' I said, 'that the answer to Alice's disappearance - and the vanishing of most of the servants - lies in Wastwater House and in that desk in particular.'

'So what is to be done? You're not thinking of breaking and entering are you? That desk is triple-locked.'

'It's time I visited our Mr Higson again,' I said. 'I want to know the history of that house. I want to know if he can arrange for me to have a gander at the deeds. He may have a copy. And I think I know how to get into that desk without using a sledgehammer.'

'How?'

'Lenny the Latch.'

'Who? Sounds like a character from *The Beano*.'

'Maybe. Leonard Jackson was the most proficient burglar in the North West for many years. My colleagues had been on his case all this time and it was only through a stroke of bad luck that he was caught. It was like something out of a cartoon. One of the reasons for his success was his amazing night vision. He could operate in near darkness. Well, ironically, he trod on a sleeping cat, which set up a fearful yowling, waking up the owner of the house who was a big man. It was all up for Lenny. In court, he admitted to a formidable string of offences and he was sentenced to several years' porridge. He went down cheerfully, vowing to go straight when he was released - and he kept his word.'

'Quite a guy,' Will said.

'Exactly,' I replied. 'Now, the secret of his success, apart from his night vision, was his capacity to pick any lock he confronted. When he came out of chokey, our poacher turned gamekeeper and, on occasion, was very useful to my colleagues, both in uniform and undercover. That's why he was known as Lenny the Latch.'

'Fantastic,' Will said. 'And you think Lenny will be able to get into the bureau?'

'He likes a challenge. A couple of pints should secure his services.'

'I can see the headline now,' Will said. 'LENNY THE LATCH UNLOCKS THE SECRETS OF THE HOUSE OF DEATH.'

I laughed.

'Tom?' Will said. 'What was it your granny said Blood Moon had told her?'

'About Ruth, you mean?'

'No, about you.'

'"He will do great works in the house of death." Is that what you mean?'

'Yeah. I was just thinking. Maybe the House of Death isn't your mortuary. Maybe it's Wastwater House?'

'Blimey,' I said, 'are you becoming a spiritualist after all?'

'Gerrout of it!' Will said. 'What do you take me for?'

19 WILL'S LUCKY STRIKE

OF COURSE I TOOK WILL as a rationalist who was pulling my leg. All par for the course.

I dropped in on Mr Higson the next day, so keen was I to get at the secrets of that bureau. Not particularly rational on my part, Will might have said - but I've already given my opinion on hunches. Often the unconscious mind has made connexions the conscious mind has not registered. Synapses explode and send fireworks racing down neural pathways even as we sleep, which is why the answer to a problem that seemed intractable at bed time pops up with the toast at breakfast.

Luckily, Higson was free, and young Nick Frost showed me through to his boss's office. The floppy blue paisley handkerchief in his breast pocket matched his tie and I thought I caught a whiff of some kind of citrus preparation from his tightly curled hair, parted neatly down the middle. I began to see what Ruth meant when she'd called him faintly ridiculous. I half-expected him to be wearing spats when he came round his desk to shake hands with me.

Still, his fascination with 'True Crime' was useful and he proved extremely helpful. The deeds to Wastwater House were currently with Mr Rafiq's solicitors but Higson and Ingham's did indeed hold a copy. There were reasons for this, he said. The potential buyer of a large property did not want to discover, after completion, that there was, for instance, a public right of way through his garden, or a disputed boundary with a neighbour. He produced the document for my inspection, from a safe in a room behind him, rubbing his hands with glee, and I threw him a few titbits of information about our discoveries to keep him onside, according to our agreement.

He couldn't allow me to make a copy but said I could make notes. I was installed in a small interview room and left to look through the files at leisure. There was a great deal of detail and thickets of legalese - *with regard to the third party of the second part, without prejudice, and notwithstanding prior notification* - that sort of thing. I used a mental machete to hack my way through all this verbiage and was able to reduce it all to a potted history of the house:

Wastwater House	Built 1873
Freeholders:	
Pickup, Cornelius	1873-1892

Geo. Hunt, Esq.	1892-1926
Colin Dodds, Esq.	1926-1939
Commissioned by HM	
War Office [EMS]	1940-1948
Winter, Richard, Dr.	1950-1980
Dariush Rafiq	1980-

A quick Google on my phone established that EMS meant the Emergency Medical Service. So the house was used as a hospital annexe, presumably for returning war-wounded. You could fit a lot of beds into those great rooms. And all the time the corpse of Adele lay walled up behind the range in the basement kitchen. And that ruddy great desk squatted, locked against time in the study.

So, what did this tell me? It told me that Cornelius sold the house to Mr Hunt in 1892, a year after the census. Why then? Alice and Mary Jane were running the house successfully in census year. Had it become too much for them? Or did Cornelius finally have to admit that the house was too big for the three of them?

And the extra-ordinary Mr Rafiq? Whenever his name came up I couldn't help thinking that it would earn at least 48 points if you could get the Q on a triple word square.

Sorry, that's no help at all.

Mr Rafiq had bought the house in 1980, had it done up twice, and never lived there. He must have been told when Adele was found but I had not been able to find any record of it at the time. His only response was to impress on Higson to keep quiet about it - though whether that was a direct injunction or whether it came from his agents wasn't clear.

As I was packing up, Nick brought me a coffee and said Mr Higson would like a word when I was finished. I said that I was quite done and gave him the papers to be returned to the safe. I pondered over my notes for a bit and returned to Higson's office.

He was keen to see my scribblings and to ask me what I thought. I saw no reason not to share my speculations, such as they were. Besides I needed to butter him up before my next request. I told him about Lenny the Latch and my cunning plan.

'Hmmm,' he said and took a plain white hanky from his trouser pocket and blew his nose noisily. Obviously the paisley one was purely ornamental.

'Hmmm,' he said again.

'Is there a problem?' I asked.

'Well, is it legal, this lock picking?'

'I admit that there may have been one or two borderline cases, but almost always, if it were a matter of gaining entry to a property, there would be a warrant. Just think: if for some reason the police needed to gain emergency access to your home, would you prefer to have the lock picked or the door battered down?'

'Well, the former obviously, but you see, letting you have access is one thing - I could easily pass you off as a genuine prospective buyer if necessary, but until the exchange of contracts and completion, the house and everything within it is the property of Mr Rafiq. Please don't ask me to do anything underhand.'

'I wouldn't dream of it,' I said. 'I merely wondered if I could ask you to write to Mr Rafiq for permission. Gaining access to the thing might conceivably be to his advantage, who knows? Just tell him as much of the story as you think appropriate and explain that anything found would be photographed and not taken away without his permission.'

'Oh, I could certainly do that,' he said. 'Indeed I would be very happy to do that. I shall do it this evening and email you a draft. I should warn you that correspondence with Mr Rafiq is very slow. The request will have to go through his agents who take a very relaxed view of correspondence. But I'll keep you informed.'

And there we left it. I came away pleased with the progress that had been made but also rather apprehensive about the time scale. What if, before Mr Rafiq replied - if he ever did - the architects and surveyors and solicitors got their act together? What if the planners granted permission to turn Wastwater House into flats? What if the conveyancing was completed and the builders moved in? We could well be denied access to the building and certainly to the bureau. Mr Higson's job would have been done and our hours of research would just dribble away. It was a depressing thought.

Days and weeks passed. Spring became summer and there was nothing but silence. I rang Higson once or twice but he seemed a bit put out and said he would ring me as soon as he had any news. I didn't like to try again.

Ruth said I should be patient. Adele had lain in her dusty cell for nearly a century. Surely she could wait a little longer?

That didn't help much either.

One evening in early June, I was sitting in the back garden with a glass of Prosecco and a bowl of paprika Pringles. I was admiring the wisteria which was in glorious bloom around the back door when I heard a cuckoo call clearly from the other side of the valley and immediately I heard the telephone ringing inside the house. I thought it might be Higson.

Ruth had got there before me, wiping her hands on her apron and picking up. I was practically hopping from foot to foot with impatience.

I mouthed 'who is it?' but Ruth shook her head and gave me a dismissive wave.

Then she said: 'Oh, Will, that's fascinating! Well done!'

I made gestures which suggested that I would strangle her if she didn't give me the receiver.

'Tom's here,' she said. 'He's wetting himself with excitement. I'll put him on.'

She handed me the receiver.

'What is it?' I said. 'What's going on?'

'Remember Mary Ann?' he said.

'The remaining domestic? Yes, what about her?'

'She was a sensitive.'

'A what?'

'She had the gift. She was psychic, a medium. She gave public séances.'

20 THE SPREAD EAGLE

'WELL! I'LL STRIP NAKED, paint myself purple and dance on the piano! I knew there were occult goings-on in that house. I knew it! How on earth did you find that out?'

'Do you remember the story of the girl who was exposed at a séance in Blackburn?'

'Miss Wood, wasn't it?'

'That's right. Her story was in *The Blackburn Times* but also in the spiritualist periodical *The Medium and Daybreak*. I dunno, maybe I was intrigued by the weird title but, anyway, I thought I'd mooch about a bit in editions from the early eighteen-nineties. I discovered that the John Rylands Library in Manchester had archive copies so I took a day trip.'

'You didn't say anything.'

'No,' Will said. 'It was a long shot and if it turned out to be a wild goose chase I didn't want to look a total div.'

'But it wasn't a wild goose chase?'

'No, I came up with this: "At a meeting of the Salford Bridge Spiritualist Group, Miss Mary Ann Duxbury, Trance Medium, Clairvoyant, and Magnetic Healer, was the chief guest." There's an account of the meeting.'

'That's our girl! Go on then.'

'I think it would be better if I scanned it and emailed it to you. Then you can look at it at your leisure.'

I agreed and we chatted about this and that, arranging to meet the following day at The Postal Order. Then I walked down to my study in the garden. It wasn't long before Will's email landed in my inbox, along with this attachment:

BLACKBURN: At a meeting of the Salford Bridge Spiritualist Society held at The Spread Eagle Hotel, Cable Street, Blackburn, on Sunday, August 3rd, 1890, at 5.30 pm, Miss Mary Ann Duxbury, Trance Medium, Clairvoyant, and Magnetic Healer, was the chief guest.

It was a pleasure to witness the cleanliness of the upper rooms at the hotel, for which thanks are due to Mrs Dinsdale, the Landlady, and to her staff. Thanks are also due to Mr & Mrs Cleaver for defraying the cost of the hire of the rooms, to Mrs Minto for the teas, and Miss Musgrave and friends for the flowers. Mr N. Duckworth (President) made a few stirring remarks in opening. Mrs Smith and Miss Kaye sang a moving duet which was greatly appreciated by the overflowing meeting. Master Paul Sutcliffe gave a creditable recitation after which our chief guest came onto the platform. She gave a very beautiful and moving discourse upon which her spirit guides gently enchanted her into a trance. Whilst she was thus absented from her body, she made several accurate clairvoyant observations concerning members of the congregation. Her guides then led her to invite members to come forward for healing. Mr Dickens later reported a prodigious alleviation of the symptoms of his gout, and Miss Collins thought there had been a diminution in the effects of her shaking fever. The service ended with prayers and a hymn. At the meeting there were friends from a number of neighbourhood societies, and we are sanguine of doing a lot of good in this neighbourhood; and we hope to do our share in expounding and promoting the glorious Cause of Spiritualism.

A second attachment was a black and white photograph of The Spread Eagle Hotel along with a few notes from Will. The pub was near St John's Church and was demolished in 1951. Cable Street itself was flattened in 1959.

The photograph is moody and very well composed. It must have been taken in the early morning or near sunset as the shadows are deep and the windows are bright. My guess is early morning as the scene is deserted. In the evening the pub would have been open and I would have expected the street to have been busier.

The light comes from the right of the image. There is a diagonal of shadow which seems to run from the height of a gas lamp on a bracket jutting from a narrow two-storey building, across the wall of a street beyond, to the doorstep of the pub.

The foreground is in gloom. Cobbles lead, via a dog's leg, to the farther street where the diagonal of shadow falls on terraced houses, the nearest of which has two steps to the door. The steps have been donkey-stoned to a standard my grandmother would have approved of.

If I am right about the timing, the western gable of the two-storey building is hit with the last of the light as are the windows of the first floor of the pub where the spiritualist meeting was held. The Spread Eagle has a stone portico with pillars. It was quite grand in its time, according to Will's notes.

The strangest thing about the image is the figure of a bird with outstretched wings on the roof ridge of the hotel. It doesn't look much like an eagle. In fact, it is nothing of the kind. It's a phoenix, the mythical bird, that is consumed by fire and rises renewed from its ashes.

Ironically, it was originally the emblem of an insurance company which was itself consumed by fire. I couldn't help thinking that it would make an uncanny insignia for the spiritualist cause with its desire to transact with a realm beyond death.

The following morning Ruth planned to benefit from half term to do a big shop at Morrison's, and was going to drive me into Blackburn to meet up with Will. We were just about to leave the house when the phone rang. It was Mr Higson. Mr Rafiq had replied and it all appeared to be very promising. Could I call in at my earliest convenience?

'Is the Pope a catholic?' I said, and made an appointment to call in later that morning.

'I don't know. You wait for ages for a bus, and two come along at once,' I said, as I was getting into the car.

'You're full of clichés this morning, Tom,' she said.

I wondered if she'd been so sarky when she taught Nick Frost.

Mr Higson was beaming all over his face when Nick showed me into his office. He was wearing a rainbow-striped bow tie - with matching breast pocket handkerchief, of course.

He had received an email from Mr Rafiq's agents saying that the wretched piece of furniture had always irritated him. If we could open it, we were welcome to the contents. It was worthless to him locked, and an encumbrance to the proposed development of the property. If we could get into it, it should be easier to dismantle it. We were welcome to take it away and sell it if it could be rebuilt. He had no interest in it at all. The luxury flats he had in mind were to be state-of-the-art modern. For all he cared, the builders could take a sledge hammer to the grotesque thing.

I said I had no interest in selling the bureau, only in getting inside it.

'Ah, but I might,' Mr Higson beamed even more brightly. 'It could be worth a pretty penny.'

'You'd have the cost of dismantling, removal, storage and rebuilding,' I said. 'And a buyer with room for it.'

'I like that kind of challenge,' Higson said.

I made an appointment to gain access to the house the following Monday, knowing that this was Ruth's day off. Higson said that Nick would meet us there as before, and asked me to remember to keep him informed.

I was in a very buoyant mood as I walked down King William Street. I popped into M&S and bought a bottle of their house champagne to celebrate the fact that things seemed to be moving fast. It was on offer but it still wasn't cheap.

I had texted Will to say I would be a little late. He was waiting for me when I arrived at The Postal Order and I gave him the good news from Mr Rafiq.

'Do you think the concentric circles are getting tighter?' he asked.

'Do bears *et cetera*?' I said.

21 LENNY THE LATCH

'NOW, HOLMES,' WILL SAID, 'what are we to make of this new information?'

'Well, Watson,' I said. 'it confirms our suspicions that spiritualism was a presence in the house. It does not confirm that it had anything to do with Adele's death.

'It does raise further questions - but that's a good thing.'

'Such as?'

'Such as did Cornelius know about Mary Ann's public performance? Was he there? Did he approve or disapprove? Was Alice there?'

'I would say possibly not.'

'Why?'

'Because a Victorian domestic would get very little time off. Especially if Mary Ann and Alice were running the household together and we know how enormous the house is. Any free time Mary Ann might have had to herself would surely have been on a Sunday afternoon and evening? She would have been at liberty to attend this meeting and Cornelius needn't have known.'

'True,' I said.

'I have a couple of questions of my own,' Will said.

'Go on.'

'Was Mary Ann paid for her performance? If so, was she managed or was she a solo operator?'

'Good point,' I said. 'Perhaps your next job should be to go back to *The Medium and Daybreak* and see if this event was a one-off or whether our young lady was chief guest at other presentations before or after.'

'I already thought of that,' Will said. 'I checked through the volumes for 1891 and 1893. Nothing. The Salford Bridge Group met often, but there was no other reference to Mary Ann. She might have entertained other groups but I found no mention. I don't mind another trip to Manchester if you want me to search further back and forward. There's an excellent pub near the Cathedral called The Mitre.'

'It shouldn't be necessary at this stage,' I said, 'but if we need to, I'll come with you and you can introduce me to your episcopal hostelry.'

'Long words again,' Will said. 'What about this bureau then? Are you sure Lenny the Latch will be free on Monday?'

'I already had him primed,' I said. 'I phoned him over the weekend. He's very keen. I'll ring him tonight to confirm. He'll be there, don't you worry.'

Ruth and I picked up Will in town the following Monday. There were two vehicles in the drive: a blue Ford Fiesta and a white Ford Transit. Nick was sitting in the car reading *The Sun* and Lenny was sitting in the van reading *The Times*. Leonard had always been a bit of an upmarket crook. The scene amused me a little. Was Lenny shy of introducing himself to a stranger - he was always one to keep to himself, a loner, a creature of the night - and was Nick cagey of an ex-jailbird? Anyway, they sat there in their respective vehicles, each trying to ignore the other.

Nick was the first to get out as we parked.

'What happened to the BMW?' Ruth said.

'Well, this is not quite as flash,' Nick said. 'But it's for my exclusive use, and not just for work.'

'Good for you,' Ruth said.

Meanwhile, Lenny climbed down from the van and I introduced him to the others. He was a short, slender man, with a winning smile now he'd been introduced, and very sharp, pale blue eyes. He had a full head of hair and seemed boyish despite his fifty odd years. And, despite the summer heat, he wore a professional suit and tie, while the rest of us were in casual clothes and sweating a bit. Nick had left his jacket in the car, and loosened his tie and rolled up his sleeves. There was not the tiniest bead of perspiration on Lenny's brow.

Nick let us in and fiddled with the alarms. Then he led Lenny and Will up the grand staircase to the study. Ruth and I followed on.

'He's not what I expected,' Ruth whispered to me on the stairs.

'What did you expect?' I said.

'I'm not sure,' she said. 'A man with a pinched face? A rat-faced little man?'

'With a striped jumper, a mask, and a bag with swag written on it?'

She gave me a little push.

'Who's being clichéd now?' I said.

'*Touché!*' she said, and laughed.

We caught up with the others as they entered the study. Lenny gave a low whistle when he saw the bureau. It was not as if you could miss it.

'You were right, Tom,' he said. 'It's a beauty and a beast at the same time.'

He went over to the bureau and bent over it, brushing away any surface dust with his fingertips and then blowing into the locks themselves.

'Shouldn't be too difficult,' he muttered.

Will couldn't bear to watch and stood looking out into the orchard, turning occasionally to look, and then turning back.

Having invested so much in my hunch, I couldn't bear *not* to watch. Ruth was fascinated too.

Lenny had brought a small tool box with him. He knelt down and reached into it, producing a metal ring with lots of tiny keys on it.

'Were those obtained legally?' Ruth said.

I gave her a dirty look.

'Asking for a friend,' she said sheepishly.

'Hush, woman,' I said. 'What you don't know...'

'Sorry,' she whispered.

Lenny began to try the brass keys in one of the outer locks one by one. After less than a minute there was a click.

'Lucky,' Lenny said.

He tried the same key in the other outer lock. It clicked.

'I thought as much,' he said.

No such luck with the central lock.

'Plan B,' he muttered, putting the bunch of keys back in his bag and taking out what looked a bit like a staple gun with a long probe.

'What's that?' Nick said. He had been leaning on the top of the bureau and watching intently. This was probably the most exciting thing that had ever happened in his life.

'Electric snap gun,' Lenny said. 'Charged via the van's USB portal. Works on most modern tumbler locks. Uses kinetic energy. Not much use with anything complicated.'

He inserted the probe at various angles and we heard the snap as compressed air rushed in. Nothing doing.

'Worth a try,' Lenny said. 'Lock's too small to get at the pins. Switch to manual.'

Lenny never used more words than he needed to.

He replaced the gun in his tool box and produced a cloth wrap which he unrolled. There were cloth pockets which contained a selection of picks in decreasing size. They reminded me of the horrible thing that dentists use to scrape about between your teeth and stab your gums. He chose one of the smallest and began to probe, listening with his ear to the lock.

Five agonising minutes passed. I felt forced to watch now. A siren wailed somewhere and faded.

At last there was a click.

'Job's a good'un,' Lenny said, standing up.

'Genius, Lenny!' I said.

'All in a day's work, mate,' he said. 'Here, take hold of the other side, kid,' he said to Nick. Together they lifted the sloping panel down. Four bars shot out from beneath to support it as the panel came down. There was a writing surface: a rectangle of green leather with a border embossed in gold. There were masses of little drawers with little brass tags. There were open pigeon-holes for stationery and correspondence. Lenny pressed a lever hidden in one of the compartments and an ingenious wooden reading stand swung out at eye level. It swivelled so that you could adjust the angle in order to consult your book comfortably as you wrote. There was an identical mechanism at the other side.

Another catch caused a shelf to shoot out on which you could stack other books as you studied. Yet another caused the leather writing desk to spring up with a twang so that the surface was at a comfortable angle for writing.

But it was empty. Its emptiness howled at me. I tried the little drawers. Empty. Every single one.

'I am so sorry,' I said to the others. 'I could have sworn we'd find something. What a waste of time.'

'Hang on, mate,' Lenny said. 'Lenny the Latch isn't done.'

He took a tape measure from his tool box and made some measurements of the side of the bureau from front to back. Then he measured from the back of one of the compartments to the front of the writing desk. Grunting softly, he began to grope in the pigeon-holes. I noticed how tiny his hand was.

'Yes!' he shouted suddenly. He had found a catch, and there was a twang. He lifted a whole bank of pigeon-holes from the bottom, and they swung up on invisible hinges. Behind was a hidden compartment containing a number of bound volumes.

'Had to be a private cache there,' Lenny said. 'Measurements didn't tally.'

I took out one of the volumes. It was bound in maroon leather and embossed in gold. On the front were the words:

Cornelius Pickup
Journal
1875

PART TWO

When falsehood can look so like the truth, who can assure themselves of certain happiness?

Mary Shelley
Frankenstein

THERE WERE EIGHTEEN VOLUMES IN TOTAL, from 1875 to 1891, and I took them all away with me. The entries are continuous and each entry does not correspond to a particular year. Cornelius simply continues until the volume is full and then begins another. I studied them over a number of weeks and have transcribed any passages relevant to our research. Ruth has been typing them up.

What follows here is not the whole text. There is a great deal about business and various financial transactions, even after his retirement, which is tedious in the extreme and irrelevant to our enquiries. There is also a great deal about his social connexions, which, though fascinating in itself, is not pertinent to the case either.

I reproduce the transcriptions here without commentary. I believe Cornelius Pickup's story speaks for itself.

1875

November 28

It being Advent Sunday, we are but newly returned from church. The sanctuary and chancel at St John's looked so beautiful: the altar front being changed to violet, purple flowers adorning the chancel, and great bouquets of purple blooming before lectern and pulpit.

Louisa's heart and mine were swollen with pride as Fanny and Charlotte approached the lectern and gave readings from Jeremiah and Luke in clear bell-like accents, so angelic did they look with their pretty golden ringlets escaping from their bonnets. Why, it would not have been the tiniest bit remarkable if they had sprouted wings there and then. Of course, they could not have seen over the lectern and so a little padded footstool was provided so that they might be observed clearly by the congregation.

Little Eliza, who was seated between us in our pew leapt to her feet, jumped up and down and clapped her hands for very delight at her sweet sisters' cleverness and grace. I stole a glance at Miss Usher, the children's governess, who was likewise blushing crimson with gratification at her charges' precocity. She had spent time coaching them for this occasion and I made a mental memorandum to commend her for her ministrations at luncheon.

At length, a sidesman brought a lighted taper to my daughters, and together, their dainty little hands conjoined, they lit the first candle in the Advent wreath. This is a time for reflection before the most Holy Birth of Our Redeemer. He is coming indeed. It is also permitted for us poor sinners to feel joy at the prospect.

For my most dear and precious wife, Louisa, that sacred prospect is further gilded by the fact that she herself is with child. It is as if the Saviour Infant That Is To Be is showering us with blessings. I have petitioned the Lord to look upon his servant, Louisa, and to grant us likewise a son, a brother to my sweet little girls. If that be pride, I am most truly sorry for it, and if it is not to be, I will humbly rejoice in the arrival in my family of another daughter. Love and protection will not be wanting.

Letting Louisa go ahead in the carriage, with Eliza and Miss Usher, I walked home through the park with Fanny and Charlotte, the servants walking behind. The air was crisp and the early morning mist not entirely lifted. The walk was bracing and I venture to say it may have contributed not a little to a healthy appetite.

And oh! What a luncheon awaited us at home. We were regaled with brown Windsor soup, a saddle of mutton with currant sauce, duchesse potatoes, haricot beans, carrots and gravy, followed by a delectable lemon mousse.

Afterwards, as ever on a Sunday afternoon, there was a time for quiet reflexion. Louisa retired to her chamber to rest; Miss Usher took the children into the salon, and there supervised their reading of some improving literature; and I, meanwhile, made my way to the library, where I turned my mind to sundry devotional texts.

It may well be that that sense of well-being that follows a well-prepared and wholesome repast contributed to my disposition - I do not deny it - but, much more importantly, it was the thought of my young family and their gifts that induced in me a sense of profound contentment with my lot.

December 17

Oh my goodness gracious, what a hurly-burly is here! What a hullabaloo! Richards, the groom, and young Peter Fell have carried the Christmas tree into the salon and set it in its tub, and now Foster and the maids are decorating it. Such gaudy baubles, such great flounces of tinsel, such little teasing parcels of sweetmeats and candies and other good things, wrapped in red and green and gold, such pretty painted rocking horses and guardsmen and gingerbread men depending from the branches. Such little posies in which candles are set, to be lit on Christmas Eve after prayers.

Now, atop a great wooden ladder which trembles slightly (though the boy Peter is trying to hold it firm with outstretched arms), Richards secures the silver star of Bethlehem at the very apex of the tree.

The children are beside themselves with glee, and caper about making suggestions until, at last, they are permitted to add little trinkets, which they have made themselves with the assistance of Miss Usher, to the lower branches.

In other years, the decoration of the tree has been Louisa's province, but today she watches from a day bed, occasionally giving directions as to the placing of a snowman or a Father Christmas.

I am worried about my wife.

In the past she has suffered from an aching back and swollen ankles, and other ailments not uncommon in the later stages of her interesting condition. She tires easily which is only natural. However, I cannot but observe that she is very pale, whereas previously I have noted a rosy bloom about her as she approached her lying-in.

Nonetheless, it is the season of hope and expectation, and we are all most solicitous for her, and she grateful and patient, dismissing all my fretting with a sweet sad smile, a humorous flick of her handkerchief, and a comical frown succeeding.

December 31

The house is quiet at last. Louisa's pains began in the night and Jane Green, her maid, who has been sleeping in her room, knocked vigorously on the door of the master bedroom to apprise me of the fact.

There was much to do, but much had been planned for her confinement. Of course, I went first to her chamber where a spasm of pain caused her to sit up in bed and then throw herself back with a groan. There was a cold sweat on her brow which I kissed and she gripped my hand tightly.

'Go now,' she said with a smile that was a little tight. 'You are not wanted here. All shall be well.'

I ventured to contradict her but she said only: 'Attend to the children, Cornelius. Jane has sent the boy for the midwife as agreed. She will be here presently. Now leave us, please. You will be in the way.'

I must confess I needed no second bidding. What is more, I soon found myself almost superfluous in my own house. Peter arrived with Mrs Dunkenhalgh, the midwife, who was to live in until the child should be safely delivered and Louisa sufficiently recovered to have no further need of her. This doughty lady firmly brushed me away and the females of my household took over as if I did not exist.

I saw Louisa, wrapped in shawls, led from her chamber, adjoining mine, along the corridor to the birthing room which had been prepared. Ordinarily it gave a fine view over the orchard but the drapes were now closed and a good fire burning. I thought I might just peer in through a chink of orange light between door and jamb, but the Dunkenhalgh closed it in my face with a scowl.

Now, however, I must turn my attention to the girls. Already the strategy Louisa and I had devised in advance was moving into action. Jane had alerted the housekeeper who had awoken the children and Miss Usher. The latter saw to their ablutions and ensured that they were prettily dressed and their hair brushed. Cook had prepared breakfast which they took in the servants' hall which was a novelty for them. At first they were full of questions but their curiosity was quelled with 'not now, dears' from cook and 'all in good time' from Miss Usher and they settled to eat their porridge quietly enough for, to be sure, they were still a little dazed by the early hour.

I alerted Richards and bade him have the carriage ready at the door within the half hour. My little ones were to be driven to my younger brother's home at Holt House on the edge of Witton Park. He and his wife, Clara, are without children - a matter of sorrow to them - and they dote on their nieces who are always accorded a merry welcome.

At length, Miss Usher had them ready in the hall and I descended to bid them farewell. How charming my little ones looked with their fur hats and mittens. I could easily imagine that they were three princesses from a story by Hans Christian Andersen.

I told them that Mama was a little unwell and that she must have peace and quiet for a day or two to regain her strength. I bade them be no trouble to Uncle Titus and Aunt Clara, and that if they were very good there would be a wonderful surprise waiting for them on their return.

When Peter opened the outer door to the vestibule, we could see large soft snowflakes falling silently in the dark. I kissed each child in turn and told them that doubtless Uncle Titus would take them tobogganing in the park and that they might build a snowman. The prospect delighted them and they climbed into the coach with Peter's help, Miss Usher following. At last, Richards set off down the road, Peter riding pillion, and I stood watching, until I could hear no more the clopping of hooves and the jingle of harness.

23 THE JOURNAL 2

December 31

Eadem die[8]

YES, THE HOUSE IS QUIET, unnaturally so, and I suddenly find myself at a loss. Banished from upstairs I take my breakfast in the servants' hall. This proves to be a mistake. I am furnished with an excellent kedgeree and good coffee but I sense that Cook is uncomfortable. It was no imposition for her to feed the children here, for she, along with every single one of the other servants, absolutely adores them. But to have the Master of the House in her domain is an embarrassment to her. She says nothing, but I feel it, and finish the dish quickly, quaff the last of the coffee in my cup, and take my leave. She bobs and says 'God bless you, sir,' as if I were a man bereaved.

---

[8] Latin: the same day

This puzzles me somewhat. I can only suppose that my countenance betrayed a certain anxiety. The truth of the matter is that I feel listless, a little lonely, and quite, quite useless. I wander from room to room aimlessly and arrive in the salon just as a tentative daylight seeps in at the window. Without the children and the mistress of the house to admire it, the Christmas tree looks all forlorn and out of sorts. Standing at the window, I see that the road and the park are overlain with snow perhaps an inch deep. The gas lamps have not yet been extinguished and the snow is tinged with orange at their feet.

Just then Richards and Peter return with the carriage, which is just as well, as the snow is still falling steadily, and the prospect of the horses not being able to make the steep gradient of East Park Road is not one which I wish to contemplate. Richards has been entrusted with a note from Titus to say that the girls are safely if sleepily arrived and have been installed in the bedroom which has been prepared for them to catch up on their lost slumbers.

This prompts me to suggest to Richards and the boy that they may wish to snatch an hour or two of sleep themselves, once the carriage is unhitched and the horses attended to. Richards says that there is no need for he is quite used to early mornings, and Peter valiantly says the same, though he is yawning despite himself. I pat him on the shoulder awkwardly and resume my perambulation from room to room. It is as if I am looking for something, although for much of the time I can scarcely tell you where I am and what, if anything, I am thinking.

I stand in the middle of the hall, looking up the stairs. I stand open-mouthed, listening intently, but no sound reaches me, which is not in the least surprising, for the walls in this house are thick; the doors substantial; and Louisa is two floors above me.

I suddenly realise that anyone coming upon me, as I stand here slack-jawed, gazing vacantly upward, would have to be readily forgiven for concluding that he has stumbled upon an imbecile, and I resolve to pull myself together.

Therefore it is that I decide to take a turn in the park to try to pass the time. There is a greatcoat and muffler on the coat stand in the vestibule, and there are gloves in the pockets, so there is no need to go upstairs. I change from carpet slippers into gumboots, and venture out. The snow has mostly stopped falling apart from the occasional flake eddying listlessly down. The crunch of fresh snow underfoot is delightful as I cross the road and into the park through the little gate opposite my house.

The scene before me is like a winter landscape painting now that the sun is up. It is still early enough for me to have the park to myself and it is a curious pleasure to look behind me and see that mine are the only human footprints, though here and there I can see the tiny prints of birds' feet. I circumnavigate the lake in an anti-clockwise direction. I understand that it was once a reservoir that served the town which was turned into an ornamental lake when I was fifteen or sixteen.

I remember vividly when the park was opened. I was a young man of thirty-four. The whole town was given a half-holiday and factories and mills closed at noon, while shops closed for business. Packed excursion trains came into Blackburn Station from Darwen, Bolton, Preston, Accrington, Burnley, and it seemed as if the whole of Lancashire had come to enjoy the day with us.

I remember a mighty procession passing up Preston New Road from the Town Hall, setting off just after two o'clock. There were several bands. Behind the first was a contingent of police, followed by two halberd bearers and a staff man, who, in turn, preceded the Mayor in full regalia (William Pilkington, I think it was). The aldermen and councillors, of whom my father was one, came next, and then their distinguished guests, including Mama, Titus and me. Then the clergy from all the parishes of the town, with their banners and flags; magistrates and beadles and bailiffs; more bands; representatives of all manner of societies and associations. There were seventy scholars from the Grammar School, where Titus and I had once been pupils, and children from other schools in the borough, including the Ragged School.

The street was lined with people cheering and waving flags. As the parade approached the triple-arched gates of the entrance, the Sebastopol cannons at the top of the park fired a volley which could be heard even above the boom of the bass drum, and the braying of the trumpets and trombones of the Darwen Temperance Band.

How very different from this frosty morning on the last day of the dying year. The snow seems to muffle everything, and there is a great sense of stillness and near silence. The lake is frozen over. The swans and most of the ducks have retreated to the island in the middle where snow has not fallen under the trees, and there is even a patch, under overhanging branches, where the water has not frozen, and where a few of the ducks bob and dive. Apart from the odd indignant quack, they are quiet too. A pair of geese walk tentatively over the surface of the ice, think better of it and take off, disappearing over the trees.

I have not dared go too far from the house. At length I come around, by the smaller lake and the statue of Flora, to the little promontory where Fanny, Charlotte and Eliza have often come with their governess to feed the ducks and swans. I look out across the ice and the snow-limned bushes and trees and wonder if, in the not too distant future, they will be joined by a little brother.

But now, the cold is seeping through my gloves; my ears and nose are stinging, and it is time to return to the house. Peter greets me at the door where I am stamping my feet on the mat so as not to trail snow into the hall. He shakes his head as if to tell me that there is no news, and then helps me remove my greatcoat and gumboots. Looking at my pocket watch, I am surprised to see that it is not yet eleven. How slowly Time slithers along when one awaits a great event.

I listen at the foot of the stairs again, and still all is quiet. And so I betake myself to the library where I try to read, but it is no use, for the words just dance before my eyes and I cannot hold the sense in my head before my mind wanders off into territory which is vague and ill-defined. When Cook sends to inquire what I should like for luncheon, I say that I am not hungry and ask that she should just send up some tea.

And so the day wears on, hour after limping hour, as if the hands on the grandfather clock in the corner have been glued to his face. Still no news from upstairs. In the afternoon I manage a little correspondence, and catalogue some new additions to my coin collection. Later, I doze off for an hour or two in the wing chair by the fire, but my sleep is fitful and my dreams disturbing, though all memory of them is gone when I awake, aching and unrefreshed. At dinner time a dish of cold game pie, a slice or two of tongue, a hard-boiled egg and some Russian salad, along with a flask of claret, are brought up to me. I pick at it and, after a while, send it back barely touched.

Shortly afterwards, the Dunkenhalgh herself appears to tell me that the birthing is proving arduous, but I am not to be alarmed. All the same, she thinks it prudent to send for the doctor.

I dispatch Peter, whom I imagine pelting as fast as his young legs can carry him through the snowy streets, to fetch Doctor Willis from his house at Four Lane Ends, hard by the inn. They are soon here and the doctor goes upstairs.

He is not gone long. On his return to the library I press a glass of whisky on him, as he bids me not to worry. He says he has given Louisa a preparation to ease her pains somewhat. He has a call to make elsewhere, he says, but he will return later.

This excellent man is as good as his word for he arrives back at a quarter to eleven. After looking in on his patient, and finding all well, he proposes a game or two of chess, to which I readily agree.

My mind is at sixes and sevens, however, and I play atrociously. It is New Year's Eve, I remember, and cannot help but think that, ordinarily, the house would have been brilliant with lights as we hosted the great and the good of the town with a reception and a ball to see in the new year.

It is when two of the doctor's knights come scissoring across the board, and I realise that in two moves they will have cornered my king with their linked powers, that Jane Green comes rushing into the library and asks the doctor to come at once. He dashes out of the room.

The clock strikes midnight and I follow into the hall.

The doctor must have left the door of Louisa's room open.

I hear the most terrible cries.

24 THE JOURNAL 3

1876

January 1st, 1876

THE SCREAMS ARE UNENDURABLE. I take the stairs two at a time but do not dare go further than the first floor for fear of the formidable midwife. Preposterous, I confess it, but my Louisa's life lies in her hands and those of Doctor Willis, and I feel I must still be patient, torturous though it may be.

And then, praise be, the cry of a child. I dither on the landing for an eternity and a day until Dr Willis comes down the stairs, his ruddy face beaming like the very sun itself.

He takes my hand in both of his and pumps it enthusiastically.

'You have another daughter, Cornelius,' he says. 'Congratulations!'

'Louisa?' I mutter.

'She is well,' he replies, 'exhausted, of course. I recommend she rest in bed for a week to ten days. I will look in from time to time. She is rather anaemic. I have prescribed iron salts and made recommendations for her diet to Mrs Dunkenhalgh. The baby is plump and hale and in fine voice, as you no doubt heard. I will take my leave now, Cornelius. I venture to think you may go up now. I believe they are quite ready for you.'

We shake hands again and I go up to see my new daughter. If I say that my joy is laced through with disappointment, I do not hit the mark exactly, for my mind at present is in turmoil. Joy there is, certainly, and relief that mother and child are delivered safely from their ordeal, but I have so hoped for a son, and for so long, that I cannot help the pang of chagrin that accompanies my higher feelings, nor the sense of shame and dishonour which issue from that pang, for is it not prideful of me to question the blessing which Almighty God has bestowed upon us, and is it not sin to wish for that which He, in His eternal wisdom, has chosen not to grant?

These unworthy thoughts vanish utterly, however, as I open the door and behold my wife, and the new life we have brought into the world. Louisa is pale. Her hair is down and still damp, I fancy, from her long exertions, but it has been brushed and neatly laid about her shoulders. She is smiling at me and I think I have never seen her so beautiful.

I move closer to the little parcel she is holding, all bundled up as if ready to be despatched to the Post Office. The baby is sleeping, her little red face screwed tightly as if trying to comprehend some curious dream. I am amazed to see that she already has a fuzz of dark hair, while the other girls are fair, like Louisa. She will have my colouring then. My heart is flooded with tenderness. I bend to kiss my wife and then my daughter's furrowed brow.

Looking up, I see that Jane Green is looking on with her hands clasped under her chin, her face beaming with such warmth I wonder she does not combust. What is more, Mrs Dunkenhalgh has a shining countenance also, and I marvel that I ever thought her a dragon.

Now, it behoves us all to get some rest.

January 3rd

I send for my other daughters and they tumble into the house along with their Uncle Titus and Aunt Clara, clamouring to see their new sister. I tell them that they must calm themselves or they will tire their mother and alarm the baby at which they put on an air of demure composure which is not entirely convincing, and we go upstairs.

The child is awake in her crib. The girls kiss their mama and go to look at their sibling. Fanny and Charlotte beg to be permitted to hold her. Mrs Dunkenhalgh lifts the bundle into their arms in turn. Charlotte puts her face close to the infant whose wandering eyes seem to focus.

'Oh, Mama, she's looking right at me,' she cries.

'Mama, she smells quite, quite adorable,' Fanny cries when it is her turn. 'I could eat her all up!'

'Pray, don't do that just yet,' I say. 'First, a name is to be thought on.'

'Oh, do not bother to think, Papa,' says pert Miss Fanny. 'Charlotte and I have already chosen a name. We are quite decided, you know.'

'Is that so?' I say, pretending to be fierce. 'I thought that the prerogative of choosing the baby's name belonged exclusively to its parents.'

'Oh no, Papa,' says Charlotte, 'that is a practice quite exploded in polite society nowadays. At present, the only proper way to set about the naming of a newborn infant is to leave the matter entirely to its sisters.'

'I see. And what name have my precocious daughters chosen?'

'Well, Papa,' Fanny says, 'you know that Miss Usher has been reading a book to us by Lewis Carroll called *Alice's Adventures Underground*?'

I do know this for Miss Usher sought my approval. I was aware (from *The Times*) that Lewis Carroll is the *nom de plume* of Reverend Charles Dodgson of the University of Oxford, and I assumed that the work of a clergyman must surely be free from harm, though I confess on glancing through it that the illustrations by Mr Tenniel are rather alarming.

'Yes, Fanny,' I say, 'I was aware of that.'

'Well. Don't you see, Papa,' she says. 'That Alice is the perfect name for baby? Alice in the book is so pretty and clever and courageous and...'

'...and *curious*,' Charlotte interjects.

'...and *curious*,' Fanny continues, 'that our sister simply must be called Alice. And there's an end.'

'Alice is a beautiful name,' my wife says. 'I like Alice.'

'Alice is holding my finger tight,' says little Eliza, and so she is. And thus is the matter settled.

January 12th

Alice was baptised this afternoon at the new church of St James, high above the town. Titus and Clara are godparents, along with Miss Garnet of Strawberry Bank, a bosom friend of Louisa's. All went well until the Reverend Whalley, the new vicar, scooped the water over the infant's head, whereupon the child set up such an indignant wailing as if the poor minister had stabbed her with a carving knife, and she began to squirm and wriggle with such energy that I felt certain that the poor clergyman must drop his tiny burden into the very font itself.

The service was concluded as hastily as was decent, but Alice did not desist from her screaming until we had quit the church and were out into the fresh air, at which time she promptly fell fast asleep.

25 THE JOURNAL 4

1877

July 22

I READ IN *THE BLACKBURN TIMES*, that a spiritualist medium by the name of Miss Wood has been exposed as a fraud at the Exchange on King William Street.

It seems that she materialised from a cabinet, apparently clothed in ethereal light and gossamer robes, when she was seized by certain men, and discovered to be no spirit but of mortal flesh, and was moreover, when the house lights were brought up on the dreadful scene, found to be immodestly clad. She affected to speak in the voice of her spirit guide, an Indian child named Pocahontas, but the game was up and she was unable to regain the credence of the audience.

I was most profoundly shocked by this disgraceful episode. It is a wicked thing to attempt to defraud the public on any matter, but to do so where great faith and tenderness of feeling are brought to the proceedings in an earnest and trusting attempt to reach loved ones who have passed through the veil of death, that is an abomination.

There are those who sneer at spiritualism; I am not of their number. There are those who claim that the followers of sensitives are credulous and weak-brained, I make no such claims. There are those who believe that death is the end of all things; I denounce such a belief as blasphemous. On the contrary, I maintain that the principles and practice of spiritualism are perfectly consonant with the Christian faith as proclaimed by the Church of England. Do we not affirm in our creed that we believe in 'the resurrection of the body'? Does not that creed assert that the Lord Jesus was 'crucified, dead, and buried,' that He 'descended into Hell', and that 'on the third day He rose again'?

Did He not raise Lazarus from the dead?

Is it not then reasonable to suppose that the spirits of the deceased watch over us as they, and we, await the awful trumpet which will announce the Last Day, when He shall come to judge the 'quick and the dead'?

August 24th

Louisa is once again expecting a child. I should rather say that *we* are expecting a child. Doctor Willis says that there can be no doubt about it, and, while I am quite naturally elated by the news, I am also not a little anxious for Louisa's health for she was a long time in recovering from Alice's birth. The Doctor finds that she continues to be somewhat anaemic and has been treating her with arsenic at which I was understandably alarmed until I was reassured that the dose is minute and extremely dilute.

She has been urged to eat dark green vegetables such as spinach, broccoli and Brussels sprouts, all of which she despises, and liver once a week, which she detests, but she dutifully submits to the regimen with humour and fortitude.

November 4th

Louisa has miscarried. We are overwhelmed with sorrow. Dr Willis has been here for some hours. There has been much loss of blood, and Louisa is deathly pale. I can't trust myself to write any more.

27 THE JOURNAL 6

1878

January 1st

IT IS NIGH ON TWO MONTHS since the Angel of Death passed silently through my door and slew with his icy touch a child as yet but barely formed and robbed me - might it not be so? - of a son.

For two months, this house has been shrouded in silence, and we have tip-toed around each other as if infected with a contagion. It has been like some castle in a fairy tale on which a wicked enchantress has cast a malign spell, so that its inhabitants drift about the chambers and stairs in a long, slow, sad dream, barely acknowledging each other.

Miss Usher has explained to the older girls what has happened; it is not a proper subject for a father to broach. Fanny and Charlotte were deeply upset and wept on each other's shoulders, it seemed for days. Eliza is too young to really understand, but has attuned herself to her sisters' grief in some manner, and has tended her dolls most solicitously since the event.

Alice has not been told, nor need she be.

Christmas was a solemn affair, Louisa continuing very poorly, and the new year comes in through fog and unrelenting rain, bringing but little cheer.

January 15th

Little by little, we return to a more hopeful course of life. Louisa has gained a little more colour and has left her bed to resume her role as mistress of the house, though a nap in the afternoons is thought prudent.

Alice continues to improve, and was permitted to join us at church this Sunday past and afterwards at luncheon, always under the watchful eye of Mrs Harflett. The upsetting of a gravy boat, I am happy to believe, was a genuine accident rather than anything wilful. Eliza is growing up to be a very winsome little girl and she and Alice are learning to play very prettily together.

May 29th
Louisa laughs at me, but I am as excited as a schoolboy at the prospect of a half holiday. A notion which germinated long ago has gradually put forth shoots in my brain, like a spring bulb growing in the darkness, and now is brought into the light to flourish and blossom.

Enough of this botanical imagery; the project is a very practical matter. It concerns the building of a desk, or rather a bureau.

When I was fourteen or fifteen years of age, my father took me to see the Great Exhibition at the Crystal Palace in London. The journey itself was a marvel: I remember the engine pulling into Preston station like some great dragon, chugging, and panting, and then, with a metallic squeal of brakes, exhaling smoke which went rolling up into the vaults of the building, and sending steam billowing across the platform.

My father read his newspaper or snoozed for much of the journey, but I could not leave the window, watching England race by at a speed I had never experienced before. We passed through industrial landscapes much like my home town, all chimneys and steeples and factories with many windows beside filthy streams under a pall of murky fumes until we reached the bewilderingly busy station at Crewe where there was a long wait, to take on water, Father said.

Soon after leaving Crewe, we burst into brilliant sunlight. And then: such green fields, such acres of stubble where stooks of golden corn stood about and haystacks, big as houses, such broad, gleaming rivers, thick woods, and rolling hills - I thought England must be boundless.

I had thought Blackburn a great city, although to be sure I had never really been anywhere else, and certainly never been further south than Manchester, but the crowds at Euston Station astounded me, nay, alarmed me even. I stayed close to my father, affronted at being jostled by these hurrying Londoners, who never apologised and who, with single purpose, seemed willing to walk right through you if you did not move out of the way. The noise of the trains behind us, of hucksters and hawkers and barrow boys shouting their wares, and of the horse traffic on the Euston Road, was deafening. I was glad when my father hailed a closed carriage to take us to our hotel in Charles Street near Berkeley Square.

The following morning we rode on top of an omnibus, an exciting novelty for a provincial boy such as I was. As we came down Knightsbridge, a fantastical vision came into view among the trees, indeed it was taller than the trees. It was the Crystal Palace glittering in the sunshine and I could not help but think of the 'stately pleasure dome' in Xanadu that Coleridge describes in *Kubla Khan*.

'Taller than the trees,' I just wrote - why, there were trees growing *inside* this vast structure. Moreover, right at the centre of the building there was a fountain twenty-seven feet high made of pink glass, and to think that I had been labouring under the illusion that the fountain you encountered on your right as you entered Corporation Park must surely dwarf any of the fountains in Rome or Versailles.

It was here that my father left me to join business associates for the day, and here that we were to meet up again at six o'clock that evening. He made sure that I had money enough to buy myself a midday meal at one of the many refreshment stalls run by Messrs. Schweppes. Otherwise, the day was mine entirely, to explore whatever and wherever I liked.

It would have been in vain to have tried to inspect all the exhibits - there were, my programme told me, a hundred thousand of them. I sauntered about the building at random, and my lack of a plan was quite unimportant as absolutely every exhibit was a uniquely compelling phenomenon. I wandered about utterly spellbound.

Half the display space was given over to Great Britain and the Empire and I felt proud of the artefacts that had been designed and built in the home country, and in Her Majesty's realms elsewhere. I saw a mechanical press that could print copies of the *Illustrated London News* faster than I could count them. There was a steam hammer that could crush an elephant or gently crack an egg; there were adding machines that could put many of my father's employees out of a job; there was a folding sportsman's knife which had been made in Sheffield and boasted eighty blades. Eighty. In one of the galleries above the principal floor, there was a wall of stained glass, more brilliant and set with more intense colours, than those of any church I had ever seen. There was ink that produced raised handwriting for the benefit of the blind.

But the Empire was not enough. As the hours went by, I wandered into other realms and territories, the more remote and exotic the better. In the United States of America, under the beady eyes of a giant eagle dressed in the stars and stripes, I was permitted to handle various firearms. In India, I sat on an elaborately carved ivory throne, and climbed a carved ladder to sit in a magnificent howdah atop a stuffed elephant.

It was in China, however, that I was perfectly enthralled. I admired beautifully painted vases featuring conical snow-topped mountains, cherry trees full of blossom, multicoloured long-tailed birds, little figures of coolies carrying yokes from which hung wooden pails, and women in silk kimonos. Some of the vases were taller than I was at the time.

Then there was a room displaying exquisite furniture lacquered in black and gold. A chinaman in mandarin robes showed me a marvellous cabinet: behind double doors were numerous alcoves, drawers and little portals. Many hidden catches caused banks of such portals to disappear, sinking into hidden recesses, or swinging outwards to left and right to reveal more shelves and secret niches. I thought it quite magical and resolved one day to have something like it, though in the form of an escritoire or bureau.

That dream has been with me ever since. As soon as I began earning a respectable income, I began haunting quality furniture stores and warehouses. It was not a piece of *chinoiserie* that I was looking for - the fashion for that kind of thing is somewhat diminished and, whilst I find it very pretty, I think I was looking for something more essentially English, in the style of Sheraton or Chippendale, perhaps. But the casing was not really the thing. What I craved was those magical compartments, moving on hinges, counterbalanced with hidden weights.

I never found what I was looking for until last week: in a warehouse in Darwen of all places, I found a roll-top desk with secret compartments. It was not on the scale I was looking for but the principle was there. Inscribed on the brass keyhole was the legend:

THOS. BASSETT & SON
CABINET MAKER

I asked the warehouseman if he knew this craftsman and had he bought the desk directly from him. The answer being in the affirmative to both questions, I sought directions, which the man readily supplied.

In brief, I have written to Mr Bassett, outlining my project and await his reply with the impatience of a small boy for Christmas Day.

28 THE JOURNAL 7

June 1st, 1878

THOMAS BASSETT REPLIED BY RETURN and a meeting was arranged for this morning. I am not sure what I was expecting - a middle-aged man and an apprentice boy, I suppose. Instead, Jane Green showed into the library an elderly white-haired man, and another man who must be approximately fifty years of age. This latter was introduced to me as Jack, the 'son' of the business. I could see the familial likeness.

They stood just inside the doorway, each clutching his cloth cap in both hands, until I made it quite clear that there was no need for deference and, sending Jane to bring refreshments, I bade them come and sit with me at the round table in the middle of the room.

I had already laid out on its surface drawings I had made of the bureau of my imagination over the years. The earliest dated from when I was barely out of my boyhood, and the plans had been refined and grown more elaborate until the most recent depicted a colossus of a desk, wide enough to seat three people. I had attempted to include in my diagrams some indication of the secret drawers and compartments that I required.

I am no draughtsman and was very apologetic about my handiwork but Thomas insisted on saying that my designs gave him a very good idea of what I was looking for. I thanked him for his politeness but insisted that he must think my scribblings very amateurish indeed. Incidentally, I have insisted on the use of Christian names, mine included, since we shall be working closely together, and because I have the highest regard for those who use their hands to create things of beauty, despising as prigs and snobs those who would prize a sculptor over a cabinet maker, or a maker of melodies over a gardener.

Over tea and seed cake we discussed the undertaking further. Thomas made little sketches based on mine - I could see how much more professional than my attempts they were - and, as he asked questions and I replied, he amended and honed his little designs. Meanwhile, Jack made notes and calculations in his own notebook. He had one very pertinent question: why so big?

I hardly know myself. I explained that while it was pleasant enough to work in the library, I was trying to raise a literate family and felt that my daughters must have access at all times, with the supervision of their governess of course. My wife, Louisa, is an insatiable reader, and likes to peruse her books by the fire in winter, or the French windows in summer, and while this is all very companionable, there are times where I yearn for a little privacy. I went on to say that I plan to retire in a couple of years' time and that I intend to turn a room on the first floor, with a pleasing prospect of the garden, into a study for my private and exclusive use.

At their request, we went up to the room, and I showed them where I wished the desk to be placed - between the two large windows. I further explained that I wanted it to be so wide because I envisaged having more than one project laid out at once: correspondence, my journal, my coin collection, my stamp collection or my scrapbooks. I would move from one enterprise to another with the aid of a chair on castors.

I did not mention that I wanted somewhere secure to secrete these journals. I do my best to trust my family and servants, but I am surrounded by females, and it is universally acknowledged that the female of the species can be seized with the itch of a curiosity far more vehement than that which killed the proverbial cat.

After further discussion - during which Jack produced a tape measure and got down on his hands and knees in order to ascertain the dimensions of the future cabinet of secrets - we returned to the library. Both men had a very serious air and I feared that they were about to tell me that it couldn't be done.

Not so. Thomas explained that a piece of those dimensions could never be got up the stairs and through the door of my future study, and so they would have to build it in sections in the workshop and assemble it in the room. He proposed that he and his son should call at the same hour in a week's time with technical drawings and a quotation for work and materials. I said this would be highly agreeable.

I saw them out myself an hour or so ago, and now I am already quite beside myself with impatience.

June 8th

The plans with which Thomas & Son presented me this morning are exquisite. With meticulous detail, the inner workings of the bureau are laid out from several angles, their various secret mechanisms, catches and levers, weights and counterweights, exposed to view. The designs are ingenious to the last degree and I could not be more delighted. Thomas tells me that it can be prepared in his workshop within a month, and that it will take several days to be built in my study.

Jack now shows me several possible designs for the marquetry on the exterior of what I have until now been calling the 'lid', but which I am assured should be called the 'writing flap'. It seems that this is Jack's speciality. I have chosen an elaborate lotus blossom to be worked in ash, cherry, and maple. The interior will feature a green tooled leather writing surface with a gold leaf border.

When all is settled, Thomas presents me with his estimate which is nothing if not remarkable. Notwithstanding, the good Book bids us recognise that 'the labourer is worthy of his hire' (Luke 10, 5), and I have, myself, requested that the very best materials be used, and so it is agreed that I shall immediately pay a certain sum to cover the cost of materials, the balance to be paid on completion.

August 11th

To the seaside with Alice and Eliza, Miss Usher in attendance. Alice has been told that if she misbehaves, we shall turn around and come straight home. The girls have never been on a train before and are enraptured, standing at the window and pointing out cows and sheep, which, until now they have only encountered in books.

In Lytham they are delighted by the windmill, and totally transported by their first glimpse of the sea. Taking a carriage to the new town of St Annes-on-the-Sea, we pass Fairhaven Lake and arrive at the pier, where we take a stroll and the girls are treated to ices.

It is pleasing to note that throughout the day, Alice has been a proper poppet, and only on the train back to Blackburn was she a little crotchety.

September 21st

My bureau is complete. I have watched its assembly all week, marvelling at the workmanship of its authors. No nails or screws have been used in the construction, but only painstakingly prepared joints. I was dimly aware of tongue and groove and mortise and tenon joints, but, over the last few days, I have learned of butt joints, rabbet joints, dovetail joints, dado joints, mitre joints and spline joints. Thomas and Jack seem happy to explain to me the terms of their art; I do not think they can be accustomed to a client who watches them exercise their craft in a state of admiration nigh unto awe.

And now it is done, the tools packed away, sawdust swept from the floor, a Chinese rug laid down, and the bureau polished to a deep shine. The men are paid and depart.

A rather nasty smell of fish glue hung about for a while, but I have been burning candles scented with bergamot, and the odour has almost gone.

Louisa thinks the bureau is hideous, but it is no matter because the family are to understand that my new study is out of bounds to all but myself. Jane Green will be admitted to clean the room periodically, though only under my supervision.

29 THE JOURNAL 8

1880

February 13th

I am most concerned about the behaviour of little Alice. It contrasts very unfavourably with that of her older siblings when they were two years old. They have always been sweet, biddable girls, whose only shortcoming has been a tendency to be a little pert, but Alice? Alice is, at times, as a creature possessed by demons.

She will throw her dolls out of her perambulator in the public street or in the park, and when Miss Usher retrieves them, out they go again.

She will refuse to eat her food, and then, after playing with it, tip it on the floor, upon which she will steal food from her sisters' plates.

If she does not get her own way she will throw a tantrum, hurling herself to the ground, screaming in ecstasies of grief and rage, and squirming about in furious paroxysms until she is quite exhausted.

She is acquiring the power of speech rapidly, as did her sisters, and already has vocabulary enough to lie, blaming others, and Eliza in particular, for her misdemeanours. What is more she will vehemently deny misconduct of which she is patently guilty, as when she deliberately pulled a jug of milk from the dresser and was to be found sitting in the spillage and surrounded by the shards of the shattered vessel, saying: 'it wasn't me'.

She will, when caught in the act of some infant felony and told to desist, continue to offend while staring at you defiantly, right in the eye.

Miss Usher and I are at a loss. However, I do not believe in raising a hand to girl-children and will not permit others to exercise corporal punishment on them. With a boy it might be different. One can only hope that this is but a tiresome chapter in Alice's development and that it will pass. Needless to say, Louisa never witnesses any of this recalcitrance, and will scarce believe it when she is told about it, for Alice is perfectly angelic in her presence, and consequently is spoiled quite shamelessly.

What is passing strange is that my love for this contrary little imp is not one whit diminished by her deplorable capers. I do most diligently believe that a parent should not have a favourite amongst his offspring, or, at the very least, should refrain from revealing any such favour, but, try as I might, I cannot help but adore my lastborn even more than her more demure and complaisant sisters.

April 4th

Alice's continued misbehaviour grieves me deeply, and it is distressing to learn that her doting sisters have had cause to complain to me about many thoughtless or even spiteful incidents. She has been known to steal and hide Eliza's toys; it seems she deliberately spilled water on to Charlotte's watercolour painting of the conservatory in the park, and she scribbled all over Fanny's common-place book, damaging the beautiful pressed flowers within its pages.

Worst of all, a tearful Miss Usher came to me this morning to say that she wishes to give in her notice as she feels the child of whom she has charge has become ungovernable. I asked if there was anything specific which had brought her to this pass, and, horrible to relate, she told me that Alice had just bitten her. Rolling back her cuffs she showed me a contusion just above the wrist. I told her that I could not accept her resignation as I not only valued her work, but considered her to be almost one of the family, and, promising that something must be and will be done, bade her bring Alice to me in the library.

Crabby and sullen, the little demon presently arrives, dragging her feet and trying to break free of her governess's grip.

'Did you bite Miss Usher?' I say.

'No,' says Alice, staring straight at me. 'She'd taste horrible and she is a gobbling turkey and she tells big fat lies.'

I pick her up bodily, and with the wriggling imp under my arm, I go out into the hall, round the staircase, and through to the service stairs.

Below them is a cupboard in which I deposit the child, lock the door, and leave her there, screaming in the darkness.

April 5th

YESTERDAY, I LOCKED MY LITTLE DAUGHTER in the cupboard under the stairs and she screamed and screamed in anguish while I stood trembling with rage and guilt on the other side of the door.

In truth she cannot have been in there for more than ten minutes, but I waited until the screaming stopped and, when I opened the door she emerged scowling, and kicked me in the shin with all the force she could muster. Miss Usher stood by wringing her hands as Alice rushed past her and up the service stairs.

'Do not disturb your mother,' I shouted after her.

'I hate you,' she shouted back. 'I hate you all.'

Miss Usher was staring at me with an expression of reproach.

'Well?' I said, still trembling with passion. 'You have something to say, Miss Usher?'

'With the greatest respect, sir,' she replied, 'I think that that was very wrong.'

My anger ebbed on the sudden, leaving only remorse and shame.

'You are quite right, Miss Usher. The act was beneath me, and I am very sorry indeed that you had to witness it. However, I am sure that we both agree that the situation cannot be allowed to continue. I must discuss with Mrs Pickup what is to be done, though I am loath to trouble her at this time. But first, you must assist me in persuading her that the predicament is real. I fear her indulgence does not help the matter.'

'Most willingly, sir,' was the estimable woman's reply.

'I am grateful,' I said. 'We shall broach the matter tomorrow morning immediately after breakfast, but now I must find my child and apologise to her.'

Upstairs I encountered Jane Green who informed me that she had just chased Alice away from Louisa's door because she was sleeping, and that she thought Alice had gone up to her own room on the floor above.

I went up and tapped gently on the door. There being no answer, I pushed it open, and went in to find her lying on her bed and staring at the ceiling.

'I am sorry, my sweet heart,' I said, humbling myself. 'It will not happen again.'

Alice turned her face to the wall and did not reply.

May 2nd

I have just concluded a conference with my wife and the children's governess about what is to be done about Alice and her misbehaviour, and I have to record that it was with considerable difficulty that Louisa was persuaded that there was any problem at all. Miss Usher and I presented her with so many examples of Alice's disobedience that she had to concede that we were not fabricating the case. I had suggested to Miss Usher in advance that there would be no point in upsetting my wife with an account of the exhibition of myself I made yesterday and she was most obliging as ever.

It was agreed that corporal punishment was out of the question for I believe the injunction in Proverbs 13:2 not to spoil the child by sparing the rod applies only to sons. I proposed that some system of correction must be devised wherein insufferable conduct would be met with penalties.

'And reformation of conduct suitably rewarded,' added Louisa whose smile, albeit sweetness itself, was nonetheless quite absolute.

I replied that that must naturally be the case. What I had in mind after a night of reflection and prayer was a table of forfeits where the punishment should be appropriate to the offence. This might mean the denial of treats, replacing Cook's excellent fare with plainer dishes, extended periods of study, confinement to the house while her sisters play in the park, confinement to her room, separation from her sisters, and maybe even her mother.

'Oh, I cannot allow that,' says Louisa.

'Only for the most egregious naughtiness,' I say - and then, in order to soothe her - 'However, if there is the prospect of an amendment in her behaviour, various prizes might be dandled before her: a strawberry ice, some ribbons, a new bonnet, a visit to the circus, the Easter Fair in Market Square, or an excursion to Lytham or to the pier at Southport.'

'That is all very well, Cornelius,' says Louisa, 'but who is to administer this enlightened régime?'

'Somebody must be employed.'

'You cannot be thinking of replacing Miss Usher? I won't hear of it.'

'Of course not, my dear. That is indeed unthinkable. No, someone must be employed in addition to Miss Usher, who, I fear, has had to endure a quite unfair burden of late. To be responsible for the welfare of four girls, one of whom is our little perisher - that is to ask too much, and I wonder we did not recognise it before. No, Miss Usher will continue with the education of Fanny, Charlotte and Eliza. This new person will undertake the exclusive care of Alice.'

'But how is this new person to be found?' asks Louisa, and I have to acknowledge that I have not the faintest idea.

It is now that Miss Usher says that she might be of some assistance. She tells us that there is a woman on the books of the agency, from whom I obtained the services of Miss Usher herself, who is noted from Griffin Park to Intack for being both fierce and kind.

In due course, we take our leave of Louisa, fearing that our discussion might have tired her, and lead Miss Usher to the library where I take down details of this nonpareil among women, and immediately compose a telegram making inquiry about her availability. Then I ring for Peter to take it to the Post Office at the top of Shear Brow with all haste.

July 8th

What a change in my little Alice! I cannot pretend that she has become a paragon for all the little girls in the kingdom to emulate, but there has been such an improvement in her manners and comportment as is truly wonderful.

Certainly, the transformation is not complete, not by a long way, and yet, there is much less malice in her mischief, she can sit still for more than ten minutes, she is much more polite to Miss Usher, and, on occasion, affectionate towards me. I am told that she is showing great aptitude in her schooling and appears to be of fine intelligence. I have promised her that we shall go to the pantomime at Christmas time if she continues to be a good girl.

And who is to be credited with bringing about this miracle? The answer is one Aurora Harflett, a widow from Rishton, who arrived in my house in her own uniform of dark grey serge, buttoned to the chin and already fully armed with a plan of action. I think I had expected a hatchet-faced martinet, but here was a matronly figure with a winning smile, on which I commented.

'You are very kind, Mr Pickup, but it is not a smile that Miss Alice is likely to witness for some time to come,' she said. I thought it best to say nothing further, simply assuring her that I would endorse whatever methods she might deem appropriate. All she required, she said, were two things: a spacious day room, where visitors would be excluded, save my wife and me, and a bedroom which she and Alice would occupy. Meals would be taken in this suite, until Mrs Harflett thought Alice ready to dine with others.

I said that the nursery might be for her use exclusively, while the older girls and Miss Usher would use the schoolroom. There would be no difficulty in turning an adjoining room into a bedchamber.

How very fortunate we are that this good fairy, as I may call her, was available to join our household and how blessed we are that she continues to work her daily miracles.

August 3rd

It is so very disappointing. Alice will have to be confined to the nursery for a week with only her tutor for company. Meals high in nourishment but low in interest will be taken up to her, and extra schoolwork has been prescribed. These are the penalties decreed by Mrs Harflett and I have assented without demur. I cannot have her interfering with the work of my servants in such a disruptive manner.

She was caught by the gardener, tearing up bedding plants he had only just set into the borders and the *parterres*. Not only had she ripped them out of the ground but she had thrown them around willy-nilly. This inexplicable act was not only distressing for Richards who had to report it to me, but inexpressibly vexing to me personally, for I have of late expended considerable time and thought on planning the evolution of the garden.

Louisa pleaded ardently on behalf of the child, but I was not to be moved and I am very much afraid that harsh words were said on both sides, an occurrence so rare in our marriage as to be profoundly unsettling when it does happen.

I am very much out of sorts.

30 THE JOURNAL 9

[UNLESS I'VE MISSED SOMETHING, there is nothing in the journals over the next few years that throws light on our researches concerning the body in the cellar. Cornelius Pickup continues to prosper financially, and his family continues to flourish with Louisa's health showing signs of improving. The census for 1881 shows the family at the peak of its affluence and comfort.

The journal for 1887 begins with an audit of Cornelius Pickup's personal fortune. Over a number of tedious pages, he assesses the value of his stocks and shares, various bonds, rents from properties he owns, and other incomes. He finds himself to be very rich indeed, and, at the age of 50, he decides to retire. He retains an honorary position on the board of the bank, is a member of a number of philanthropic organisations, is a governor of St John's Church of England School, and is elected town councillor.

In that year, there are significant calls on his wealth. - TC]

1887

February 26th

From this house, my dear, clever, reliable Fanny was married this morning, in St James's Church. Louisa and I had considered St John's where we ourselves were married, but St James's is nearer and we became members of the congregation once it was built. Since St James's is a kind of daughter parish to Blackburn's oldest church, there is perhaps a kind of felicity in my own daughter's being married there.

I suppose there is a point in every father's life when he realises, with a shock, that his little girl has become a young woman and, in Fanny's case, a very beautiful one at that. Of course, Louisa has seen to it that both Fanny and Charlotte have been introduced to the best society in this part of the county, and they have attended dances, more formal balls, concert parties, and the theatre. I have myself often been of the party.

It was at a soirée here at Wastwater House last Christmas Eve that I became aware that Fanny was now quite grown up. It was at that event that young Arthur Gleeson, a mill owner from Manchester, asked for my daughter's hand in marriage. We had done business with his father at the bank, and I had met the young man several times and found him very personable. When I asked him about his prospects, he said that later in the year he was going to move to Lille in order to run an enormous textiles factory there.

I heard this with a terrible pang. There was no possibility of my standing in the way of their happiness. However, I was conscious that I was not only to lose a daughter through marriage, but that the loss would be compounded when they became *émigrés*.

And so, this morning I gave away my eldest daughter in church. She looked radiant in white silk with a bouquet of orange blossom, and Charlotte and Eliza were bridesmaids. We were not sure that Alice could be trusted but she was bribed with a new dress and a little bouquet of her own and caused no undue embarrassment.

The reception and wedding breakfast were held at Wastwater House and cost me a pretty penny, not a farthing of which was begrudged.

Much good champagne was drunk, many veal pies and much cold chicken were consumed, the cake was cut and shared around, and many pretty speeches were made. If I may say so, the guests were gracious enough to be amused at the little pleasantries with which I ornamented my own oration.

At last, the happy couple left in the carriage which would take them to the railway station and thence to their honeymoon in Paris. It had been decorated with many white ribbons, and Richards and Peter had tied white crêpe around their hats. Just as she was handed into the carriage, Fanny threw her bouquet into the crowd of guests in the drive and it was caught by Charlotte with an alacrity that suggested the manoeuvre had been thoroughly rehearsed.

Back in the house, the carpet in the salon had been taken up and there was dancing, and to begin, the Best Man and Charlotte led a quadrille. The aforesaid gentleman was the Rev. Simon Street, vicar of St Chad's in Rochdale, who had been a close friend of the groom since they were both at Oxford.

Later in the evening, I saw, across the room, Louisa, Charlotte and the gentleman in earnest conversation, with frequent glances in my direction. At length, I saw Louisa urge him to come towards me, which presently he did. I should have sensed a conspiracy.

The Rev. Street begged the indulgence of a word in private, and still I was dull enough not to discern what was afoot. I obliged him by taking him across the hall into the library where he asked for Charlotte's hand in marriage. Dumfounded as I was for a moment, how could I not give my consent, for, although Charlotte is but seventeen years of age and very lively, she is a very commonsensical sort of a girl and her suitor a man of the cloth with a good living to boot? In addition, it did not fail to cross my mind that Rochdale is a good deal nearer home than Lille.

Back in the salon, Charlotte read her fortune in our beaming faces and my wife took me in her arms and kissed me. It has been an eventful day: I am pleased and proud. But, as ever, my joy is tinged with sadness.

March 6th

Mrs Harflett told me something quite remarkable this evening, and it was this: it transpires that Alice has formed an attachment to the between-maid, one Mary Ann Duxbury. She told me that Alice frequently goes down to the kitchen to talk to her and follows her about the house as she goes about her duties. Feeling quite reasonably that there was a decided impropriety in a situation wherein the eleven-year-old daughter of a good family is thick as thieves with a junior servant of twenty, she determined to put a stop to it, upon which Alice became very fractious.

The remarkable thing, she told me, was that the friendship appears to be wholly beneficial. Alice is becoming more obedient and more tractable by the day, and, on the whole, despite the friendship being a little too secretive for her liking, she feels that there is no harm in its being indulged. Nonetheless, she thought I ought to know.

I thanked her and said I would give thought to the matter. Now, I find Duxbury to be a personable, courteous and extremely diligent young woman, and, if it is true that her friendship with my daughter is making her more placid and compliant, I see no reason to interfere, despite their very different stations in life.

May 1st

To St James's Church to see my little Alice crowned May Queen after morning service. I thought my heart must burst with pride. She wore the white dress bought for her for Fanny's wedding and a red cloak trimmed with white fur, and accoutred thus she was crowned in the chancel.

There followed a procession down to the fields at Pleckgate, led by a brass band, the vicar and choir, and next a phaeton bearing her diminutive majesty and her little ladies-in-waiting. Another carriage bore last year's May Queen, wearing a blue cloak. Next came the Mothers' Union with their banner, and finally the rest of the congregation.

Once arrived at Pleckgate, we were regaled by a right royal picnic. A memorable day.

May 21st

This morning, in bright spring sunshine, I gave away my second daughter, Charlotte, to the Rev. Street in St James's Church. As with Fanny's nuptials, no detail was overlooked, no luxury denied, no expense spared. Alice was trusted to perform the duties of a bridesmaid, and she and Eliza carried them out very prettily.

It gladdened my heart that Fanny and her husband were able to travel from France to be with us. I was grateful to note that she has all the lineaments of settled happiness.

Once again, the wedding breakfast was held at home: the buffet was lavish, the cake was a cathedral among cakes, and the speeches glittered with wit.

Charlotte and her clergyman were about to depart for their honeymoon in Lyme Regis, when she turned and threw her bouquet into the crowd of guests. There could have been no rehearsal this time, for it was caught, on a reflex, by Miss Usher, who coloured so vividly that a pickled beetroot would have looked pale by comparison. She was teased by the young people about this for much of the evening, fiercely denying that she had any matrimonial plans whatsoever, until Louisa, seeing that the poor woman was pained and embarrassed by this teasing, bade them desist.

May 22nd

Mrs Harflett came to me this morning to say how proud she felt of Alice's deportment at the wedding, and declared that she felt that her work was completed. She proposed to leave my employ at the end of the month.

I said that there was no need for her to leave on my account but she would not be gainsaid, and declared indeed that she was ready to retire on her modest means, and proposed to join her sister in a cottage near Todmorden, where the Lancashire-Yorkshire boundary runs through the town hall. I intend to pay her a substantial honorarium for all the fine work she has done. She will be missed.

How my household appears to be shrinking.

31 THE JOURNAL 10

December 17th, 1887

CHARLOTTE IS HERE ON A VISIT. We have made it plain that she and her husband are always welcome, but, of course, Simon's Advent duties tie him to St. Chad's, and as Christmas approaches she will need to be by his side, much as we would love to have her here for the festivities.

She and Louisa are gone into town. Eliza begged to go with them and it was agreed that she might do so. They plan to do some Christmas shopping and no doubt they will visit the Thwaites Arcade which was built between Church Street and Lord Street a few years ago. It really is most salubrious. There are some twenty-four shops with plate glass frontages and ladies may peruse their lavish displays, whatever the weather, under a tented glass roof. And gentlemen too.

They will, no doubt, visit the shoe makers, the milliners, and Miss Ashworth's fancy goods shop, and no doubt Eliza will drag them into the confectioner's shop. I have myself bought gloves at Gallagher's. I understand that their plan is to take afternoon tea in the Spanish Room at the Old Bull Hotel, and then to take a hansom cab back home.

Alice looked a little dejected at not being invited to join the expedition, but Louisa said, quite rightly, that she would only be bored. In compensation, I promised that I would take her to feed the swans in the park, to inspect the conservatory, and, if she were very good, I would buy her tea and cakes and an ice at the café by the bowling green. In the event, she was quite impeccably behaved, and I fancy she greatly enjoyed having her papa to herself.

December 22nd

Our peace is disturbed. Charlotte has come down with a most virulent fever, and has taken to her bed. Doctor Willis has been sent for, but has not, as yet, been able to form a diagnosis. Nonetheless, he has recommended that she be isolated as a precaution. The children must be kept away, and given Louisa's history of imperfect health, any visits should be short and infrequent. Miss Usher insists on nursing her, despite the possible risk to her own health, and I am most grateful.

I have sent to Simon to inform him of the case and have promised to send him frequent bulletins concerning his wife's condition.

What a reversal from our happiness at the beginning of the week. Charlotte is constantly in our prayers.

December 23rd

The fever continues and my poor child is suffering from terrible headaches and abdominal pains. I cannot begin to imagine what she is suffering. If prayers can relieve her agonies, they shall not be wanting. Dr Willis is still not able to offer a diagnosis. Louisa and the children are being kept away as a precaution.

Christmas Eve

Alarming changes are visible today. Charlotte's skin has become dusky in a most unnatural way and pustules have begun to appear. She is conscious but does not eat, taking only sips of water.

Dr Willis fears that it may be smallpox though he is puzzled by the colour of her skin and has returned home to consult his books.

I was most vexed this afternoon. Miss Usher tells me that Eliza sneaked into the sick room whilst her back was turned, saying that she could not bear to be parted from her dear sister a moment longer. This, despite my most earnest prohibition.

There can be no thought of punishing her, under the circumstances, but nor can there be any thought of celebrating Christmas this year.

Christmas Day

Dr Willis has terrible news. After a further examination of Charlotte he suggests that we retire so that he can impart it. I lead him into my sanctum where he tells me that he believes that Charlotte has indeed been infected by smallpox and of a specifically vile kind. He says that the discolouration of the skin and that some bleeding at the base of the pustules confirm his diagnosis of haemorrhagic smallpox. He bids me prepare myself for the worst - the disease is invariably fatal.

I can hardly prevent myself from railing at the injustice of it. How on this most holy of days, when the Christ Child came into the world to save us all, can it be that my beloved child receives her death sentence?

I find it hard to pray, except to ask God to take me and spare my beautiful child.

December 26th

I asked Dr Willis why Miss Usher and I, who have been with Charlotte almost constantly have not been infected, and he confessed that he did not really know why some fall prey to contagion whilst others receive mercy.

Nonetheless, he urged that my family should be evacuated to some safe place. Consequently, I sent to my brother, Titus, to ask if he were willing to offer sanctuary and he replied immediately that his home was at their disposition. At the same time, I sent to Charlotte's husband at St Chad's with the ghastly news and urged him to come at once since not many days may be left to Charlotte.

But now, horror upon horror! As the carriage is got ready, and in all the bustle of hasty packing for the sojourn at Holt House, Eliza complains of a headache, and, placing her hand on the child's forehead, Louisa declares that the poor girl has a fever.

There follows an awful fracas. If Eliza has contracted the sickness, she cannot be allowed to go to my brother's. I have not told Louisa of the lethal nature of the pestilence, hoping against hope that Dr Willis is wrong. She begs to be allowed to stay with her daughters, and so I have no option but to take her aside and tell her the terrible truth. I urge her, for Alice's sake, to quit this house of pestilence immediately.

December 27th

Eliza has the marks upon her, a darkening of the skin and some few pustules. It is all too clear that she has been infected with the same plague as her sister.

Dr Willis has helped me move a bed into Charlotte's room as I don't want Peter or Richards to be exposed to infection. It makes sense to have the two girls together in one chamber so that Miss Usher and I can take turns to watch over them both, and thereby allow ourselves occasion for rest, although, to be sure, I don't think I have slept properly during these last grave days and nights.

Dr Willis says that Miss Usher and I may be presumed safe from the disease because sufficient time has passed since Charlotte was first infected and he believes we may have survived the incubation period. This is precious little solace. I would gladly perish rather than see my children suffer so dreadfully.

Indeed, Charlotte grows worse and cries out in her torment. The doctor explains that there is extensive bleeding under her skin. Soon there will be bleeding from her internal organs and it can only be a day or so before they fail and she passes from us. Eliza will suffer the same end, sooner rather than later.

He administers an opiate to both girls and they seem calmer, though who can know what hideous dreams haunt the stupor which the drug has imposed on them.

Eadem die
9 o'clock
Simon, the Rev. Street, my son-in-law, has just arrived, having left his parish in the care of a curate. Naturally he wishes to see his wife directly, though I warn him with great solemnity how very catching the disease can be, and how unrelentingly mortal.

Despite the difference in our years, he chides me as if I were an ignorant schoolboy. It is his duty, he says, both as a husband and a man of the cloth, to be with his wife at her departing. It may be that he can offer solace to her soul at the final hour - but if God wills that he contract the sickness - why, so be it. We are all in His hands.

After an hour or so in the sick room, we retire to the library. He accepts a small glass of Scotch whisky whilst I, normally a very temperate man, consume rather more. Indeed, in a very short time, to my shame and consternation, I see that the decanter is half empty.

The operation of the spirits on my brain dispels all inhibitions and I begin to rant. How can a loving God, I cry, inflict such suffering on two innocent girls? What sins can I have committed that I should be so afflicted. Surely none so grievous as to invoke such a punishment? How then can God be a just God? If God there be.

Simon is calm in the face of this blasphemy. He merely says in an even voice: 'Cornelius, think on the words of the psalmist, *The fool hath said in his heart, There is no God.* Come, Cornelius, let us kneel together and pray.'

He takes my hand and we kneel there on the carpet before the dimming ashes of the fire and say The Lord's Prayer together.

There is solace of a sort, however dilute.

32 THE JOURNAL II

December 28th

I FELT RATHER CRAPULOUS this morning after my consumption of whisky last evening and I am sorry to say that not only was I short with Miss Usher, but I actually struck Peter as he brought the morning post into the library. And why? Because I judged his fingernails to be dirty.

I could feel shock and disapproval emanating in waves from my son-in-law, but far worse was the hurt in the poor boy's eyes, and I knew immediately that I had been a brute. Peter has never been anything but a loyal and cheerful servant, ever willing and uncomplaining. I apologised profusely with tears in my eyes, but this only seemed to embarrass him.

Simon said nothing but I felt a chill between us and an air of reproach in his demeanour.

I fear my mental equilibrium has been upset by my daughters' sickness, especially since many more pustules have appeared on Eliza's skin, while Charlotte's breathing has become raucous, and at times, it seems that she is struggling to breathe at all.

Dr Willis calls in three times a day, but he says there is nothing more he can do, except to alleviate the pain a little. This morning he did not even speak, but shook his head, and looked at me with infinite sadness in his eyes.

Eadem die
7.15 pm
My darling Charlotte has passed away. I was in my study when I heard Simon, whose watch in the sick room it was, calling out to me to come immediately. Miss Usher and I arrived together and we were just in time for Charlotte's passing. I held her hand but there was no recognition in her eyes and the death rattle was terrible.

Eliza, lying nearby, was in an opium trance, and had no notion of what had just taken place.

Stricken with grief as I was, it was some comfort to kneel by the bedside, as Simon read prayers in a steady voice, reminding us that today was the day we remember the Massacre of the Holy Innocents. It was almost a relief to know that Charlotte was at rest. In my anguish, I became forcibly aware that this young man, intoning so calmly, was at the bedside of his wife of just a few months.

December 29th
Eliza continues unchanged except that the fever has abated a little. Her skin is still murky and the pustules bleed. Dr Willis thinks it cannot be long.

My son-in-law is proving a strength to me. Despite his own grief, he is stoical and calm, as befits his calling. Charlotte's funeral is to be thought on, and, on the doctor's advice, Eliza's too.

An undertaker was sent for this morning. He took measurements, attended to Charlotte's corpse, and will return with the coffins tomorrow evening.

I wondered at the man's willingness to enter what is, in effect, a pest house, until I reminded myself that it is as much his profession to take such risks as it is the vocation of my friend the doctor and my son-in-law the priest.

December 31st

Eliza continues to hold on to life, drifting in and out of consciousness. She does not seem to be seized with the intolerable agonies that accompanied Charlotte's end and sometimes she is sufficiently aware to talk a little, albeit in a voice that seems remote. She speaks of dreams of meadows full of flowers, where children play forever, and the leaves of the trees are pure gold, and there is a vast, glassy lake where blue swans drift. Doubtless, these are hallucinations caused by the drug. They give her some relief until a spasm of pain racks her and I cannot refrain from weeping.

The old year is passing, unlamented, and the new year brings no promise of hope or regeneration.

1888

January 1st

It is done. Shortly after midnight, Eliza died in my arms. There was not the anguish of Charlotte's passing. She began to cough, and I lifted her to ease the congestion in her chest. She looked straight into my eyes, managed to smile, and then simply stopped breathing.

I sent for Doctor Willis who issued the death certificate. Simon and I discussed the funeral plans into the early hours of the morning. The undertakers will be sent for and the bodies will be prepared and laid in their coffins which have already arrived. Charlotte will be laid to rest in her wedding dress and Eliza in the party dress bought for her on the shopping expedition they undertook before Charlotte fell ill. Was it really only a fortnight ago? It feels like another epoch.

Because of the nature of the illness which has robbed me of my daughters and Simon of a wife, we have decided to eschew my original plan to ask for the funeral service to take place at St James's. We wish to avoid any superstitions about the transmissibility of the disease through oak caskets, which members of the congregation might be foolish enough to entertain. Instead, Simon will conduct a short service at the house, attended only by the servants and ourselves.

The funeral cortège will then travel into town, up Penny Street and Larkhill, and on to the Cemetery on Whalley New Road. The service for the Burial of the Dead will be conducted by Simon at the family vault. Louisa and Titus will join us there, although Alice will remain with her Aunt Clara. There will not be time for Fanny to attend, but I have written to apprise her of the tragedy which has befallen our house.

Louisa will not return to Wastwater House just yet. Bedlinen and clothing from the sick room must be burned and the whole house fumigated before I can even contemplate their return.

It did cross my mind to ask Simon if he would prefer his wife to be taken to St Chad's, but he said that no-one could tell where his vocation might take him in the years to come, and that he had oftentimes felt the stir of a calling to a mission abroad, perhaps in China.

Meanwhile, it was better that Charlotte should lie with her sister, and later, other members of her family, to await the resurrection on the last day.

I cannot fault his wisdom.

January 3rd

I cannot write much. I am exhausted and my spirits are sunk. We buried our daughters today in the aching cold, with sleet flurries whirling around us.

Louisa acknowledges intellectually the reasons why I deemed it impossible for her to return to the house, and yet, in her heart, she holds it against me that she could not be with her children at the hour of their death.

Moreover, I know she is not happy to be forbidden her home until I am content that it is safe and ready.

Again, she understands my reasoning, but is resentful nevertheless.

My son-in-law returned by train to his parish in Rochdale this afternoon. Notwithstanding his silent censure of my barbarous treatment of Peter some days ago, I believe that adversity has made us friends: I have promised to correspond regularly, and assured him that he will always be welcome at Wastwater House.

33 JOURNAL 12

January 5th

I HAVE BEEN THINKING about certain words in the funeral office so solemnly delivered by Simon two days ago in the biting wind and dull grey sleet. I am troubled because I cannot square them with other texts in Holy Writ and in the *Book of Common Prayer*.

It was the phrase 'sure and certain hope of the resurrection' that began to disturb me: surely a hope is unsure and uncertain? It is a wish, not the confirmation of an event, is it not?

Then, in our creed, we say that we believe in the 'resurrection of the body'. Now surely my daughters will not arise as they perished, wasted, blackened, pustular, like medieval portrayals of witches? No, there is comfort in St Paul in a passage from the first epistle to the Corinthians, which Simon asked me to read at the interment:

So when this corruptible shall have put on incorruption, and this mortal shall have put on immortality, then shall be brought to pass the saying that is written, Death is swallowed up in victory. O death, where is thy sting? O grave, where is thy victory?

But again, it is not apparent to me when this will be. The creed says the dead shall rise at the Second Coming when Christ will judge the 'quick and the dead', so do we but sleep till then? Are there dreams, as Hamlet surmised? Or just blackness until 'the trumpet shall sound' and we awake eternally? But then, why does Jesus on the cross say to the Good Thief: 'Verily, I say unto thee, this day shalt thou be with me in Paradise'?

I cannot reconcile these texts. I must put these questions to Simon when next I write.

No doubt these musings arise because I cannot resign myself to the idea that my children are lost to me for ever and ever. Nor can I believe that they are in the process of becoming no more than insensate dust. Something deep within tells me that they are still alive, either already with Jesus, or perhaps they are sleeping the long sleep until the Day of Judgement. Or perhaps, they are alive as spirits, beyond the veil, 'on the other side'.

Oh, it would bring such solace to my weary soul if I could believe that.

January 6th

Men have been to fumigate the house, and there has been a bonfire of bedding and anything else that might be considered capable of carrying infection. I have locked the sick room and I very much doubt if any of us will ever wish to set foot in there again.

Louisa and Alice are arrived home, along with Titus and Clara, who are to dine with us. Instinctively, Louisa and I know, without words, that this day must be given over to Alice who is, since Fanny now lives in France, our only remaining child. Although my brother and sister-in-law made some attempt to celebrate Christmas Day with her, it was necessarily a subdued affair. Her birthday, on New Year's Day, was Eliza's death day, and so that could not be celebrated at all.

She is just turned twelve, and, though she is old enough to understand the enormity of what has happened, her natural spirits are irrepressible - she may be quiet and thoughtful for long periods at a time, but, at others, she forgets her grief and is bright and ebullient.

The Christmas tree is still up in the salon which has not been used at all during our long sadness. We all repair there and the candles on the tree are lit as we attempt to celebrate a belated Christmas.

Despite her barely concealed excitement, Alice refers to a commonly received notion.

'But Papa, should we not be taking the decorations *down* today? Isn't it unlucky to leave them up after Twelfth Night?'

'Some people say so, but I believe that in all the great houses of England, decorations are not taken down until Candlemas or Lady Day, which is the second of February. What is more, I believe that is the rule at Osborne House, where Her Majesty the Queen celebrates Christmas, and it shall be the rule at Wastwater House this year also. However, as a concession to my darling daughter's superstition, I shall blow out *one candle* on the tree.'

Alice laughs and claps her hands. She is a sunbeam in a house of shadows.

'And here is another interesting fact for you, child,' I say. 'Today is Epiphany, and what does the Feast of Epiphany celebrate?'

'The Coming of the Kings bringing gifts to the baby Jesus,' says Alice.

'Indeed, that is so. What a knowledgeable child it is,' I say, 'And in Spain, and in other countries too, the exchange of gifts takes place on the Epiphany rather than on Christmas Day. Shall we follow their example?'

'Oh yes, Papa,' says Alice. 'I had quite forgotten about presents.'

I don't believe this for a moment.

'Well,' I say, laughing. 'The presents are under the tree still. It shall be your task to distribute them.'

First of all she finds the presents she has bought from her allowance, which is not meagre, nor yet so profligate as to spoil her. And, bless her, she insists on giving her presents first, before receiving her own. Who would have thought that this sweet child was a demon when she was younger.

For Louisa there is a phial of cheap scent which she will wear in Alice's company, but not in public; Aunt Clara has a tea cosy, which I know Alice knitted herself; Uncle Titus has a cigar; Miss Usher has some fragrant writing paper, and for me, there are handkerchiefs, monogrammed in blue with an elaborate 'C'. Alice's kindness touches us all.

Louisa receives a brooch from me, set with amethysts, and from her I have a very handsome fountain pen, 'for your study', she says. 'It is a Waterman, and I had to send to New York for it. I hope you approve.'

I do indeed approve. It has a beautiful tortoiseshell barrel and cap, and it is trimmed with gold. It takes in ink through capillary action and is a most ingenious contrivance.

'But Alice, Alice,' I cry. 'What about you? Go on, open your presents.'

She tears into the packages and finds toys and candies, chocolate mice and a peppermint pig, nuts and a tangerine, and declares herself thrilled.

'Ah, but that is not all, my treasure,' I say. 'Come with me, Alice - and everyone!' We troop across the hall and I throw open the door, bidding Alice to come forward.

At the far end of the library, is the most enormous doll's house I could find. I have opened it out so that Alice can see that all the rooms have miniature furniture, and tiny figures are going about their business in the kitchen, the drawing room, and the maidservants' quarters in the garret rooms. She is enraptured as she kneels to play, moving the figures about.

For a moment, witnessing Alice's glee, I almost forget that there is a boxwood wreath on the front door of this house, tied with black crêpe, and that the curtains in every room are drawn to announce to the world outside that this is a house of mourning - a world which impertinently goes about its business as if nothing has happened. For a moment only, for with a guilty tug, I am brought back to the realisation that there are yet presents under the tree which will never be opened by their destined recipients, and presents which they gifted which no-one will have the heart to open.

We will have to decide what is to be done with them.

At last, we have to tear Alice away from her magical house, where all is ordered and cheerful, back to her real home, where all cheer is merely confected by us grown-ups.

It is time to go up to dinner during which we attempt to be festive. To be sure we begin with Christmas crackers containing sugared almonds, little trinkets and paper hats. The ladies are crowned in violet, green and orange, while Titus and I are pirates. Alice squeals with laughter, whilst we adults, I know, feel guilty about our mirth.

There is not the usual panoply of good things which normally adorns my table at this time of year, but there is a handsome goose with all the usual accompaniments, followed by a plum duff with glossy white sauce, and some superlative Lancashire cheese both mild and tasty. Titus and I drink an excellent Margaux, while the ladies have opted for hock.

We try to chatter; we try to be mirthful; Titus, dear genial soul that he is, tries to rally us with jests and riddles, but, after the bursts of forced laughter, there follow long silences.

Fruit and nuts are brought in. There are figs and dates and port and madeira. The ladies do not retire as we are so few. But alas, when we are all served, I propose a toast to 'Our dear departed', and Louisa can bear it no longer. She flees the room, and Clara and Miss Usher escort Alice to her own room, to comfort and console her.

I fear it has all been a ghastly charade.

July 8th

Louisa is in half mourning. There are those who consider this to be rather early to come out of black but I am one of those who believe that Her Majesty's grieving for Prince Albert has been excessive and the fashion for wearing black for fifteen months similarly needless and disproportionate. Let those who think me radical in this keep their opinions to themselves. We carry our griefs in our hearts and there they will stay; they are not forever to be a matter of public display.

Alice has also had dresses made in grey or lavender, which she thinks are very pretty, and while that is not the point, I think it right that her young life should not be deformed by heartbreak.

Little by little, we begin to venture out and to receive visitors.

[There are few entries in the intervening months before Cornelius takes up his journal again in earnest, and none material to our researches. No doubt he and the family continued to try to come to terms with the deaths of Charlotte and Eliza, especially after the sorry attempts at Twelfth Night jollifications. However, October of that year brought a radical move towards fresh beginnings. - TC]

34 THE JOURNAL 13

October 5th

LOUISA, ALICE AND I, along with Miss Usher, have travelled to Lille, to stay for a month with Fanny and her husband. I have to concede that my son-in-law, Arthur, is master of a most opulent household and that my daughter is most handsomely provided for. He can afford to live in the grand style here in the countryside just outside the city because his textile factory within the city itself is successful in the highest degree.

The house resembles a small château: beyond the gates an avenue of lime trees leads to a courtyard, where on three sides there are many windows with louvred *volets* or shutters painted a grass-coloured green. Three steps lead up to a heavy door. The rooms in the interior are spacious and light, though more sparsely furnished than is to the English taste. However the furniture is good and mostly in the style of Louis XVI.

Alice is enchanted by everything and she and Fanny take long walks in the nearby woods, returning with baskets of mushrooms and other edible fungi, or with apples and pears from the orchard.

Meanwhile I get to know Arthur better. He gives me a tour of his factory and I am mightily impressed. It is not unlike the many mills in Blackburn, though I would venture to say that it is bigger than the Imperial, Albion Street and Brookhouse Mills, and possibly even bigger than the India Mill in Darwen. I admire the efficient management, the well-ordered running of every aspect of the enterprise, and the laudable ambition of my young son-in-law.

We also make frequent sallies into the city *en famille*. The central square or *Grand Place* is magnificent, with majestic buildings on every side, especially the *Vieille Bourse*, or Treasury, and there are many busy cafés where the ladies of my family take coffee and pastries.

The expedition was planned as a diversion from the sense of tragedy with which the very fabric of Wastwater House seems to have become infused. On the surface, it appears to be successful: we strive to enjoy our novel surroundings, and the new friends we make from Arthur and Fanny's acquaintance, but each of us has his or her private grief, which, if contained, is yet very strong.

Fanny and I often take a turn in the garden and talk of our loss. She berates herself for not being there at the end, but I reassure her that poor Charlotte recognised nobody in her extremity and that Eliza's consciousness was severely limited by narcotics. Moreover, there was always a risk of transmission. She seems a little comforted by these observations; at any rate there is a wordless compact not to trail our unhappiness back into the house, where we find occasion to praise Alice's embroidery, or her growing proficiency in French. Or we cry out at the fancy package containing a *tarte tatin*, or some macaroons that Arthur has brought back from a pâtisserie in Lille.

But there is no escaping my dreams. One in particular keeps recurring and is exquisitely painful. I am in my study, adding a new stamp to my collection. It is circular and bears an image of the lunar disc with the head of The Queen in a corner. It pleases me that the moon has become a new Dominion in the Empire.

There is a tap on the door.

'I'm busy!' I cry, finding solitude the best palliative for grief.

Again the timid little tapping.

Exasperated, I get up and open the door, and there on the landing are Charlotte and Eliza, as hale and as exuberant and as beautiful as in life. Eliza is laughing, and Charlotte, though always demure, is smiling broadly, and there are familiar dimples in her rosy cheeks.

'Oh Papa!' Eliza cries. 'You didn't really think we were dead, did you?'

'It was just a dream, Papa!' says Charlotte. 'And now you have woken up!'

I take her in my arms and kiss her forehead and those pretty dimples, and then I pick up Eliza and lift her in the air to look at her and look and look. Their bodies are warm and palpable.

And then I do wake up, and none of it is true, and I am more desolate than ever I was before.

October 10th

Yesterday, I made an excursion to Ostend by train. I wanted to attend a lecture by Mme Blavatsky, the noted theosophist, who was visiting from London. I had read about her in *The Medium and Daybreak*, the spiritualist magazine to which I have been subscribing for some months now. I wanted to know if she had anything to say about contacting the spirits of the dead. I suppose I was looking for some kind of affirmation, some kind of authentication from this woman who had captured the imagination of the world's intelligentsia. I was to be disappointed.

That she is a spiritualist, there can be no doubt. She has travelled the world and seems to have developed an eclectic personal philosophy derived from a number of major religions, chiefly Hinduism. She had much to say about reincarnation, which I cannot contemplate, and it remained unclear whether she embraced the belief or not, though she seemed to believe that it inspired morally upright and compassionate behaviour. The idea of Charlotte returning as a cow and Eliza as a cockroach does not appeal. Even if they were expected to return as women of the Brahmin caste, or as Empresses of India, the doctrine does not appeal. This was not what I was looking for.

I contrived to have a few words in private with the great lady after the lecture, and she was most gracious. She has a squarish slavic face, and one might take her for a peasant woman, but that her blue eyes are intellectual and piercing. She wore a plain dress of bombazine black, as if she were in mourning herself, but her hair was pulled back tightly from her face, and over it was a magenta coloured silk shawl, embroidered in many colours with exotic birds and flowers.

In answer to my questions, she agreed that her personal philosophy owed much to many sources, Hinduism, certainly, but also Buddhism and other religions of the East, along with Persian Zoroastrianism, and the writings of Plato. What they have in common, she said, was an intense spiritualism, an intangible world beyond physical phenomena, which manifests itself in the rituals and ceremonies of the occult. But, no, she said sadly, taking my hands into hers, no, she did not believe that this spiritual world was inhabited by the spirits of the dead.

I stayed that night in an hotel which was rather seedier than its publicity - or its exterior - had led one to believe, and returned to Lille by train, conscious of the very itchy bite of a bedbug on my left buttock with which that establishment had accorded me a souvenir.

The ladies, accompanied by Arthur, had in the meantime made an excursion to Paris to see the sights, and inevitably to visit the shops. They laid their expensive and frivolous purchases before me, and laughed and cooed with such seeming light-heartedness that I could not begrudge them their diversion.

October 31st

Though I was disappointed by my interview with Mme Blavatsky, I am becoming more and more convinced that the spirit forms of Charlotte and Eliza are not beyond our reach. I know Louisa shares this growing intimation that they are not wholly lost to us. We still attend St James's Church, and occasionally Sung Eucharist at St John's, and while it is true that the consolations of Scripture and Divine Service are not inconsiderable, I think we both feel that there is something wanting.

I read an advertisement this evening for a meeting at the Spiritualist Temple on Johnston Street, on November 2nd, where a Miss Maisie Entwistle, a 'new and puissant sensitive', would be conducting a public séance. Two things intrigued me: firstly, that November 2nd is All Soul's Day, and secondly, that Miss Maisie is only ten years of age.

35 THE JOURNAL 14

November 2nd

THE SPIRITUALIST TEMPLE on Johnston Street is not particularly impressive. There is a Grecian portico over the entrance, like many a Methodist church, and double doors freshly painted in a bold red. It is a street of terraced houses, occupied by working class people of the decent sort, judging by the clean lace curtains and well-scrubbed doorsteps. There are a number of shops at the Montague Street end, many of them still open: a butcher's, a greengrocer's, a baker's, a hardware shop, a post office. There are a number of public houses. The temple does not stand out; one might easily have mistaken it for a slightly grander private house.

Our destination is not far from Wastwater House, and not wanting to arrive in an ostentatious kind of way, and it being a mild night for the time of year, Louisa and I decided to walk down through the park. The walkways and the wide avenue down to the gates on Preston New Road are well lit by gas lamps - nonetheless, we seemed to have the park to ourselves. Louisa was delighted to see rabbits frisking under the trees to our left.

When we arrived at the temple, the double doors were open, and folk were filing in. A middle-aged woman with a flamboyant pink bonnet was handing out leaflets, and she greeted us warmly.

'Is it your first time, love?' she asked Louisa, who was evidently surprised and amused by the familiarity.

'Indeed, it is,' Louisa said.

'Only we don't often have gentry pay us a visit, you see,' the woman said. 'Hey up, our Ronnie, come 'ere, lad!'

Ronnie appeared instantly as if from nowhere. He was a pustular youth whose hair stood on end as if he'd just received a terrible shock.

'Show this lady and gentleman to a nice seat,' the woman said. 'And don't pick your nose.'

Ronnie left his nose alone and led us to excellent seats on the front row, quite near the stage. The interior was something of a surprise, given the modest frontage of the building. It was large - a cross between a church and a playhouse. There were fixed seats as in a theatre, and a raised stage, but there was also a pulpit-like structure at the right-hand side of the dais. Or was it more like the Master of Ceremonies' podium in a music hall? There were small stained glass windows. I could not work out their subjects because it was dark outside, though one was illumined by a street lamp and appeared to be a scene from *Revelation* - the descent of the New Jerusalem. There was a large but plain cross at the centre of an arch above the stage, and the legend *I am the Resurrection and the Life* in gold letters.

There was not the hush in the auditorium you would expect in a church, rather the animated chatter you would expect before a play. However, everyone settled down when a tall thin man in a simple grey cassock went up into the 'pulpit' and announced a hymn which was sung lustily. It was one we did not know; its words spoke of a day 'when radiant angels shall draw back the veil.' The hymn was accompanied by mighty chords from a harmonium to the left of the stage which I had not noticed before. I found it strangely uplifting.

There followed a series of prayers, not the sonorous prayers at the beginning of a Church of England service, but more like the bidding prayers before the sermon - in simple English, naming specific people. Then came another hymn, very well known to both of us, and we joined in with the beautiful melodies of *Abide with Me*.

The man in the cassock, the Rev. Bratt, gave a short talk, mostly about the success of healing missions in the previous weeks: a Mrs Betty Croasdale who had been suffering from fading eyesight found she could see again after a séance held earlier in the month.

'The scales literally fell from her eyes!' the reverend cried and the audience applauded warmly. Dorothy Barker had been suffering agonies at the base of her spine, causing her to stoop, but the prayers of the assembled faithful had been efficacious. At the weekend, she suddenly felt a great healing warmth in the place and was able to stand upright. Further applause.

After more of this kind of thing, the Rev. Bratt announced that Miss Maisie Entwistle would now conduct a séance. There was a charged silence as ushers went about the audience and the stage, turning down the gaslights till the whole place was in near darkness. In the gloom, we could just about perceive a wing chair being brought on and placed carefully centre stage. One of the attendants came forward and turned on certain footlights which illuminated the chair.

We could now dimly discern that there was a child, a little girl, curled up in the chair. She seemed to be wearing a nightdress and she carried a fan. She seemed to wake, stretch, shift in the chair and then, unblinking, she scanned the barely lit faces of the audience, her gaze coming to rest at last on Louisa. She stared at her for a long time as my wife took hold of my arm and clung to it tightly.

'Hello, lady,' the child said. 'I'm Maisie.'

'Hello, Maisie,' Louisa said faintly.

'What's your name, lady?' the girl said.

'I'm Mrs Pickup - Louisa.'

Why she picked out Louisa needed no special explanation at this point. There was an overspill from the footlights which meant that her features were more clearly delineated than those of the rest of the congregation. Moreover, she was wearing pale grey half-mourning which would have stood out from the dark clothing of the working class people who surrounded us. No doubt many of them, just like my wife and I, were hoping to make some kind of contact with deceased relatives and friends, but these good people were not in a position to purchase garments to mark the different stages of mourning.

'Well now, Mrs Louisa Pickup,' the girl said. Her accent was that of the common people. 'What brings you 'ere, eh? You lost somebody recent-like, didn't you? A loved one? A child.'

'Two. Two of my children. I was wondering if...'

'Patience, Mrs Louisa, patience, lovely lady.'

The child then addressed three or four other members of the congregation who had recently lost children, and one man whose wife had passed away last week. She asked a few brief questions of each. She then looked up at Mr Bratt and said: 'I am ready, sir.'

'Ladies and gentlemen,' Mr Bratt said to the audience, 'I must require you to be absolutely silent. The séance begins here. I pray you join hands with your neighbours and concentrate. Think of your dear departed. Miss Maisie Entwistle will now go into a trance.'

The child sat deep in the chair - her feet didn't even touch the ground. She sat with her hands on the arms and her head thrown back. For two minutes perhaps nothing happened. The silence was profound.

Suddenly the child appeared to go into a fit. From behind the chair there was a series of blinding white flashes and smoke came rolling from the back of the stage towards the front and over the edge. As our eyes recovered from the flashes, we could see a tall figure standing to the right and slightly behind the chair. This apparition was covered from head to foot in a black veil so that it was scarcely visible. The girl's fit ceased.

She turned in the direction of the figure, spread her fan in front of her face, and said: 'Is it you, Star Shadow?'

The girl closed her fan, faced the audience, and said: 'I am Star Shadow.'

The voice was not her own, though it seemed to come from her - it was that of a grown man, and there was something distant about it, as if the spirit were struggling to articulate.

'What do you ask of me?' the spirit voice said.

The girl's eyes searched the audience and lighted on my wife again.

'Mrs Louisa,' she said in her own voice again. 'Your child - his name was Charlie, was it not?'

'Well, not quite. She was, *is*, a girl you see - a woman when she passed. Her name is Charlotte.

'Of course, Charlotte, that's right,' Maisie Entwistle said. 'And there is another. A sister called Elizabeth, I think.'

'Oh yes, we called her Eliza,' Louisa cried. She squeezed my hand and there were tears in her voice. 'She passed away within days of her sister. Oh, please, Miss Entwistle. Can you reach them? Are they safe? Are they happy?'

The girl did not answer but turned in the chair again and unfolding her fan appeared to commune with the shrouded figure. Then she turned back and spoke in the man's voice again.

'Eliza and Charlotte are here, on the other side. They are playing in a beautiful garden with roses, fountains and flamingos. They are very happy. They think of you often and pity your lives in this vale of tears. But, they do not grieve - they know you will join them soon.

'Enough. It costs me pain to reach through the veil.'

Star Shadow passed messages to other bereaved souls in the congregation until he was reduced to begging the child to let him go, and when she finally gave permission, there was another dazzling white flash, and the spirit guide disappeared. The girl curled up in the chair and went to sleep, evidently exhausted by the experience. She was carried off at last in the arms of Mr Bratt.

When we stepped outside, a bitter November wind had sprung up, and we were very grateful that Richards was waiting for us, as arranged.

Inside the carriage, Louisa hugged me in floods of joyous tears.

36 THE JOURNAL 15

November 3rd

I WROTE YESTERDAY THAT STAR SHADOW had communications for other members of the congregation, but I hope an objectionable degree of selfishness will not be imputed to me if I say that I heard what was said, but registered none of it in my consciousness, for I was so surprised and elated at proof positive that my darling daughters have not perished, but dwell in ineffable happiness in a world that co-exists with ours, though divided by a veil. There they reside as spirits in bliss, while we are clad, for now, in this 'muddy vesture of decay'.

Louisa and I talked through to the small hours, and I know she feels the same.

I am not unaware that there may well be some who would call us gullible. But it is not so, and I am persuaded that if such doubters *had been there* last night they would have had to abandon their accusations of credulity.

I had moments of scepticism, I will freely admit. I was mindful of the article I read some time ago where a grotesque fraud was perpetrated on a credulous public, here in Blackburn, where a girl was caught in a state of shameful undress, whilst pretending to be a manifestation of a spirit. I was shocked and angry then and I am shocked and angry now. However, the case is clearly different.

For one thing, the age of Maisie Entwistle is material. She was not old enough to have put on such a spectacle on her own account, and yet the masculine spirit voice definitely came from her own throat. As the psalm says: 'Out of the mouth of babes and sucklings hast Thou ordained strength.'

Most importantly of all: how could she come to know the names of our daughters, or as near as makes little difference? She had never met either of us; we did not know her. Moreover, we knew no-one at the venue; nor did anyone there know us.

The world of banking, in which I toiled successfully for many a dull but fruitful year, is a hard-headed one. It encourages caution and scepticism to the highest degree.

No, I do not think I am a gullible man.

November 6th

Louisa and I have been discussing whether or not we ought to tell Alice about the séance at the temple on Johnston Street. I argue that she should not be denied the relief and solace that we ourselves have enjoyed. Louisa, however, argues that she is yet very young and accepts without question the traditional comforts of Christianity. She believes that her sisters are now 'with Jesus'. Miss Usher concurs with my wife. 'Let sleeping dogs lie,' she says, and I am content - for now.

November 8th

Alice's friendship with the servant girl Mary Ann continues, and I see no harm in it at all, though recently Miss Usher has expressed reservations to me. She claims that the girl is becoming rather flighty and has been impertinent towards her. I mentioned this to Louisa who laughed and said that, invaluable as Miss Usher has been to us, especially in the nursing of Charlotte and Eliza, there are times when she is a little frosty with the lower servants. Moreover, Louisa says, she fears that our treating Miss Usher as a member of the family may have given her notions above her station. She was employed to care for and to educate the children and has no jurisdiction over our other employees. Perhaps she may need to be gently reminded of this. I quietly resolve to do no such thing.

Rather more alarming is Miss Usher's suggestion that Alice has picked up some coarse language from Mary Ann. I ask her to be specific about this 'language' but she merely blushes, and says she cannot repeat it.

I say that I find this hard to believe. Mary Ann has been raised at Wastwater House, where she cannot possibly have picked up any lewd expression. Mrs Foster, my housekeeper, a woman of exemplary character, would not allow it.

'I hope, sir, that you are not implying that I am lying,' says Miss Usher.

'Indeed, I am implying no such thing,' I say. 'Perhaps you misheard.'

Miss Usher says nothing, but gives me a chilly look.

December 25th
Christmas Day
At last we are able to celebrate Christmas as the birth of our Saviour should be celebrated. Titus and Clara are here with us and will stay until New Year's Day. We have feasted and exchanged gifts and there has been dancing in the salon. Louisa danced a reel with Richards, who proved surprisingly light-footed, while I took the floor with Miss Usher, who was not. Alice danced with Peter who had a new velveteen waistcoat with shiny buttons.

'Do you not think him remarkably handsome, Papa?' she said afterwards.

'Who, my treasure? Who is remarkably handsome?'

'Why, Peter of course.'

'Is he?' I said. 'Is he really? I can't say I'd noticed.'

'Don't be such a tease, Papa. He is quite beautiful.'

I managed not to laugh out loud. To hear our boot boy, stable boy, gardener's boy, and all out factotum boy described as 'beautiful' was most amusing. To me he looked a very ordinary boy with a small nose and big ears.

I sent a mental memorandum to myself. Soon it would be time to think of raising her sights. We could not have her married to the 'boots' with a tweeny as bridesmaid. I do not think you could accuse me of snobbism, but I think we can do better than that for my youngest.

Later
Titus and I have retired to the library, he to drink brandy and I to take port. I do not touch spirits since the occasion when I forgot myself and behaved abominably - an occasion I would prefer not to remember.

I judged it time to tell my brother about the astonishing séance on All Soul's Day and how his nieces communicated with us through a child medium and her spirit guide. He was not as impressed as I had hoped.

'I am very glad for you, brother,' he said. 'But I must caution you to beware. There are charlatans about, who are only too ready to separate those who grieve from their money.'

'Oh, but you don't understand, Titus. No money changed hands. There was no entrance fee. It was wholly gratis.'

'Was there no voluntary collection?'

'Well yes, at the exit. But only like the collection in church. And it was entirely voluntary.'

'But you gave generously?'

'Well, yes. I threw a few sovereigns into the hat. Who wouldn't under the circumstances?' I said. 'Look here, are you saying that you don't believe the proceedings were genuine?'

'I am saying nothing of the kind, Cornelius. I quite understand the happiness that you and Louisa experienced. I am only urging caution.'

'Well, I must say, you are a wet blanket, and no mistake.'

'I am sorry. I simply do not wish you to be hurt. Have there been other such occasions?'

'Indeed there have. Louisa and I attend the temple whenever there is a guest medium, which is usually weekly.'

'But you still attend services at St James's?'

'Certainly. We attended Christmas Eucharist this morning before you arrived. We see no incompatibility.'

'Good. And have these attendances at the temple been successful?'

'In contacting Charlotte and Eliza?'

'Just so.'

'Once or twice, yes. But separately - never together since that first time. The message is always very much the same. They live in a bright world where there is neither dawn nor dusk, no winter or summer, but perpetual spring. There is no pain and there are no tears. And they think of us often and are certain we shall be reunited.

'Much depends on the medium, you see. They are known as sensitives, and they are mostly women, perhaps because the emotional temperament of the female is more easily attuned to vibrations from "the other side".

'Alas, the most especial sensitivity of that female child at our first visit has not been repeated with the same intensity. And she seems to have disappeared. She has advertised no further séances in the town, the vicinity, or anywhere for that matter.'

'How would you know?' Titus asked. 'Where would you expect to see such advertisements?'

'I subscribe to *The Medium and Daybreak*. It is the foremost periodical of its kind, Titus, and contains not only advertisements for séances and healing sessions, but scholarly essays on spiritualism and the occult, in addition to testimonials from people of stature, probity and intellect. There are issues on that table in the corner going back almost a year. Do feel free to peruse them.'

'And their contents will dispel the clouds of my scepticism, will they?' Titus said with a smile.

'If you have an open mind.'

37 THE JOURNAL 16

1889

January 6th

YESTERDAY WE HELD A TWELFTH NIGHT BALL. The cream of Blackburn Society was in attendance: the Hornby's, the Thwaites's, the Baynes's, not to mention my very good friend, the current Mayor, John Rutherford.

The Rev. Whalley from St. James's joined us, as did Doctor Willis and his wife. Titus and Clara were here again, but best of all, Fanny and Arthur travelled from France to be with us.

It was a grand affair, quite outdoing the family celebrations at Christmas. It was just like the hospitality for which we were noted in the borough before our bereavements, for we were determined to shed all of the inward and outward insignia of mourning. Our essays into spiritualism allowed us to do this. We thought of the poor miscarried child every single day, and of Charlotte and Eliza, but with steadfast hope rather than anguish.

May 8th

Because Louisa takes such delight in the garden, I am constantly looking for ways to improve it. To this end, I have employed a local builder to construct a summer house at the end of the gravel path which leads to the orchard. Louisa herself made a drawing of how she would like it to look, and Mr Sparrow, who insists we call him Derek, complimented my wife on her drawing skills, and said that there would be no problem in creating a gazebo entirely to her taste.

There is to be a brick wall at the back to minimise draughts, and then, almost to waist height, brick walls, curving to form a circular structure. Rising from these walls, and on either side of the entrance, there will be a number of pillars, also of brick, reaching up to a thatched roof in the rustic manner. Inside, there will be ample room for wicker chairs and a table for tea things and the like.

'And I shall read in there,' Louisa declared, 'or sew, or just watch the bees in the lavender, and the sparrows on the bird table, all summer long.'

A week or so ago, Derek laid the concrete foundations for Louisa's retreat. This completed, he said he would return in a week's time to commence building. The concrete needed to set hard.

He arrived this morning, along with an apprentice boy called Wilfred, and Peter showed them around the side of the house and into the garden. I went out to watch.

I think I may have written elsewhere of the pleasure I take in watching a craftsman at his work. I had thought that building a wall was not a very complicated matter - just one brick on top of another - but I was wrong.

I came upon them as they had just finished stacking their materials from their cart: sacks of cement, sharp sand, and piles of deep red Accrington brick. While Wilfred mixed the mortar, I watched as Derek laid a length of timber along the ground where the back wall was to be built. This would ensure that the first course of bricks would be perfectly aligned.

When this had been laid, he checked the evenness of the course with a spirit level, then, sinking pins into the mortar and extending string around them, he created a level line. This would ensure that the next course of bricks was even on the horizontal plane.

He began the second course by breaking a brick in half using a chisel and club hammer and it split with a single blow. Everything he did was precise but relaxed and self-assured. He laid mortar on top of the first course for about three bricks along, feathering it to the edges with his trowel. Then he took hold of the half brick, slapped mortar on one end, and laid it on top, tamping it down with the wooden end of his trowel. Next came a whole brick and so on, building up an easy rhythm as he worked.

When the wall was at knee height, I could resist it no longer and begged Derek to let me lay a few bricks at least. I thought he seemed a little reluctant at first, rather as if I'd asked Leonardo da Vinci if I could attempt one of the disciples at The Last Supper. He agreed readily enough after his moment of doubt and I sent Peter, who had been watching, to ask Cook if I might beg the loan of a serviceable apron to protect my clothes.

As I set to work I saw, out of the corner of my eye, Peter and the apprentice boy exchange a smirk, but I said nothing for I was aware that I must have cut quite a ludicrous figure in the overall that Mrs Foster had supplied, bedizened as it was with images of roses and violets.

Despite their mockery I did very well. I had at first a tendency to overload my bricks with mortar, but Derek showed me how to feather away the excess with the trowel so that the amount of mortar on each brick was the same. Naturally, I worked more slowly than he had, but quite soon, with Derek checking from time to time with his spirit level, I had laid a whole course, all save the last brick, which he said was 'tricky', and at this point he took over again. My efforts were greeted with polite applause from the boys which I think was unfeigned. I stood back to admire my handiwork and I have to say I was not displeased myself. It is true that there were one or two places where a little too much mortar had squeezed out between the bricks, and others where little cavities had appeared where I had not applied enough of the mixture, but these Derek quickly repaired.

'And now, sir,' he said, 'perhaps you'd like to leave your mark?'

'What do you mean?' I said.

'Well sir, in the business we like to leave our mark - our initials perhaps, or a symbol - just like the masons of old did in great public buildings such as cathedrals. Look, here's mine!'

And sure enough, on the face of one of the bricks lower down the wall was the image of a little sparrow.

'What a splendid idea. Only you must do it. I have no skill in the art. Just my initials if you please.'

With a few strokes effected with a tiny chisel and small mallet, Derek etched my monogram into the brick, the P nestling neatly within the curve of the C.

'There you are, sir,' Derek said. 'You can show this to her ladyship and say it was all your own work.'

May 9th

There have been tiresome altercations this morning. It seems that Mrs Foster discovered that Alice has stolen a seed cake destined for Louisa's tea table in order to feed it to the ducks in the park. This she is alleged to have done with the connivance of Mary Ann Duxbury. The matter was referred to me, but I found it petty and irritating and referred it to Louisa, who referred it in turn to Miss Usher, who flew into a dreadful bate, and said it was all beyond her competence and burst into tears.

There has been much slamming of doors, and the matter has been referred back to me after all. I spoke to Alice and said that nothing would be denied to her if she but asked for it politely, and wasn't bread enough for the ducks?

'Indeed, Papa,' the little minx replied, 'but not for the swans.'

Consequently, I sent my diminutive Marie Antoinette to her room, with the admonition that if she insisted on stealing food meant for others, she could go without her supper. In order to appease Cook, whom I cannot afford to lose, I have docked 6s 8d from Mary Ann's wages.

With Louisa present, I then interviewed Miss Usher, who said that her outburst had been the result of frustration. Alice might appear to be a saint to us, but when in her sole charge, she was very changeable - mostly obliging but at times a little vixen. Why, only the day before, she had discovered that her governess' Christian name was Letitia, and had skipped around the schoolroom chanting 'silly old lettuce' at her.

Louisa only just managed to turn an involuntary shriek of mirth into a sneeze.

38 THE JOURNAL 17

May 11th

I HAVE MADE NO FURTHER CONTRIBUTIONS to the building of the gazebo, but I have followed its construction with keen interest. Besides, once curved bricks were brought into play, I knew immediately that my newly acquired skills would not be equal to the task.

Over the last few days, I have been out to watch as the wings of the structure curved round so that the building was circular apart from the back wall. Sometimes I found Peter beside me watching in awe, and I refrained from shooing him back to his work in the boot room or the stables, for I thought it was no bad thing for him to learn the importance of craftsmanship.

This afternoon, Derek and his boy began work on the circular pillars that will support the roofing. He asked me if I would like them covered with stucco to create a classical look, but I said that I would prefer a more rustic appearance, and that I would ask Richards to train ivy up the brickwork, and that maybe we should look to have briar roses clustering over the entrance.

Tomorrow, they start work on the timber roof frame, and when that is completed, the thatcher can set to work.

I have ordered rattan furniture and bright rugs, and cannot wait to see Louisa installed within her bower.

May 13th

Louisa has persuaded me that we should take Alice along to the next meeting at the temple on Johnston Street. The child has been pestering us for some time now and I cannot help thinking that her curiosity is quite as extraordinary as that of her fictional namesake. I was about to say no, but Louisa faced me down with a scowl, and I was forced to concede.

Miss Usher was invited to accompany us, but declined, rather haughtily I thought, saying that the liturgy of the Church of England was quite good enough for the likes of her. On hearing this, Alice begged that Mary Ann Duxbury be allowed to join the party instead. Once again

I was about to object but Louisa looked at me under her brows, and once again I gave in with a sigh.

We walked down through the park in the evening sunshine, having made arrangements for Richards to collect us in the brougham after the service, as before.

The guest, according to *The Medium and Daybreak,* was to be a Miss Clarice Thornberry of Wakefield in Yorkshire, who would give a demonstration of spirit writing, otherwise referred to as automatic writing, which I had not witnessed hitherto.

The service commenced much as usual, with familiar hymns and prayers, and, needless to say, there was an expectant buzz as Miss Thornberry was introduced to the congregation by the Rev. Bratt. She was a tall thin spinsterish woman with spectacles, grey hair in a bun, and a high-bosomed black silk evening dress adorned with a multitude of jet beads.

Centre stage was a writing desk with many branched candelabra placed on either side. The Rev. Bratt led her to the table at which she seated herself, and the said gentleman made a number of mystic passes over her, upon which she went into a staring trance.

She held this position for some time and then, still staring sightlessly into the congregation, she took up a pen and began writing furiously, without looking at her script at all.

Page after page she covered in this mechanical fashion, dropping each page to the floor as soon as it was complete, immediately beginning another. We watched in silent awe, until at last, with a strange, bird-like cry, she closed her eyes and her head fell forward onto the desk, quite overcome with exhaustion.

And then the Rev. Bratt led her, as one might lead someone who is sleep-walking, to a *chaise longue* at the side of the stage, which I had not noticed before. There he laid her down and she appeared to go into a deep sleep.

Now attendants - like stage hands in the theatre - rushed onto the platform and removed the desk; one collected the scattered sheets of paper and handed them to the Reverend; others erected a gigantic screen at the back of the stage, and yet another wheeled on a strange contraption on a kind of trolley.

This, Rev. Bratt explained, was an epidiascope, a wonderful contrivance, which could, by means of limelight and a reflector, project Miss Thornberry's inspired scribblings onto the screen. He then ignited the limelights and placed the first sheet on the plate and adjusted the focus until the writing was illuminated before us all, miraculously enlarged.

I had pressed a threepenny bit into Ronnie's sticky hand when we arrived and the pimply youth had led us to excellent seats, which was as well, because Miss Thornberry's handwriting was not easy to read - hardly surprising considering the prodigious speed with which she had covered the sheets. It was mostly gibberish, a stream of words without rhyme or reason, grammar or syntax, but every now and then there would be a passage which was recognisably English, though rarely coherent for long.

Proper names cropped up often and there would be sudden ripples of conversation within pockets of the audience in response to mention of a Bessie, a Herbert, a Jimmy, or a May. The Rev. Bratt left the projections up on the screen long enough for the slowest reader to scan them, and then he would replace the sheet with the next page. I found this frustrating as I was keen to move on, and Alice, who was sitting next to me, was clearly exasperated too, judging by her fidgeting.

I think it was on perhaps the sixth or seventh page that she clutched my arm in excitement. From Louisa there came a little cry and Mary Ann said out loud: 'Sweet Jesus!'

On the screen before us were these words:

alice's sisters dwell at the bottom of a well

under a sycamore there is a door

which leads into a rose garden

here are rainbows but no rain

Then the script dissolved into just a wavy line before degenerating into gibberish again.

The page was replaced, and then again and again. At length, the house lights were relit. Miss Thornberry awoke and stretched. The Rev. Bratt showed her the scripts but she merely smiled and shook her head as if to deny any knowledge of them. Prayers were said, and we sang a hymn before going out into the street where Richards and Peter were waiting for us.

In the carriage, Alice was subdued, but then, as we turned out of Montague Street onto Preston New Road, she said: 'But what does it mean, Papa?'

'I think the well must be a metaphor,' I said. 'It's like "the veil", or "the other side".'

'O Papa, it's not Hell is it?' Alice said in sudden panic.

'Hush darling,' Louisa said. 'Charlotte and Eliza are in the rose garden.'

'I think that must be the Garden of Eden,' Mary Ann said. Alice had insisted that she be allowed to ride with us rather than on top with Richards.

'Why, Mary Ann,' I said, 'you are almost right. If you remember your Bible, you will recall that Adam and Eve were expelled from the garden by an angel with a fiery sword. But if you also recall, we are promised through

Our Saviour's sacrifice, that a place is being prepared for us in Paradise instead.'

'If we are good,' Alice said.

Louisa laughed.

'Yes, Alice, if we are good.'

'And Paradise originally meant a walled garden,' I said.

'Like ours?' Alice asked.

'Like ours but infinitely more lovely.'

'With a gazebo?'

'Thousands of them.'

'Made of gold and silver? And precious jewels?'

'Without the shadow of a doubt,' I said, and held my remaining worldly daughter close to me.

May 17th

The thatcher has finished his work, the garden furniture has arrived, Richards has trailed ivy up the pillars, which will thicken over the years, and so the gazebo is finished. I have kept my mark on the brickwork along the back wall a secret until now but at last I showed it to Louisa. It is clearly visible although the wall has been whitewashed. Louisa declared herself delighted with her bower and astounded at my cleverness.

August 21st

My wife and I came out to the gazebo after dinner, and

Mary Ann has brought coffee and liqueurs. The little Chinese lanterns which Louisa has hung about our little retreat have been lit, and moths are attracted and brush against the coloured paper. Just now one managed to get inside one and banged about inside.

'O save it, save it,' Louisa cried, but I couldn't see how, until the poor creature flew into the flame it worshipped, and perished with a brief fizz.

Louisa was close to tears and to divert her I proposed that I should read to her, perhaps something from Mr Dickens or Mr Thackeray.

'It must be something cheery,' she said, 'especially tonight. I think *The Pickwick Papers* might be just the thing.'

I did not ask her what might be special about the evening but went indoors to fetch the volume from the library. When I returned and was looking for some drollery concerning Sam Weller and his master, Louisa laid her hand on mine and said she had something important to tell me.

We are to be parents again and I rejoice at it. There are greater risks as a woman gets older, but Louisa is fitter and healthier than I have known her. She has spent much of the summer outdoors, here in the gazebo or walking in the park. Her appetite is good and her complexion blooming. Hope is a Christian virtue, and I embrace it.

Despite the hour, there was a sudden noisy squabbling of geese in the park. We burst out laughing at the absurdity of it.

'I feel sure it will be a boy,' Louisa said.

'Don't tempt providence,' I replied.

Nevertheless, I have often observed that women know things hidden from the eyes and minds of men.

[There are few entries between August and March and they contain nothing new. Cornelius seems content with a life of apparent fulfilment and the progress of Louisa's pregnancy. Perhaps he feels that he has nothing much to record - until, that is, the following sudden item. - TC]

39 THE JOURNAL 18

1890

March 5

My God, my God, why hast thou forsaken me?

My wife and son lost to me in the space of less than four hours! What foul sin, in thought, word or deed, must I have committed, in my past, unknown to my conscious mind, that He should punish me with such anguish?

Louisa went into labour late last night and it soon became clear that all was not well. We all knew it was too soon. Dr Willis was sent for immediately and he bade me prepare myself for the worst, and that the Rev. Whalley should be sent for.

My son was born at three of the clock and my darling wife perished in delivering him into the world. He was tiny, but so very beautiful.

The vicar arrived post-haste. There was no time to send for Titus and Clara and for Fanny's husband, Arthur, who were the intended godparents - Dr Willis, Richards, and Miss Usher agreed to stand in their stead.

There, by the bloodied bed, in which Louisa lay lifeless, I held my little boy in my arms as the vicar christened him: 'Horace', the name Louisa and I had chosen for him.

Two hours after opening his bewildered eyes on the world, Horace closed them forever.

I howled like a wolf until his little body was taken from me.

March 14th

St John's Church was packed for the funeral as Louisa was popular and well-loved in the town and beyond. I chose the church where we were married rather than St James's because it was larger though, even so, the gallery was full, and many well-wishers had to stand.

Women wept at the appearance of Louisa's coffin with its purple pall and its charge of lilies, but even grown men shed tears when Horace's little white casket, surmounted with a posy of violets, came into the church.

Fanny had been fetched from Lille by Titus and she and Alice sat on either side of me in what had been our accustomed pew. I had penned the eulogy, blotted with many tears, but I could not trust myself to deliver it, and the vicar did it for me.

I had requested that the interment at the vault in Blackburn Cemetery be attended only by family and invited friends, and this was complied with, though many people walked behind the funeral cortège as far as Bastwell and beyond, out of respect for Louisa and compassion for the child, and then they faded away at the gates.

As the burial service was read out, I was filled with silent rage, for the sun was shining and there was some spring warmth in it; daffodils were everywhere and purple crocus; birds were singing, and a robin was hopping about inside a rose bush which grew just by the door of the vault. How dare the world continue as if nothing had happened? How dare the sun shine on my desolation? How long before my worthless remains passed through that door to lie with the bodies of my abolished wife and children?

For me, it could not be too soon.

July 15th

I attend the services at the Spiritualist Temple on Johnston Street with constancy. I attend spiritualist meetings elsewhere where the guest medium is of repute. I have attended gatherings in Manchester and in Leeds. At none of these has contact with Louisa been attained, and I have heard nothing of Charlotte and Eliza for many a long month. Nevertheless, I become more and more convinced that the spirit world is no illusion, and that it is no less *real* because of its lack of materiality.

July 20th

Apart from spiritualist meetings, I spend much of my time in my study because I cannot really bear to be with other people - Alice alone excepted - and even with her I am often short-tempered. She is the only living member of my ruined family apart from Fanny, who is so very far away. Alice deserves more than ever my love and nurture, having lost, not only siblings, but her mother. However, she is also a living and constant reminder that my son, for whom I waited so long, lived but a bare two hours, and the injustice of it makes me hate her and then I repent me of my hate.

I no longer attend services of the Church of England, because they bring me no comfort. The Rev. Whalley has called on me more than once, presumably to ask why I no longer cross his threshold, but I would not see him.

I read *The Medium and Daybreak* and nowadays I also write articles for them. I have bought quite a collection of volumes by spiritualist writers and devour them.

My collection of ancient coins can occupy my mind for an idle hour or two, and I have composed contributions for a numismatic periodical. I take no delight in my butterfly collection, however - I think of the moth that perished in the flame on the evening that Louisa told me she was expecting Horace, never dreaming that she would be extinguished likewise and so soon.

My relations with the servants are fraught, and they tippy-toe around me, no longer with respect, but with fear. More than once, I have cuffed Peter for no better reason than that he is always polite and bears no grudges. I have sent perfectly good food back to the kitchen out of sheer cussedness and I have found fault with Jane Green's cleaning of my study where no fault exists. And then I feel agonies of remorse and I apologise, or - more often - I fail to apologise and the perverse resentment grows.

It is with Miss Usher that my frustration is most intense. She exudes a self-righteousness which irritates me. She tries to make me feel that I am under a sense of obligation to her and that she is necessary to me and to the household. She looks down on me - she seems to find me inadequate somehow - she has the audacity to *pity* me.

She comes to me to tell tales about Alice: how Alice refuses to obey her in anything; how respect has turned to insolence; and how love and affection have turned to contempt and defiance. I say that I do not wish to hear such tittle-tattle, but she replies that Alice's delinquency is all down to that hussy, Mary Ann, who is leading her astray. I find this all very tiresome and tell her that I am beginning to wonder why I employ her when she lays difficulties at my feet which it is *her* duty to resolve.

We played out this ugly scene again this afternoon, on the upper staircase, where Miss Usher made quite an exhibition of herself, claiming that I was ungrateful for the service and self-sacrifice she has given to this house over many years, the unqualified love she has given to my children, and the risks she has undertaken in nursing members of my family in the sick room. I fear that recent events have unbalanced her mind for she raised her voice to me in a most improper manner.

I made it perfectly clear that I was in no wise ungrateful for her devotion, but that she appeared to have forgotten that she was nevertheless 'in service', albeit in a distinct and more elevated position than the other servants. If she had chosen at times to go beyond the terms of her employ, that was her affair. I would not, however, be harangued by her in a public part of my house, and she would do well to remember it, or to conclude that she might be happier elsewhere.

'Indeed, I have no doubt that I should be happier elsewhere, sir,' she said. 'Nor will I stay where I am not treated with the respect due to my station and my performance.'

Though her cheeks were washed with tears, her tone was defiant and she brushed past me up the stairs to her room.

I retired to the library, expecting her to appear at any moment to apologise, and plead with me to be allowed to keep her post.

Much later, I was going up to my study with books I had selected when I encountered Miss Usher on her way down the stairs. She wore an overcoat buttoned to the chin, despite the hot evening, and was carrying a cardboard suitcase and an ancient carpet bag.

When she reached the hall, she took an envelope from a pocket in her coat, and held it out to me.

'Here is my letter of resignation, Mr Pickup,' she said. 'Since I will not be serving out my notice, I do not expect any outstanding stipend. I shall be staying with my sister in Oswaldtwistle. The address is enclosed. I should be grateful if you would send on my things. There is not much, but it is of sentimental value, and it is already packed. I shall of course refund the cost of carriage.'

If she thought this histrionic display was going to incline me to beg her to reconsider, she was mistaken. Nevertheless, I put my books down on the stairs, descended, bade her put down her bags in the hall, and follow me into the library. There I wrote out a cheque for two months' wages.

'I shall forget any insubordination in recent days,' I said, 'and remember only the times where you have served the family well. To that end I will write you an open letter containing an excellent character, which I will send to your sister's address.'

This unnecessary generosity was met only with silence and a frigid nod, though she accepted the cheque readily enough. Refusing any help with her bags, she stepped into the balmy evening and out of our lives.

40 THE JOURNAL 19

July 23rd

IT WAS TWO DAYS before Alice made any enquiry about the disappearance of Miss Usher. I told her that her governess had chosen to leave of her own accord. Alice showed a remarkable lack of curiosity (for her), and when I said that I supposed I must look for a replacement, she queried why there should be any such necessity. She was, she said, almost fifteen, and beyond the need of any governance.

'And as for schooling, dearest Papa,' she said, 'are not you yourself most eminently equipped to supply any omissions in my learning. Besides, there are no little ones for her to care for. I think you might spare yourself the expense. I am quite capable of looking after myself, you know, and will be no trouble to you.'

Her mention of 'little ones' gave me a pang, and I thought of Horace with heartache. On the other hand, there was much sense in what she had to say, and all I said was: 'We shall see.'

July 25th

Jane Green came to see me this morning to say that she had been reflecting on Miss Usher's sudden departure and that she wished to give in her notice. She admitted that she and the other servants had not been particularly fond of Miss Usher, and that they had found her to be 'hoity-toity' at times, but that, all the same, the house was not what it was, and that, begging my pardon, she was minded to look for another position while she was still young.

This saddened me. Green has been a loyal and cheerful servant, trusted to a very high degree, the only member of the household permitted into my sanctum in order to clean it. It is Jane Green who brings me my meals on a tray, in the library or the study, now that I prefer to eat alone. Alice eats with her friend Mary Ann in the servants' hall and is happy to do so. I see no reason to complain.

I told Green that I should be very sorry to see her go, but that I would not stand in her way. Indeed, I said that she can expect an excellent character from me in due course. Blackburn is a flourishing town nowadays and even the lower middling classes are able to employ a servant.

However, in the end I persuaded her to a compromise. In return for a liberal increase in her wages she agreed to stay with me until the end of the year.

I go out only to spiritualist services. I receive nobody. Even Titus, who expressed a wish to visit, has been dissuaded. I take tea with Alice in the library for three quarters of an hour each afternoon. We both read, and do not converse much. Alice likes to read *The Medium and Daybreak* when I am finished with it. Sometimes we play chess, but I fear my concentration is not what it was, and of late she has been able to beat me quite easily.

August 3rd

Alice did not appear for tea this afternoon, but I thought nothing of it, until Jane Green came to me in the library to say that she had not appeared for supper either. She and the other servants had searched the house without success. Mary Ann Duxbury was missing too.

Alice has been guilty of many little misdemeanours in her girlhood but she has never played the truant like this. I remembered Miss Usher's complaining that the Duxbury girl had been leading her astray, and I wondered if there was perhaps something in it.

I was about to summon Richards and Peter, and to begin a search in the park when Cook came to me in the library to say that Alice and Mary Ann had just tumbled into the house through the tradesman's entrance, laughing and clutching each other as if intoxicated. I thanked her and asked her to send Alice to me directly.

In a few minutes Alice arrived, extremely buoyant, almost giddy, and quite oblivious to the anxiety she had caused. I told her that I was extremely vexed and had been on the point of scouring the town for her, desperately afraid that she might have absconded or been abducted.

'Oh Papa,' the impertinent girl replied. 'Don't be absurd. Mary Ann and I have only been to a séance at the Spread Eagle. Mary Ann is a sensitive, didn't you know?'

'I only know that the Spread Eagle is one of the lowest dives in town.'

'That it is not, and Mrs Dinsdale is a very respectable woman.'

'And who may she be?'

'Why, the landlady, of course.'

'Be that as it may, how dare you visit such a low den, without my leave, without informing anyone, and without a chaperone?'

'I'll have you know there were many other respectable ladies there other than Mrs Dinsdale, and it should be perfectly obvious to you why we told no one that we were going to attend.'

'And why is that?'

'Because you would have forbidden it.'

'I most certainly would have done so. You are impertinent, Miss. What is this nonsense about Duxbury being a sensitive?'

'It is not nonsense, Papa. She is one of the most powerful mediums that ever was, and you are being blind and stupid.'

I might have struck her at that very moment for her unconscionable impudence had she not said: 'Papa, she spoke to Mother, and had news of little Horace.'

I held back my hand.

After a while, I said: 'Where is she now?'

'In the servants' hall, I think,' Alice replied.

'Go and find her, and bring her here.'

The two girls returned forthwith, not in the least abashed. Indeed, Mary Ann's eyes sparkled with bravado.

'What do you mean,' I said to her, 'by taking my daughter to a mean public house in a most unsavoury part of this town, without my permission? Such places should not even be open on a Sunday evening.'

'Begging your pardon, Mr Pickup,' she said, 'Sundays is my day off when I've done my morning chores, and I may do what I like, and besides, the Spread Eagle may be a public house, but they be private rooms where the meeting was held, and there were very respectable people in attendance, and Mr Duckworth, the President, is a Justice of the Peace.'

I knew the name and it gave me pause.

'President of what?' I said.

'The Salford Bridge Spiritualist Society. I have been attending on Sundays for a long time now, and you can't stop me.'

'We shall see about that,' I said. 'Now, tell me, what makes you think you have the second sight?'

'I don't think it. I know it. And Mr Duckworth has been bringing me on, like, since the gift came to light. It were him as organised the meeting today, and it went down a treat, didn't it, Alice?'

'Certainly. The audience was most appreciative, Papa.'

'And how did you come to know that you had "the gift" as you put it?'

'It were at a meeting in the upper rooms of The Fleece on Penny Street. Well, the séance was well under way when the medium, Bessie Walmesley, said that her spirit guide sensed that there was another psychic in the room. I felt this strange tingling run right through me, and I passed out.

'Only, I didn't pass out. They told me afterwards that I'd gone into a trance, and that I'd stood up like, with my eyes glazed over like, and that I'd walked through the crowd - and it were packed, believe you me - and that I'd walked onto the platform and joined old Bessie.'

'Go on. What happened?'

'Well, apparently I said some things about some members of the audience that I couldn't possibly have known, seeing as I'd never met 'em in my life afore.'

'What things?'

'I don't know, do I? You never remember anything that's said and done when you're in a trance. Nobody does.'

'So you started running public séances on your own?'

'Oh no, sir. Today were the first. But I done loads of private séances. Mr Duckworth, see, he were that impressed that he started taking me to séances in private houses. I've been in some posh places, I can tell you. Just as posh as here.'

'Really? I wish to hear of what was alleged to have been said about my wife and child. But not now.

'Alice, you are yawning in a most unladylike manner, and it is late.

'You can give me your account tomorrow, Mary Ann, or as soon as I have been able to make contact with Mr Duckworth and invite him to confirm the truth of what you aver. I wish to spare myself any further heartache, in case what you say, whether wilfully or under some delusion, turns out to be baseless fantasy.'

'Are you saying you don't believe me?' said Mary Ann in a saucy tone. 'I don't take kindly to that.'

'You can please yourself,' I said, 'and if you speak to me like that again, I shall throw you out down the front steps of this house, before you can draw another breath.

'Now, both of you, leave me. No, not another word.'

41 THE JOURNAL 20

August 7th

THOUGH I WAS MOST UNWILLING to quit my reclusive life, financial affairs, which I could neither ignore nor postpone, obliged me to travel to Manchester for the first few days of this week, and it was not until today, Thursday, that I was able to waylay Duckworth at the Magistrate's Court. We repaired to the Ribblesdale Hotel, where, over a glass or two of porter, I made my enquiries. I was already known to him in my capacity as town councillor, a position which I have neglected rather since Louisa's passing.

He seemed reluctant to discuss his connexions with spiritualism at first until I convinced him of my own interest, and explained to him something of my tragic family situation. He confirmed that he had indeed witnessed Mary Ann Duxbury's psychic powers, that he had encouraged her, and that he had convened the meeting at the Spread Eagle where the girl had displayed remarkable psychic insight.

'But have you not seen yesterday's *Medium and Daybreak*?' he said, producing a crumpled copy of the periodical from his briefcase. 'There is a very favourable write-up, if I can but find it.'

After a brief search he found what he was looking for, and handed me the paper, pointing to the following paragraph:

[This is the review which Will found, and which is reproduced on p.159 - TC]

'This is most impressive,' I said. 'I am sorry I doubted the girl. You are quite sure there was no back-stage sharp practice involved, no skulduggery?'

'My dear Pickup, I vetted the performance myself. I can assure you that I hold the Salford Bridge Spiritualist Society's reputation for integrity very dear. There are plenty of people out there who are deeply sceptical of our beliefs. We would not survive even the merest whiff of scandal. This is why an endorsement by *The Medium and Daybreak* is very precious to us.'

'Quite so. May I ask if any payment was made to the girl in respect of her performance?'

He named a sum.

'It is not much,' he said, 'but membership of the society is by subscription. We feel this deters mockers and those of bad faith. It also allows us to pay our mediums for their service and for the expenditure of their spiritual energies. As I'm sure you know, these psychic encounters can often leave a medium quite exhausted.'

Eadem die

I caught one of the new trams up Preston New Road to the bottom of the park. I must say they are wonderful contraptions and I am not ashamed to say that I felt the same excitement a young boy might feel at riding on the upper deck.

On arriving home I repaired to the library and ordered tea to be brought, and for Alice to be found and sent in to me. She appeared and poured tea for us. I told her that I had been able to confirm that Mary Ann had been telling the truth and that now I wished her to tell me what she had learned of my wife at this meeting.

'Oh Papa,' she replied, 'we *told* you she wasn't lying, and you *wouldn't* listen - but leave that be. After she had gone into her trance she gave messages of comfort to several members of the audience from the other side. And then she gave me the surprise of my life when she said, in a strange voice: "Why, here is Lulu. Hello, Lulu, who are you looking for?"

'And I stood up and shouted: "Me, she's looking for me! Lulu, it's me, Alice!"

'Mary Ann couldn't have known that that was what I called mother when I was very small. She couldn't have known that, could she, Papa?'

'No child, she could not. And then what? Did Louisa speak again.'

'No. Not out loud. But then, Mary Ann asked in her own voice if I had any message for her, and I said: "Tell her I love her. Tell her I will always love her."

'Mary Ann said: "She is fading now, but she knows. She wants you to know that she is reunited with the children and that they are all very very happy."

'And with that Mary Ann let out a little cry, as if she had pricked a finger while sewing, and said: "She is extinguished. The veil has fallen. We will not reach her again today."'

By now we were both weeping tears of relief.

'Go and compose yourself, my darling girl. And then send Mary Ann to me. I wish to speak to her alone. We will reach out to your mother again. I am sure of it. Go now. Dry your eyes.'

Mary Ann arrived so promptly that I thought she must have been hovering nearby. I explained that I had sought independent confirmation of her honesty and wanted to apologise most humbly for what I had said the day before.

'Oh, that's all right, sir,' she said. 'That's very handsome of you to say so, to be sure, and I am not saying as I didn't deserve it neither, for I have to admit I were a mite contrarious meself, if truth be told. I apologise humbly an' all.'

Thus reconciled, I went on to say that I had a proposition for her, and it was this: that if she were to give up any public performances in shady public houses, in order to protect the reputation of *my* house and family, I would remunerate her accordingly with much more than she could possibly have earned through such ventures. Moreover, if she would consent to conducting *private* séances here at home, she would be rewarded most generously.

She accepted the offer, as well she might, because it was very liberal. I asked her when it would be convenient to meet for our first session and suggested this very evening, but she demurred and said she would like to meditate for twenty-four hours or so in order that she might be in a state of optimal receptiveness. As to where, I proposed that we meet here in the library, but Mary Ann suggested that the nursery might be better, the aura of the place being more charged with memories. I agreed and will order for a fire to be lit today and for it to burn until any mustiness be consumed, the room having been unused since Louisa's passing. It had been re-decorated, of course, in anticipation of Horace's arrival, but no more of that.

I said that I wished no-one to be present save Alice, and Mary Ann herself, and she agreed that this was a propitious suggestion which she had been about to propose herself. We settled on ten o'clock tomorrow evening.

And so we parted, Mary Ann to meditate, and I to pray.

42 THE JOURNAL 21

August 8th

AT THE APPOINTED HOUR, the gas lights in the nursery were dimmed almost to nothing, the curtains drawn tight, and two candles lit and placed on the mantelpiece. A round table, brought in from elsewhere, was set in the middle of the room, and three chairs set around it. A velvet cloth of midnight blue covered the table, and on it lay a pair of gloves of Louisa's, a bracelet of Charlotte's, a lock of Eliza's hair, and a pair of blue bootees which had been knitted for the baby.

We sat around the table and Mary Ann bade us hold hands. I took Alice's soft hand in my right and Mary Ann's roughened hand in my left. We sat in silence for a very long time, and there was no sound but each other's breathing. Eventually, Mary Ann began to breathe through her mouth. Her breathing slowed and became very deep until she scarcely seemed to breathe at all. Her hand felt cold in mine. I looked into her face, and, dim though it was in the room, I could see that her eyes were wide, bright and unblinking.

'Spirit of the North,' she said. 'Are you in this house? Come into this room. Come through the veil.'

There was a pause of some minutes, and then Mary Ann repeated her invocation. Suddenly, she laughed - a laugh which seemed unnatural in the darkened room.'

'He is here,' she said. 'Chibiabos is here, standing behind you. *Do not turn around.*

Chibiabos, welcome.'

It may have been just a draught, but the two candles on the mantelpiece flickered and then appeared to burn brighter.

'Chibiabos, Spirit of the North,' Mary Ann said. 'We seek knowledge of loved ones who passed to the other side from this house. We seek to know of Louisa, mistress of this house, of Charlotte and Eliza, daughters of this house. We wish to know of baby Horace, who lived but a few hours in this house.'

Mary Ann, turned her head to one side, as if listening intently, and then she stood, letting go of our hands, gazing at a spot a few feet behind Alice and me.

Mary Ann's face it up with something like rapture.

'Chibiabos says he knows them,' she said. 'They are happy at being together again. When he last saw them, they were sitting together on the bank of a beautiful river, overhung with willow trees. Charlotte had made a paper boat for Horace while Eliza was making a daisy chain coronet for her mother, who was singing. Horace was chasing butterflies.'

I could not stop myself. I turned around to ask how Horace could be chasing butterflies when he was only a couple of hours old at his passing. There was no-one there.

At the same time I heard a little scream and turned around again to see Mary Ann slumped across the table.

'O Papa,' Alice said sadly. 'You have broken the charm.'

I moved round to Mary Ann who appeared to be in a deep sleep, and was about to shake her awake when Alice cried out.

'No, no. Don't touch her Papa. It would be very dangerous for her if you were to bring her to consciousness while she is in a realm halfway between the living and the dead. We must let her sleep it out.'

With this she took Mary Ann by the hand and led her like a sleepwalker to the window seat where she laid her down. Alice sat beside her, stroking her forehead.

'You should go now, Papa. I will bring her to you in the library when she awakens.'

I confess I was very shaken by this turn of events, but I saw the sense in what my daughter said and went downstairs to the library where I tried to read.

It was two hours later before Alice knocked on the library door and came in to inform me that Mary Ann sent apologies but felt that she needed to take to her bed for now as the séance had exhausted her. However, she would be sure to attend on me after breakfast tomorrow morning.

August 9th
Mary Ann Duxbury has just left me. To my very great surprise I feel quite discomfited, for what she had to say to me felt very like a rebuke, though it was delivered in such a sweet and gentle tone that I could not take offence at it.

She said that I may have irrecoverably shattered the fragile rapport between herself as a medium and her personal spirit guide. She explained that such confidences are built up over time, and that the bond is maintained only through fierce concentration on the part of the medium. The guide is not easily seduced into relinquishing his bliss in the other realm in order to traverse the invisible boundary into the world of the living, and many have attested that the guide endures some kind of pain whilst in the shadowy province between life and death. She said she feared he might avoid any future contact.

She said that I had to imagine that it was like searching through an innumerable crowd of beings all coming towards you but not lingering long enough to be identified.

Did this mean, I asked, that she would no longer be able or willing to make future attempts? Not so, she replied, but she felt some time should be allowed to elapse before making any further attempt. How long? I said. Perhaps a fortnight was her reply. I said that I would follow her direction in all things and try to possess myself in patience.

'But one thing more,' I said as she turned to quit the chamber. 'You said in your trance that Horace was chasing butterflies.'

'Did I?' she said.

'How could that be, Mary Ann, when Horace died a babe in arms?'

'Ah, that's easy, sir,' she said. 'On the other side, a spirit don't necessarily stay at the age when its body gave up the ghost, so to speak. How could a spirit be in bliss at ninety-two? Or at two hours old? Why, a new-born infant is only beginning to learn to see and hear, let alone understand the world around it, so how could it appreciate the beauty of the spirit world unless it developed somehow?

'No, sir, as I understand it, each spirit grows into the age best suited to it in the after life. There's no old people there, and there's no infants. I've been told that the spirits of most deceased persons reverts to the time of their prime, which is around the age of thirty-two - that's the age at which Jesus died.'

'I believe that I've read something of the kind,' I said.

'It don't apply to everybody,' Mary Ann said. 'People as dies in old age loses years as a spirit. Stands to reason, but them as dies young, stays young, or if they died in the cradle, they *gain* a few years. That'll be why Horace has the spirit of a young boy now, Cornelius. In time, it might be possible to speak to him.'

I declared that this would bring me inexpressible joy. Mary Ann proposed a day and time for another séance just over a week from now, and then she left me to ruminate on these things.

It was perhaps an hour or so later that I realised that she had addressed me as 'Cornelius'. Ordinarily, this would have been a deed of such effrontery as to merit immediate dismissal. Yet I had not noted it at the time.

I decided to let it pass.

It is a token of how very much I depend on this girl's powers.

August 17

We met in the nursery for a séance this evening at eight, but it was fruitless, and we gave up at a quarter past nine. Mary Ann said that she sent her spirit out to find her guide but that there was much confusion at 'the crossing'. She said that it was like electrical discharges, a kind of crackling interference, which would not let her spirit reach through the veil.

October 4th

We have held séances at roughly fortnightly intervals for some time now, without much success - until tonight. The divide between the quick and the dead is not as permeable as it was.

Chibiabos was able to make an appearance behind Alice and me, albeit very briefly. I did not turn around having learnt my lesson at considerable cost. I thought of Orpheus and Eurydice and kept my eyes fixed on Mary Ann.

She asked Chibiabos why he had shunned the house for so long and he told her that the aura of Wastwater House was fuzzy and that the psychic vibrations were too agitated. Mary Ann asked him what he meant by this. He didn't answer the question, but he did say that he had a message from Eliza. Before he could tell us what the message was, he disappeared. At the moment of his vanishing, the candles on the mantel went out.

October 17th

Mary Ann's spirit guide made an appearance as soon as summoned, and he stayed some time. However, no sense could be made of his utterances. He had much to say, and Mary Ann relayed it to us, but it was all the most tangled mumbo jumbo imaginable. The nonsense verses of Edward Lear are nothing to it.

As in Mr Lear's poetry, the individual words are current and recognisable, but combined they are gibberish. Mary Ann relayed sentences like: 'Frogs and newts climb the rainbow to reach the jewelled casket', and 'the mist on the lake is woven by the owl out of surplus twilight.' And much much more of this ilk.

If this were code, I could see no key. When she awoke, Mary Ann could not interpret it either. Alice merely said that it was very silly of course, but rather beautiful all the same.

This is all so frustrating, but I will not give in.

43 THE JOURNAL 22

October 20

ALICE AND MARY ANN HAVE PUT A SUGGESTION to me which is, on the face of it, outrageous. Mary Ann is of the view that a principal reason why our correspondence with the spirit world is so tenuous is that Wastwater House is too 'busy'. There are too many people in service here who are sceptical or even antagonistic to the precepts of spiritualism.

'I have even heard Cook tell Richards as it's all so much fiddle-faddle and eyewash,' Mary Ann said. 'Oh, they may all be as sweet as sugar plums to your face, sir, but you should hear what they say below stairs. Young Peter says he's not sure he wants to work in a haunted house and Jane Green says summoning the dead is agin the true religion. Is it any wonder, sir, as Chibiabos has trouble paying a visit to a nest of unbelievers?'

I replied that I was not happy to hear such things about people who have been in my service for many years, and who have proved loyal to me, even in the most trying of times.

'To your face, sir,' Mary Ann said. 'You mind what I say.'

'But Papa,' Alice said at this juncture. 'Let us think rationally about this. Our family has dwindled to two. We inhabit just a few rooms. We do not visit. We do not receive. Why do we need troops of servants? In my view, you should close down those parts of the house that are not in use and reduce the number of those in service accordingly. It would represent a considerable easing of expense, Papa. I could be your housekeeper and Mary Ann knows everything necessary to provide for your comfort. She has learned to be an excellent cook and has always proved diligent.'

'And the aura of the house would be purified,' Mary Ann said.

'No,' I said. 'I will not hear of it. Whatever you say, these people are not dispensable.'

And yet, when the two young women were gone, I was not so certain.

October 22
So near, and yet so distant. A séance held this evening, proved so very tantalising. We sat for a long time in silence after Mary Ann had gone into her trance. Suddenly there was a loud rap that seemed to come from the window. The street lamp outside was out of order and consequently it was pitch black outside. As a consequence we had forgotten to close the heavy drapes as was our usual custom. Mary Ann continued to stare into the distance, but Alice and I turned to the window. Nothing. Then another rap, and a child's voice, which seemed to come from outside, said: 'Papa, it is I, Horace. Why do you not speak to me?'

Then I saw, or thought I saw, a small boy's face at the window, pale and large-eyed, with dark hair, a lock of which fell across his forehead. The vision was there but a moment, and then instantly vanished.

October 23rd
My distress at the transience of last night's vision, combined with the hope that it might be repeated at greater length, has inclined me, after all, to think positively about closing down much of the house and dismissing the servants.

However, it cannot be in 'one fell swoop'.

October 25th

I called all the members of my household into the salon today. The very room looked desolate and I could not help but remember occasions when, with my wife and family about me, we made merry for one occasion or another, with old friends and distinguished guests.

I began with a prayer, after which I explained the situation which was met with such a stony-faced reception that I suspected that it was not news to them, and that the intelligence had leaked through Mary Ann, or possibly even my daughter. I felt a certain selfish relief at this: they would have had a little time to accommodate themselves to the facts, and I would not have to suffer the embarrassing consequences of delivering a terrible shock.

I made it perfectly clear that I would provide each one of them with an excellent character and an advance on their wages, sufficient to tide them over until they might be placed elsewhere. I said that I would endeavour myself, by consulting friends and acquaintances, and by consulting agencies dedicated to the recruitment of domestics, to ensure that each of them found a decent situation before Christmas. Indeed, my brother Titus had already agreed to take Peter into service at Holt House. I announced that I have already spoken to Richards, who had been thinking of retiring, but had consented to continue working for me as part time gardener.

Nevertheless, I said that I wished to have my house to myself and my daughter by November 30th. I asked if there were any questions. Since there were none I bade them go about their business.

As they left, I heard Cook say to Jane Green: 'He's going barmy, the master', and Jane replied: 'Off his rocker. It's the grief what's doing it.'

Naturally, this wounded me. Especially to hear Jane Green speak of me like that, a woman I had respected and advanced in her career.

However, I quickly reassured myself that I had never done a saner thing in my life.

November 30th

The house is quiet. You can almost hear it breathing - with relief perhaps.

The servants have all been placed to their advantage. Millicent Foster, my housekeeper, is gone to take up that role with the Ribchester Walmsleys. Her sister, hitherto my cook, has been placed as head of the catering brigade at the Town Hall. Finally as a governor at St John's school, I was able to find Jane Green a post as supervisor of the school's domestic staff.

My house will be run by my daughter with Mary Ann Duxbury as cook and general domestic.

Now that Peter is gone and Richards on diminished duties, the carriage will be put under dust covers, and the horses sold. I shall miss them, but it is but a short walk into town, and there are cabs and trams in inclement weather. Besides, I propose to venture out as little as possible.

We shall do very well.

December 2nd

Our first séance under the new régime was a great success, Chibiabos appearing almost immediately when summoned. When Mary Ann asked how my family were, he said that they were close by him. She asked if she could speak to them, and he replied in the affirmative. I urged Mary Ann to ask about Horace.

'The boy is blithe and carefree,' Chibiabos said through Mary Ann, 'and always smiling. He is as much loved in the spirit world as he was in yours. We are in a woodland glade, where sunlight is dancing through the leaves, by a stream which runs over coloured pebbles. Would you like to speak to him? I can be your intermediary.'

The strange thing was that it was Mary Ann who was speaking, though she was in a trance. She was conveying the words of her spirit guide, who in turn, would be relaying Horace's words. I would be speaking to my son at two removes as it were. But that didn't matter - I was excited beyond measure.

'Are you there, Horace?' I said. 'Do you know me?'

'Of course I do. You are my papa. I do not remember ever seeing you, but we will meet soon, and forever.'

'Are you content, Horace?'

'Oh yes, Papa. There is no unhappiness here. There are lovely sunsets, but no night, for the dawn follows directly. There is rain sometimes but it refreshes us and does not wet us. We are eternally awake.'

'And how are Mama and your sisters?'

'They are happy too. We are going to have a picnic - there will be milk and honey and manna.'

'Please tell them I love them.'

'Oh they know that, Papa. But I shall tell them anyway.'

'What are you doing at the moment, my boy?'

'I am riding Mayfly along the bed of a stream. She is my spirit pony. Eliza is holding her bridle, and Charlotte and Mama are walking alongside. Charlotte is gathering bulrushes.'

'Ask if I can speak to my wife,' I said to Mary Ann.

There was a long pause.

'He's tiring,' Mary Ann said. 'He wants to go. I cannot hold him.'

'Then let him go,' I said. 'He has brought joy enough for now.'

With a sigh, Mary Ann closed her eyes and slept. Alice and I guided the somnambulist to the window seat and laid her down tenderly. We gazed, smiling, into each other's faces, but we did not speak.

Our hearts were too full.

44 THE JOURNAL 23

1891

March 23rd

AT FIRST, I THOUGHT IT MIGHT BE A DIRTY CLUSTER of spiders' webs hanging from the ceiling, but the smudge was too dark against the white paint, and so I concluded that it must be black mould.

However, on closer inspection I perceived it to be writing. The letters were ragged and clumsily formed to be sure, but the message was clear enough: 'Father weep no more'.

I was surprised and thrilled in equal measure. How could this be? Now that Jane Green was gone, no-one has access to my study but me. I often take my meals in here but the tray is left outside. Kindling, logs and coal are also left outside the door at my request, and, though Mary Ann has protested, I light the fire myself.

It is true that dust is accumulating and that the windows are becoming grimy, but that is no hardship. I keep the surface of my desk clear and that is all that matters. I live only for the séances. Apart from my daily time with Alice, I see no-one. I have received any number of letters from Titus who is solicitous about my welfare, but I have not replied, and I have given up reading them.

What is most astonishing about the writing on the ceiling is that it is clearly addressed to me, and that it is from my children. The ceilings in this house are high; only a spirit could have delivered these words, without the presence of a medium or any other intermediary.

Since the servants left, our séances have become more consistently successful.

I feel the presence of my family, though I cannot see them yet. It is a consolation rich and deep.

March 24th

There was more writing on the ceiling today, this time in several places towards the centre. They appear to be zodiacal signs which appear in strips of seven symbols. It occurred to me that they might represent some kind of occult cypher or cryptogram. I have consulted several of my books on the occult but so far I have been unable to unravel any secret meaning. Besides, the combination of hieroglyphs is different in different places.

I will persevere.

March 25th

Today, there appeared above me the inscription: 'Mt 1914'. I saw immediately that this was a biblical reference and recognised it as the passage where the disciples try to turn the children away from Jesus and he rebukes them. The meaning is abundantly clear. Death means to keep my children from me but the Lord will not permit it.

I praise his beautiful name.

March 28th

Writing has continued to manifest itself on the ceiling of my study. There have been two more biblical references, both to do with children. Arcane symbols which I do not recognise have also appeared: Persian perhaps? Or Egyptian?

There have also been clusters of words and phrases which I cannot convene into meaningful sentences and I find this tantalising. It is like the nonsense that Mary Ann's spirit guide sometimes puts into her mouth in less fortunate séances. It resembles occasions when one is abroad and attempts to communicate in French or German, say. One's best efforts are met with a friendly but uncomprehending shrug, followed by a stream of talk from one's interlocutor in which one recognises individual words but can construe no meaning.

April 1st

It is beyond extraordinary. I stumbled from my bedroom to my study, still half-dazed with sleep, to find a merry little fire crackling in the grate. I shouted down the stairs to Alice and Mary Ann to come up and behold this miracle for I could not believe the evidence of my own eyes.

The girls were less dazzled by this apparition than I expected. I say apparition, but it was really nothing of the kind: I saw it, I heard it, I felt its warmth. It was in the material world.

Alice said that for some days now, they have risen early and come down to the kitchen to find jugs of hot water ready on the kitchen table. Mary Ann said she had witnessed a jug of water sailing up the stairs of its own accord towards my bedroom. I was at first disinclined to believe this, but remembered that I had read about many instances of 'levitation', whether of objects or persons, in *The Medium and Daybreak,* though I have never personally witnessed such an event.

Alice said that she and Mary Ann had found fires, which they had neither laid nor lit, burning in other rooms, including their bedrooms and the library. They have, they say, found their beds made by unseen hands.

At length they left me to marvel at these things. It was only when they were gone that I noticed that there was new writing in a fresh corner of the ceiling which read: 'We watch over you'.

It cannot be but that the spirits of my dead wife and children now inhabit this house frequently and at will. It is as if they issue backwards and forwards through a rent in the veil. It is as if the house itself has become a portal through which they can leave the other side and manifest themselves to my aching soul. It is as if Death no longer has dominion in them, and that our communion becomes more profound and more tangible with every passing day.

I know that the day will come, be it sooner or later, when my time is come and I too become a spirit dwelling with them on the other side, until that last prodigious day, when we shall be reunited in the flesh and time shall be no more.

April 6th

Writing continues to appear on the ceiling almost daily. When intelligible, the messages are reassuring and expressive of deep love, emanating like warmth from the other side. They instil in me a sense of content glowing like a coal inside me. I have no need of the material world. Meals are left uneaten and I fear I have allowed myself to become a little unkempt. I ought to send for a barber. But not yet.

I find I am unwilling to admit an outsider lest he contaminate the aura of the house, lest it leach out through the open door as he comes in, to dissipate in the outside world into nothing.

Another biblical reference has appeared on the ceiling. It is from the very end of the Gospel according to Matthew:

'Lo, I am with you always, even unto the end of the world.'

45 THE JOURNAL 24

May 1st

THE NIGHT WAS BEEN UNSEASONABLY HOT and I slept badly. I awoke from troubled dreams of shipwreck to the sound of heavy rain on the window panes and splattering from blocked gutters onto the paving below. Thunder was grumbling in the distance. I opened the hunter on the table by my bed and saw that it was a little after four.

I could not get back to sleep. I lay there for an eternity, twisting and turning, the pillow damp on my face. At length the rain passed, and a thin strip of sunlight leaked from a gap in the curtains. Birdsong announced the coming dawn. It must be around five-thirty then, and still sleep eluded me, though I felt quite exhausted.

Thinking that if I were to read for a little while I might eventually drift off, I rose from my tangled sheets, and put on my dressing gown, intending to go along to my study and select a book. I collected the key from a hook behind my bedroom door.

On the landing, I was surprised to see that the study door was ajar, though I was confident that I had locked it the night before as I always did. A splinter of light spilled out on the landing carpet. I could hear stifled giggling from within.

Flinging the door open, I encountered a dreadful sight.

Mary Ann Duxbury was standing on the highest step of the library ladder writing on the ceiling with a paint-brush attached to a broom handle. Alice was standing at the foot of the ladder with a pot of paint.

In a rush I knew everything. I had been duped. I was a blind, credulous fool. It had all been a fraud from start to finish, the séances, the spirit guides, the props, the theatrics - all, all a gaudy hoax. And I had swallowed it whole: hook, line and sinker. I had been seduced by party tricks that would not have deceived a slobbering imbecile. And I had fallen for all the poppycock in that silly rag *The Medium and Daybreak*, and its tall tales fit only for senile old maids and children.

I had allowed a mere servant girl to corrupt my own daughter, and for both of them to turn me into an object of ridicule.

A scorching rage ensued. I pulled Mary Ann from the ladder and hurled her to the floor. Then grabbing Alice by the arm, I dragged her from the room, locking the door behind me. I hauled her down the stairs, and when she fell several times, I tugged her to her feet. Oblivious to her screams I lugged her across the hall to the front door where I threw her into the street. I stood for a long time as she pounded on the door, but I was unmoved. She was nothing to me.

My daughters are all dead.

I continued to stand in the vestibule for perhaps an hour after the pounding stopped, thinking and feeling nothing. And then I remembered the Duxbury girl, and went upstairs to deal with her.

When I opened the door, she was trying to open the window, but they had been fitted with locks long since, and there would be no escape for her that way. I turned her around and held her by the wrists while I fired questions at her: how long had this been going on? how had she ensnared my daughter? Who had taught her her repertoire of tricks?

She would not answer but struggled to escape my grip, turning her head violently from side to side so as not to look me in the face.

'It were dead easy, Cornelius. You're dead soft, you are. It were like being let loose in a toffee shop.'

Then she vented a stream of appalling abuse in language which would have shamed a Liverpool docker.

This was intolerable. I grabbed her by the neck and squeezed. It did not take long, for she was slight of frame and her neck was slender, and fury made me strong.

When I was sure that the life had gone out of her, her eyes bolting and her tongue protruding, I dropped her to the floor, and opened up my bureau where I sat down to add to this journal.

As I write, I see what must be done.

In one of the outhouses there are bricks left over from the building of the gazebo. There is also cement and sharp sand.

[There are no further entries - TC]

PART THREE

Epilogue

Omlet, ek is de papa's spook.
'Hamlet, I am thy father's ghost'
(in Afrikaans)

45 SPIRIT PONY

'SPIRIT PONY?' Will spits out the words. 'Spirit pony? How naive can you get?'

'Oh come on, Will,' Ruth says. 'Are you made of granite? Look what the poor man had to endure - the death of everyone dear to him, not to mention a daughter who betrayed him for fun. No wonder he lost his marbles.'

'And became a murderer,' Will says.

'He has a nice turn of phrase though,' I say. '"You can always count on a murderer for a fancy prose style." I read that somewhere.'

We are in the garden in Mellor, enjoying a lunch of cold cuts and salads. We have all read Ruth's transcript of the journals.

'So our Adele was really Mary Ann all along,' Ruth says.

'Didn't you see that coming?' Will says. 'I thought it was pretty clear from early on, and it was obvious she and Alice were up to no good.'

'It did begin to dawn on me quite quickly,' Ruth says, 'but I would never have guessed the details.'

'I knew Alice would turn out to be a wrong'un when he locked her in the cupboard,' Will says.

'Oh, come on,' I say, 'if you'd had kids yourself, you wouldn't read too much into Alice's tantrums. Par for the course.'

'Tom,' Ruth snaps. 'That was uncalled for.'

'Oh, sorry mate,' I say. 'Tactless.'

'Don't worry about it,' Will says. 'There's time for me to learn yet. Charlie Chaplin had a child at 73.'

'He did not,' Ruth says.

'He did so,' Will says. 'Look it up.'

'I'll pass,' Ruth says.

'Anyway,' Will continues, 'What gets me is how a man as obviously literate and intelligent as Cornelius falls for all this. I mean, I know it was all a part of the spirit of the times, to coin a phrase - and I know family tragedy drove him from despair to extravagant levels of hope, but all these séances. Really? They're all much the same as your hoax at Cambridge, Tom. Just on a more sophisticated level.'

'A more professional one too,' I say. 'Don't forget, there was money involved.'

'What about Mary Ann's private séances though?' Ruth says.

'I reckon she learned the tricks of the trade from that magistrate chap, Duckworth was he called?' Will says.

'I thought he seemed a bit shady,' Ruth says.

'Many of the tricks are easily explained,' I say. 'Remember the child medium, Maisie Entwistle, and the appearance of her spirit guide with a veil from head to foot? Do you remember that before he appeared there was mist rolling across the stage?'

'And a blinding flash of light,' Ruth says.

'Exactly,' I say. 'The mist is easy. We used the trick when I played Prospero in *The Tempest* at school. You drop a lump of dry ice into a bucket of water and the mist comes rolling out of the bucket.'

'And the flash?'

'Also easy. Do you remember Ben Westwell at school, Will?'

'The one who got sent down for arson?'

'Yeah, him. He used to nick magnesium tape from the master in Chemistry and ignite it. There would be a brilliant white flash and we would all cheer. He got caught every time of course, especially when he set fire to the wastepaper bin, but he said it was worth it.[9] Now, if you just upgrade the principle you have a flashbomb...'

'...which dazzles the audience so the spirit guide can just walk on!' Ruth says.

'Exactly,' I say, 'and all these tricks were common enough in the theatre and the music hall. Ventriloquism played a large part. Cornelius himself says that the

[9] *Northern Flames*, p. 140

temple on Johnston Street was like a cross between a theatre and a church.'

'And you think all the mystical stuff can be explained as practically as this?' Ruth says.

'Probably,' I say.

'And what about identifying strangers in the congregation?'

'Insider information,' Will says. 'When I went to the séance on St Peter Street, I'd already given the woman on the door my name and profession, so it was no surprise when the medium called it out. Again, think of Mary Ann's public séance at the Spread Eagle. She had plenty of information from Alice that she could use. It was a double act.'

'And the rest,' I say, 'is to do with misdirection - the conjuror's ploy. You throw out a name experimentally, and if somebody picks up the ball, you run with it and improvise. Remember Maisie trying "Charlie" and "Elizabeth", near enough to "Charlotte" and "Eliza" for Mrs Pickup to be taken in.'

'What about the healings then?' Ruth says.

'Auto-suggestion,' I say. 'Haven't we seen often enough that people will believe what they want to believe? There's plenty of evidence that psychosomatic symptoms can disappear just as readily as they appeared in the first place. So if you find yourself in an atmosphere heavily charged with a will to believe, then miracles can happen.'

'What about the miracles inside the house then?' Ruth says.

'Fires lighting of their own accord?' I say, 'and jugs of water floating upstairs?'

'Yes, that kind of thing.'

'Well,' I say, 'as for the jugs of water, had you forgotten that dumb waiter?'

'My God,' Ruth says, 'straight up from the kitchens to the salon - which is on the same floor as the study.'

'Right,' I say. 'As for the self-igniting fires, well, I think the girls must've been getting up very early whilst Cornelius was still asleep. Remember that it's just after dawn when he catches them producing the spirit writing on the ceiling.'

'That's another thing that gets me,' Ruth says. 'How did the girls get access to the study in any case? Didn't Cornelius have the only key?'

'But Alice is his housekeeper now. She would've inherited the keys from Mrs Foster, the outgoing housekeeper, and don't forget that Jane Green also had a key in order to clean the study. It stands to reason that she would've passed on that key to Alice as the new housekeeper, and there was no reason why Alice should've said anything about it to her father.

'And if you think about Mary Ann's séances within the house, it's hardly surprising that she should make such a fuss about Cornelius' not turning round at the appearance of Chibiabos.'

'Because there was no one there,' Ruth says.

'Precisely,' Will says.

'All the same,' Ruth says. 'I can't get out of my head the image of little Horace at the window pane saying: "why do you not speak to me father?" It's heartbreaking.'

'Well,' I say, 'doesn't Cornelius himself write "I saw *or thought I saw*" this apparition? By now it's clear he's extremely suggestible.'

'If not completely potty,' says Will. 'The other servants obviously thought so. I think there are signs from very early on that Cornelius is unstable, and I think there's a gradual decline of his grip on things. He's not eating; he's not socialising; he's not sleeping. Pretty unhealthy if you ask me. And over a number of years there are instances of serious lack of control over his temper. I think nowadays we might be inclined to think of him as psychotic.'

'Well,' I say. 'I'm not entirely sure that his symptoms would fit the clinical definition of psychosis, but sure, he was pretty deranged by the end.'

'Poor Horace,' Ruth says. '

'Poor everybody, I say. 'It's a pretty grim story, fit for a penny dreadful, and in Blackburn too. Who'd a thowt it?'

We sat there for a while in the afternoon sunshine, musing.

'We should have a gazebo, Tom,' Ruth says suddenly.

'Where?' I say.

'There, in that corner - we could demolish that ugly shed.'

'That ugly shed is my study. Nothing doing. Besides, I don't have the brick-laying skills of Cornelius Pickup. And even if I did, it would be a constant reminder of Mary Ann walled up in her tomb of Accrington brick in the kitchen of Wastwater House.'

'I suppose so,' Ruth says. 'Now, who would like some raspberries?'

'I would,' says Will.

'And me!' I say. 'My English master at QEGS used to say that there were only two things that could induce him to believe in God: raspberries and giraffes. He said that raspberries were so improbably delicious and giraffes so utterly absurd that only an omnipotent God could've invented them.'

46 ALICE

I BROUGHT OUT ANOTHER BOTTLE OF WINE and Ruth served up raspberries with clotted cream.

'What are we going to do about these journals?' I say.

'What do you mean?' Ruth says.

'Well,' I say, 'I know that Mr Rafiq said that he had no interest in the contents of the bureau, and that we could keep anything we found, but somehow I don't feel that we have any right to them. I think we should show them to Mr Higson as we promised, but I'm not sure he can be trusted with a printout. I did think of leaving them to the history department in the Library. With the proviso that they should not be accessed by the public until a certain date?'

'I don't see the point of that,' says Will. 'They've been locked in that bureau for over a hundred years, and all the people involved are long dead.'

'That's true,' I say. 'Well, whatever we decide, I will need to report our findings to the police so that they can finally close the case, and I suppose we might just as well hand over the diaries to them and let them decide what's to become of them.

'One thing I think we ought to agree on is to keep the story from the press. I've always regretted letting them have the story of "the Skelly in the Bog", and the temporary notoriety it gave us. Do you agree, Will?'

'Well, as a former journalist, part of me says publish and be damned, but I take your point.'

'Oh yes,' Ruth says, 'for heaven's sake, let them all lie in peace.'

'Sure,' says Will, 'though I can't help but wonder what happened to them. I suppose Alice ended up in the workhouse - or on the game.'

'Possibly,' I say, 'but my guess is that she turned up on her uncle Titus's doorstep. He and Cornelius had become estranged, remember, and Titus had a great affection for his nieces.'

'Could be,' says Ruth. 'Maybe she even ended up marrying Peter.'

'Who was found to be the heir to a vast estate? I don't think so. Too like a Dickens novel,' I say.

'And Cornelius,' Ruth says, 'what do you suppose happened to him?'

'Well,' Will says, 'his corpse ended up in the family vault a few years later, and the house was sold. Somebody must have arranged all this. Do you think he might have gone over to France to his eldest daughter and her husband?'

'Fanny?' I say. 'It figures, I suppose.'

'I think the most horrible part of the story,' Ruth says, 'is the *why?* Why should these two girls unite to torment Cornelius in such a dreadful way?'

'There's such a thing as *folie à deux*,' I say, 'where two people combine to commit crimes which they would not even contemplate as individuals. There was the sheer devilry of it, and maybe they half-believed in what they invented.

'Mind you, it's clear that Mary Ann was very clever. Did you notice that she spoke in a working class Lancashire accent, but not when she was in a trance? And what about that reference to Alice's sisters being at the bottom of a well?'

'Oh, I see! The Mad Tea Party!' says Ruth.

'Right,' I say. '*Alice in Wonderland*. The dormouse says that Elsie, Lacey and Tilly live at the bottom of a well. Alice Pickup had been sharing her favourite books with Mary Ann.'

'So it was a little joke between them?' Will says.

'I think so,' I say. 'And Chibiabos? Do you remember doing *Hiawatha* with Mrs Ainsworth at St John's, Will?'

'Definitely.'

'Chibiabos was Hiawatha's friend. He was a singer, the tribe's bard, historian and truth teller.'

''Ecky thump! I'd forgotten him.'

'Well, Mary Ann paid dearly for it all at any rate,' Ruth says. 'Oh look, I think we're in for some rain. Help me clear up.'

And sure enough the sky is blackening over the fells.

Suddenly, Will stands up with a loaded tray in his hands.

'Just a minute,' he says, 'that girl medium - what was her name, Maisie Entwistle? Tom, wasn't your grandma called Maisie?'

'Ah, I see what you're getting at,' I say. 'but no. Nearly though. She was called Daisy. I used to get the giggles when the aunties used her first name.'

'It was the fan that made me think of it,' says Will. 'Didn't your grandmother have a fan as one of her props?'

'She did,' I say.

'Oh my goodness gracious me!' Ruth says suddenly, nearly dropping the tray she is holding and setting it back down on the table. 'Tom, Maisie was your *great* grandmother. You remember the letter from her husband from the Somme.[10] I'll bet she became a clairvoyant after the war - to get in touch with Daniel. Spiritualism was the thing at the time, wasn't it?'

'And she passed on her skills, or her tricks, to her daughter, your granny?' Will says. 'Tom Catlow, what is it about your family? Your ancestors seem to have left their signature on at least two horrible deaths.'

'Shut up, Will,' I say. 'You've just sent shivers down my spine. You know that expression: "somebody just walked over my grave"?'

'Superstition,' Will says.

'And rain,' I add.

As we rush inside, the Lancashire skies open and the rain comes sheeting down.

---

[10] *The Northern Elements*, p. 200

ACKNOWLEDGEMENTS

AS EVER, I AM GRATEFUL to my sage and percipient editors: Peter Cheshire in London, and Julie Dexter, who lives under the shadow of a volcano on far away Hawaii. They have been my midwives throughout this series, and my thanks fall short of what they deserve.

Once again I should like to thank Mary Painter of the Blackburn with Darwen Library Service for encouragement and helpful research. This book is dedicated to that Library which, at its former site on Museum Street, contributed so much to my intellectual development through my childhood and teens.

The members of three Facebook groups have been extremely helpful: *Blackburn and District in the Past, 1960's Blackburn - Where Are You Now?* and *Memories of old Blackburn.* I am so grateful to their moderators for their support: Frank Riding, Barbara Whewell Lawrence and Fee Fleming respectively.

The events and characters depicted in my stories are entirely fictional. As for my portrayal of the town, it is charged with memories that are real enough, though it too has been shaped into fiction. I hope many of the scenes I have conjured up will send echoes down the cobbled streets of my readers' memories too.

Lincoln
March 2023

Printed in Great Britain
by Amazon